H.G. WELLS (1866–1946) was born in Bromley, Kent, the son of a shopkeeper and professional cricketer and a lady's maid. Although he left school at thirteen, he was awarded a scholarship to study for a degree at the Normal College of Science (now Imperial College London). Regarded as a prophet and a father of science fiction through best-selling novels such as *The Time Machine* and *The War of the Worlds*, he was a prolific writer of other types of fiction and became equally famous for his social commentary and essays, books and articles on politics and history. He was several times nominated for the Nobel Prize for Literature.

MR.
BLETTSWORTHY
ON RAMPOLE
ISLAND

MR. BLETTSWORTHY ON RAMPOLE ISLAND

H.G. Wells

Being the Story of a Gentleman of Culture and Refinement who suffered Shipwreck and saw no Human Beings other than the Cruel and Savage Cannibals for several years. How he beheld Megatheria alive and made some notes of their Habits. How he became a Sacred Lunatic. How he did at last escape in a Strange Manner from the Horror and Barbarities of Rampole Island in time to fight in the Great War, and how afterwards he came near to returning to that Island for ever. With much Amusing and Edifying Matter concerning Manners, Customs, Beliefs, Warfare, Crime and a Storm at Sea. Concluding with some Reflections upon Life in General and upon these Present Times in Particular.

PETER OWEN
London and Chicago

Peter Owen Publishers
81 Ridge Road, London N8 9NP, UK

Peter Owen books are distributed in the USA and Canada by
Independent Publishers Group/Trafalgar Square
814 North Franklin Street, Chicago, IL 60610, USA

First published by Ernest Benn 1928
Introduction © Michael Sherborne 2017

Paperback ISBN   978-0-7206-1943-0
Epub ISBN   978-0-7206-1936-2
Mobipocket ISBN 978-0-7206-1937-9
PDF ISBN   978-0-7206-1938-6

A catalogue record for this book is available from the British Library.

Printed and bound in Great Britain by
CPI Group (UK) Ltd, Croydon, CR0 4YY

Dedicated
to the Immortal Memory
of
CANDIDE

INTRODUCTION

BY MICHAEL SHERBORNE

The sea voyage that carries the traveller to a strange and challenging world is a time-honoured literary genre. Think of Shakespeare's *The Tempest* or Homer's *Odyssey*. On rare occasions it may lead the seafarer to a world that has claims to be better than his own – as is the case with Raphael Hythloday in Thomas More's *Utopia* – but if the current is running in the wrong direction, as it almost always is, then a monstrous reception is likely to imperil the voyager's life and, along with it, his assumptions about human existence.

Such is the fate of Edward Prendick in H.G. Wells's *The Island of Doctor Moreau* (1896). The shipwrecked Prendick is given a reluctant refuge on Moreau's island, but his host proves to be an obsessive vivisectionist whose idea of scientific progress involves taking a surgical knife to animals and reshaping them into people. The Ape Man, Swine Woman, Leopard Man and other products of his cruelty are a freakish parody of the human race, professing morality while succumbing to their animal cravings. In a vain attempt to preserve their humanity, the creatures equip themselves with some commandments and a religion, worshipping Moreau as their creator and fearing his laboratory as their Hell. When Moreau is killed by his latest ill-conceived experiment, the Puma Woman, the pieties prove ineffective and the creatures regress into bestiality.

Prendick escapes to England, but he has been so traumatized by his experiences that his fellow citizens now seem to him little better than the Beast People, and, like Swift's Gulliver before him, he has little choice but to become a virtual recluse.

Three decades after this *tour de force* of Gothic horror Wells decided to take his readers on another such voyage but this time in a more comical spirit. Despite his complaint in his *Experiment in Autobiography* (1934) that *Mr. Blettsworthy on Rampole Island* (1928) got a 'tepid reception', the novel seems to have been widely praised on its first appearance. The influential critic Middleton Murray, writing in the *New Adelphi*, judged that the story blended farce and tragedy magnificently. The *Observer* hailed it as an astonishingly rich and varied tale. The *New Statesman* thought the best of the satire was brilliant, while the *Times Literary Supplement* compared it favourably with *Gulliver's Travels*. The reviewers were all the more enthusiastic because the novel marked a return to entertaining storytelling from an author who in recent years had tended to dilute his tales with excessive social comment and philosophizing. Wells's previous effort, *The World of William Clissold* (1926), released in three volumes at two-monthly intervals to mark his sixtieth birthday, had been a particularly wearing example.

As *Blettsworthy* proved, Wells had not lost his talent, only changed his aim. When in 1915 he told fellow novelist Henry James, 'I had rather be called a journalist than an artist,' he was the author of a score of outstanding books of fiction but was aware that a new generation of writers was beginning to make his work look dated. At the same time the state of the world after the Great War was so precarious that he believed it was his duty to speak out for the public good. Rather than enter into futile competition with the likes of D.H. Lawrence and James Joyce, Wells decided that he would prioritize what would later be called 'consciousness raising'.

His talent for lively, subversive narration could still be deployed, however, when the occasion required. It was wonderfully present in his 1925 novel *Christina Alberta's Father* (reprinted by Peter Owen in a companion volume to the present one) and was again on

display in *Mr. Blettsworthy on Rampole Island,* which is dedicated to
'the Immortal Memory of Candide'. In a letter to Julian Huxley of
12 February 1928 Wells enthuses that *Blettsworthy* will be 'my
Candide, my *Peer Gynt,* my *Gulliver*'. Of the three references, *Peer
Gynt* (1867) seems to be the least significant. Peer Gynt travels into
strange lands and undergoes fantastical adventures, but the metrical
language of Ibsen's play and its sources in Scandinavian folklore
make it a very different proposition to Wells's novel.

Far more of an influence was Voltaire's *Candide* (1759), which
had first came to Wells's attention in his late teens or early twenties
in the library of Uppark, the country house in Sussex where his
mother was working as a housekeeper. Candide is a young man
who leads a sheltered life under protection of his uncle and is
brought up to look at the world in a spirit of facile optimism.
However, a series of misadventures, full of cynical reference to
contemporary events, leaves him thoroughly disabused of that
naïvety. The impression that Voltaire's writings made on Wells
lasted a lifetime. In his *Outline of History* (1920) he praises Voltaire's
'enormous industry' and the 'hatred of injustice' that led him to
intervene on behalf of the oppressed. Since Wells himself generally
wrote two or three books per year and spoke up for those he
considered to be victims of injustice, the Frenchman seems to have
been something of a role model. Wells describes himself in his
autobiography as having behaved in his youth like 'a Cockney
Voltaire', and in the writings of his old age, posthumously published
as *H.G. Wells in Love,* he expresses the hope that the closing years
of his life will resemble 'Voltaire's contentment at Ferney', a period
of well-deserved rest, commenting acidly on the world from the
sidelines.

Much like Candide, Wells's protagonist, Arnold Blettsworthy,
is raised by his uncle and brought up in a firmly positive spirit. The
Reverend Rupert Blettsworthy espouses an Anglicanism that can
apparently shrug off all intellectual challenges, Darwinian evolution
included, and forgive any evil, even murder. After his uncle's death,
however, Blettsworthy struggles to come to terms not only with

the dishonesty and selfishness of others but with his own rage and lust. Having experienced a nervous breakdown, he decides to try a therapeutic sea voyage, only to find himself trapped in a demoralizing series of adventures that reaches its extraordinary nadir on Rampole Island.

In *Candide* Voltaire had written about the Seven Years War between France and Britain, making particular reference to the controversial execution of Admiral Byng, dispatched by a Royal Navy firing squad for lack of determination in carrying out his duties. Wells's equivalent topics are the Great War of 1914–18 and the execution of Sacco and Vanzetti, two anarchists who went to the electric chair in Boston, Massachusetts, on a charge of robbery and murder, despite obvious flaws in their trial. Wells had been one of several prominent authors to oppose their execution. (His comments on the case can be found in a collection of his articles, published in 1928, entitled *The Way the World Is Going*.)

Alongside *Candide* in the Uppark library, the young Wells encountered another outlandish satire from the eighteenth century, Jonathan Swift's *Gulliver's Travels* (1726). Wells tells us in his autobiography that the book was an 'unexpurgated' edition. That is to say, it did not confine itself to Gulliver's voyages to the lands of little and big people which, with a few cuts, has provided suitable reading material for generations of children but also included the more adult Books III and IV. The latter features the bestial Yahoos, creatures that live in their own filth and are driven by their basest instincts. They doubtless influenced Wells's conception of the Beast People in *The Island of Doctor Moreau* and must again have been in his mind when he conceived the Rampole Islanders. These cannibal savages are extravagantly repulsive in their appearance and actions, yet at times their bloodthirsty and hypocritical behaviour has a disconcerting familiarity. Since you may be reading this introduction in advance of first reading the book, it would be unfair to reveal the islanders' secrets here. Suffice it to say that this is a tale where things are not always what they seem.

Typically, Wells's handling of his material is more realistic than that of Swift and Voltaire. In the intervening century and a half novelists had built up ways to create a fuller sense of everyday life. This gave Wells the opportunity to present the fantastic more convincingly than his forebears had done, an achievement for which he has often been praised. Joseph Conrad, for example (in a letter to Wells of 6 January 1900), called him a 'Realist of the Fantastic' and admired his 'capacity to give shape, colour, *aspect* to the invisible' as well as to convey 'the *depth* of things common and visible', suggesting the curious mixture of plausible detail and almost hallucinatory symbolism to be found in books such as *The Time Machine* and *The War of the Worlds*. Perhaps the best example in *Blettsworthy* is the account of the giant sloths or Megatheria in Chapter 3, vividly realized monsters that also come to stand for oppressive institutions and the dangers of ecological destruction.

Throughout the book Wells ensures that Blettsworthy's adventures retain a sense of authenticity to experience. Consider this passing description of life aboard the *Golden Lion*, taken from Chapter 2.

> Everything is engaged in mysteriously pivoted motions and slowly changing its level towards you. The sky outside and the horizon have joined in that slow unending dance. You get up and dress staggeringly, and blunder up the gangway to the deck and clutch the rail. Water. An immeasurable quantity and extent of water about you and below, and wet and windy air above; these are the enormous and invisible walls of your still unrealized incarceration.

The painstaking subjectivity of this description, constantly shifting the point of view and the surrounding objects in relation to each other, leaves us disorientated and beginning to feel almost as seasick as poor Blettsworthy. Reinforced by the unequal sentence structures and the pronoun 'you', the effect is to create a sense of being trapped inside an alarming world, an entirely different position from the one of detached observer generated by the brisk narration of *Candide* or *Gulliver*. We get to know Blettsworthy from the inside, drawing us into the story and leading us to sympathize with his views. Yet our reliance on him for the facts cuts the ground from under our feet when trying to distinguish the real from the delusional and the literal from the symbolic. In other words, we are placed inside the story to such an extent that, like Blettsworthy himself, we have to engage in some serious thinking to find a rational perspective on it. The above passage is in the present tense, but most of the narration is retrospective, allowing Wells to use one of Dickens's favourite devices: an older, wiser version of the main character telling us about his adventures as a naïve young man. The mature Blettsworthy's cynical tone and point of view offset the tale of an innocent abroad, allowing plenty of scope for the ironic humour that is one of the book's chief attractions.

As a trained scientist, Wells had brought to his early work the perspective of an evolutionary biologist. Stories like *The Time Machine*, *Dr Moreau* and *The War of the Worlds* are set in a godless universe where human nature and morality are exposed as insecure constructs. The Martians who invade the Earth may be monsters, but, in view of the way humans treat other species and so-called inferior races, what does that make us? Later in his career Wells offered a more encouraging doctrine of human evolution, holding out the prospect of reform and progress towards an ideal world if only people would work together for the common good. In *Blettsworthy*, however, the earlier vision returns with a vengeance to challenge such idealism. Caught in delusion, Blettsworthy enters into debate with a shark who scorns reformism. 'What price hope and fear, the desire of the human heart, its dreams of sacrifice and glory after two minutes in the gullet of Reality?' The Great War suggests that the 'land of man's supreme effort' is not the future Utopia advocated by idealists such as Wells, but the No Man's Land of war, where the science and industry of the world's leading nations, and the courage and determination of their citizens, have been concentrated to bring about a 'desolation' of craters, trenches, barbed wire and corpses. By introducing a heroine called Rowena, Wells even recalls Weena in *The Time Machine*, linking *Blettsworthy* to that earlier book which presented human existence as futile then concluded with a desperate resolve to live as though it were not so.

In the final pages of *Blettsworthy* a similar resolve – affirming that 'a collective purpose grows' – is placed in the mouth of a character of proven unreliability. This has been seen as a flaw in the book, a clumsy self-contradiction, but only because Wells is assumed to be writing simple propaganda and any element which detracts from that 'message' must therefore be the result of incompetence. Acquaintance with Wells's works will show, however, that he is a more open, dialogic novelist than his reputation suggests. In 1940's *The Common Sense of War and Peace* he tells his readers, 'please, please do not imagine you are being invited to line up behind me. You have a backbone and a brain; your brain is as important as mine and probably better at most jobs.' Wells certainly likes to show readers his preferred views, but he usually tries to build in alternatives, dissensions and ironies which require them to think for themselves.

Ultimately, *Blettsworthy* is one of many Wells stories about a man haunted – or even trapped – by a mind-bending vision, trying to distance himself from it in order to put its disturbing content into perspective and integrate it with received views of the world. Is his experience a delusion, an anomaly or perhaps a revelation? To answer such questions the Time Traveller returns from the far distant future, Bedford from the Moon, George Ponderevo from the rise and fall of his uncle's business project (the pernicious tonic Tono-Bungay) and set down their experiences so we can share and interpret them. Blettsworthy has a similar tale to tell, surely deserving of a place alongside the others.

Fifty years ago the Russian scholar Julius Kagarlitski singled out *Blettsworthy* among Wells's later works as 'an integral, forceful, deep book'. Reflecting on Kagarlitski's judgement in *The Novelist at the Crossroads* (1971), the novelist and critic David Lodge agreed that Wells's novel displays 'the startling imaginative concreteness of his best early work', deployed with 'tremendous verve', and, while not endorsing all of Kagarlitski's views, he none the less proclaimed *Blettsworthy* to be 'worth resurrecting'. Now, thanks to Peter Owen Publishers, this remarkable book has at long last been relaunched. Enjoy the voyage. But keep your wits about you; there are some deceptive waters ahead.

CHAPTER THE FIRST

§ 1

THE BLETTSWORTHY FAMILY

THE Blettsworthys, my family, have always been a very scrupulous family and gentle, the Wiltshire Blettsworthys perhaps even more so than the Sussex branch. I may perhaps be forgiven if I say a word or two about them before I come to my own story. I am proud of my ancestors and of the traditions of civilised conduct and genial living they have handed down to me ; the thought of them, as I shall tell, has supported and sustained me on some difficult occasions. "What," I have asked, "should a Blettsworthy do ? " and I have at least attempted to make my conduct a proper answer.

There have always been Blettsworthys in English life in the south and west of England, and they have always been very much the same sort of people. Many epitaphs and similar records reaching back far beyond Tudor times witness to their virtues, their kindliness, probity and unobtrusive prosperity. There is said to be a branch of them in Languedoc, but of that I know nothing. Blettsworthys went to America, to Virginia in particular, but they seem to have been swallowed up and lost there. Yet ours is a family of persistent characteristics not easily extinguished. Perhaps some American reader may know of the fate of this branch. Such chances occur. There is an alabaster figure of a Bishop Blettsworthy in Salisbury Cathedral that was brought thither from the aisle of old Sarum when that was demolished and Salisbury set up, and the marble face might have been a bust of my uncle, the rector of Harrow Hoeward, and the fine hands are like his hands. There ought to be Blettsworthys in America, and it perplexes me that I never hear of any. Something of their quality appears, I am told, in the Virginian landscape, which is wide and warm and kindly, they say, like our English downland, a little touched by the sun.

The Blettsworthys are a family of cultivators and culture. They have had little to do with merchandising, either in gross or detail, and they played no part in the direct development of what is called industrialism.

They have preferred the church to the law, and classical scholarship, botany and archæology to either, but they appear doing their duty by the land in Domesday Book, and Blettsworthy's Bank is one of the last of the outstanding private banks in these days of amalgamation. It is still a great factor in West of England life. The Blettsworthys' rest assured, were drawn into banking by no craving for usurious gain, but simply to oblige the needs and requests of less trustworthy neighbours in Gloucestershire and Wilts. The Sussex branch is not quite so free from commercialism as the Wiltshire ; it practised " free trade " during the French wars when free trade was strictly speaking illegal and a fine adventure, and in spite of the violent end of Sir Carew Blettsworthy and his nephew Ralph as the result of a misunderstanding with some Custom House officials in the streets of Rye that necessitated bloodshed, it acquired considerable wealth and local influence through these activities and has never altogether severed its connection with the importation of silks and brandy.

My father was a man of sterling worth but eccentric action. Many of the things he did demanded explanation before the soundness of his motives was clear, and some, because of their remoteness, his habitual negligence, or for other reasons, were never fully explained. The Blettsworthys are not always good at explanation. It is their habit to rely on their credit. Being a fifth son and with no prospects of a fortune nor any marketable abilities, my father was urged by his friends and relations to seek his fortune abroad, and left Wiltshire at an early age to look, as he said, for gold, looking, I admit, without any natural avidity and generally in quite unsuitable places. Gold, I understand, is extremely localised in its origins, and it is as a rule found gregariously in what are called " gold rushes," but father had an aversion from crowds and crowd behaviour and preferred to seek the rare and precious metal among agreeable surroundings and where the ungracious competition of unrefined people did not incommode him, subsisting meanwhile upon the modest remittances afforded him by his more prosperous connexions. He held that though this line of conduct might diminish his chances of discovering gold, it gave him a prospect of monopolising any lucky find that occurred to him. He was more careless about marriage than is usual in the Blettsworthy strain, contracting it several times and sometimes rather informally—though indeed we are all rather unguarded in our assent to contracts—and my mother happened to be of mixed Portuguese and Syrian origin, with a touch of the indigenous blood of Madeira, where I was born.

My birth was entirely legitimate ; whatever confusion there may be in my father's matrimonial record came later and as a consequence of the extremely variable nature of marriage in tropical and subtropical climates.

My mother was, I understand, on the testimony of my father's letters, a passionately self-forgetful woman, but she did not altogether eliminate herself in my composition. To her, I think, I must owe my preference for inclusive rather than concise statement, and a disposition, when other things are equal, to subordinate reality to a gracious and ample use of language. " She talks," wrote my father to my uncle during her lifetime. " You never hear the last of anything." Meaning that she felt things so finely and acutely that she resorted instinctively to the protection of a felt of words and that her mind could not rest satisfied so long as a statement was in any way incomplete. She fined; she retouched. How well I understand ! I too understand how insupportable inexpression may become. Moreover I surely owe to her something even more alien to the Blettsworthy stock in my sense of internal moral conflict. I am divided against myself—to what extent this book must tell. I am not harmonious within; not at peace with myself as the true Blettsworthys are. I am at issue with my own Blettsworthyness. I add to my father's tendency to a practical complexity, a liability to introspective enquiry. I insist I am a Blettsworthy, and you will remark that I insist. That is what no twenty-four carat Blettsworthy would do. I am consciously a Blettsworthy because I am not completely and surely a Blettsworthy. I have great disconnected portions of myself. Perhaps I am all the more loyal to my family traditions because I can be objectively loyal.

My mother died when I was five years old, and my few memories of her are hopelessly confused with a tornado that ravaged the island. Two clouds of apprehension mingled and burst in dreadful changes. I remember seeing trees and hours most shockingly inverted and a multitude of crimson petals soddened in a gutter, and that is associated confusedly with being told that my mother was dying and then dead. At the time I believe I was not so much greived as astounded.

My father, after some futile correspondence with my maternal relations in Portugal and a rich uncle in Aleppo, succeeded in entrusting me to an inexperienced young priest who was coming from Madeira to England, and requested him to deposit me with an aunt in Cheltenham, Miss Constance Blettsworthy, who in that manner first became aware of my existence. My father had armed his emissary with documents that left no doubt of my identity. I have vague memories of mounting the side of the steamship at Funchal, but my recollections of the subsequent sea passage are happily effaced. I have a distincter picture of my aunt's parlour in Cheltenham.

She was a dignified lady in what was either a blonde wig or hair skilfully arranged in such a fashion as to imitate one ; she had a Companion similar to herself but larger, an unusually large person in fact, whose bust impressed my childish mind profoundly ; and I remember they both sat up very high above me while I occupied a hassock before the fire, and that the conversation with the young priest was sufficiently momentous to leave a strong impression on my mind. They were clearly of opinion that he had been wrongly advised to bring me to Cheltenham and that he ought to take me on at once at least a further hour's journey by rail to the home of my uncle, the rector of Harrow Hoeward.

My aunt said repeatedly that she was touched by my father's confidence in her, but that the state of her health made her feel unequal to my entertainment. She and her Companion furnished the young priest with such facts about her state of health as were suitable for him to hear and even, I fancy, with additional particulars. They must have felt the emergency called for decisive treatment. In spite of the commiseration his profession demanded from him, he was manifestly anxious to waive these confidences in so far as they might be considered relevant to the business in hand. My father had said nothing to him about this brother at Harrow Hoeward, having concentrated his directions upon my Aunt Constance, the elder sister of his upbringing and a pillar of strength in his memory. The young priest did not feel justified, he declared, in varying his instructions. The trust was discharged, the young priest maintained, by my delivery into the hands of my aunt, and he lingered only for a settlement of certain incidental expenses upon the voyage for which my father had made no provision.

For my own part, I sat stoically upon my hassock and, with an affected concentration regarded the fire-place and the hob, which were of a type unknown in Madeira, listening the while. I was not very anxious to stay with my aunt, but I was quite eager to see no more of the young priest, so that I wished him well in his efforts to relinquish me and was pleased by his success.

He was a fat white young priest, with a round face and a high strangulated tenor voice more suitable for praying aloud than ordinary conversation. He had begun our acquaintance with the warmest, most winning, professions of affection, and I had shared his berth on board at his suggestion, but my inability to support the motion of the vessel with restraint, and a certain want of judgment in my disposition of the outcome, had gradually embittered a relationship that had promised to be ideal. By the time we reached Southampton we had conceived a mutual distaste which was mitigated only by the prospect of a separation that promised to be speedy and enduring.

In short, he would have no more to do with me. . . .

I stayed with my aunt.

Cheltenham was not a very happy refuge for me. A small boy of five is sedulous in pursuit of occupation, tactless in his choice of entertainment, and destructive in his attempts to investigate and comprehend the more fragile objects of interest with which life teems for him. My aunt was addicted to collecting Chelsea figurines and other early English china; she loved the quaint stuff; and yet she failed to recognise a kindred passion in me when my eager young imagination would have introduced conflict and drama among her treasures. Nor did my attempts to play with and enliven the life of two large blue Persian cats who adorned the house please her maturer judgment. I did not understand that a cat, if one wishes to play with it, should not be too ardently pursued, and is rarely roused to responsive gaiety by even the best aimed blows. My doughty exploits in the garden, where I dealt with her Dahlias and Michaelmas daisies as though they were hostile champions and embattled hosts, aroused no spark of approval in her.

The two elderly domestics and the crumpled gardener, who ministered to the comfort and dignity of my aunt and her Companion, shared their employer's opinion that the education of the young should be entirely repressive, so that I was able to go on existing at all only in a very unobtrusive manner. A young tutor was engaged, I seem to remember, to take me for walks as prolonged as possible and give me instructions as inaudible as possible, but I have no distinct recollection of him except that he was the first person I knew who wore detachable cuffs, and my impressions of Cheltenham are of a wilderness of endless spacious roads of pale grey houses under a pale blue sky, and of a Pump Room, bath chairs and an absence of bright colour and exhilarating incident in the extremest contrast with Madeira.

I note these months at Cheltenham—or perhaps they were only weeks, though in my memory at least they are months of a vague immensity— as a sort of interregnum in the Void before my real life began. Above and outsic₂ the sphere of my attention, my aunt and her Companion must have been making the most strenuous efforts to place me among other surroundings, for against the dim background to these Cheltenham reminiscences there come and go a number of still dimmer figures, Blettsworthys all, scrutinising me without either affection or animosity, but with a rapidity crystallising disposition to have nothing further to do with me. Their comments, I believe, fell under three main headings; firstly, that I was *good* for my aunt because I should take her out of herself —but clearly she did not want to be taken out of herself, and indeed who does ?—or, secondly, that I had better be returned to my father, but that was impossible because he had left Madeira for an uncertain address in Rhodesia and our imperial postal system will not accept little boys addressed to the Poste Restante in remote colonies ; or, thirdly, that the whole thing, meaning me, ought to be put before my uncle, the Rev. Rupert Blettsworthy, the rector of Harrow Hoeward. They were all in agreement that I promised to be rather small for a Blettsworthy.

My uncle was away in Russia at that time, with various Anglican bishops, discussing the possible reunion of the Anglican and Orthodox churches—it was long, long before the Great War and the coming of Bolshevism. Letters from my aunt pursued him, but were delayed and never overtook him. Then suddenly, just as I was growing resigned to a purely negative life in a household at Cheltenham under the direction of a tutor with detachable cuffs, my uncle appeared.

He resembled my father generally, but he was shorter and rosier and rounder and dressed like the rich and happy rector he was, instead of in loose and laundry worn flannels. There was much about him too that needed explanation, but the need was not so manifest. And his hair was silver-grey. He came right out of the background at once in a confident and pleasing manner. He put rimless glasses on his nose and regarded me with a half smile that I found extremely attractive.

"Well, young man," he said in almost my father's voice; "they don't seem to know what to do with you. How would you like to come and live with me ? "

"Please, sir," I said as soon as I grasped the meaning of the question.

My aunt and her Companions became radiantly appreciative of me. They cast concealment aside. I had never suspected how well they thought of me. "He is *so* lively and intelligent," they said ; "he takes notice of everything. Properly looked after and properly fed he will be quite a nice little boy."

And so my fate was settled.

§ 2

THE GOOD BROAD CHURCHMAN

WITH my establishment at Harrow Hoeward my life, I consider, really began. My memory, which has nothing but gleams and fragments of the preceding years, jumps into continuity from the very day of my arrival at that most homelike home. I could, I believe, draw maps to scale of the rectory, and certainly of the garden, and I can recall the peculiar damp smell of the pump in the yard beyond the out-house and the nine marigolds at equal distances against the grey stone wall. Year by year old Blackwell, the gardener, replaced them. I could write a chronicle of the cats, with sketches of their characters. And out beyond the paddock was a ditch and then the steep open down, rising against the sky. In the snowy winter or the hot summer I used to slide down that on a plank, for the dry grass in summer was more slippery than ice. In the front of the vicarage was a trim lawn and a hedge of yew, and to the left of us were Copers Cottages, and then at the notch in the road the Post Office and the General Store. The church and churchyard was our boundary the other way.

My uncle took me there a small indeterminate plastic creature, which might have become anything. But there inevitably I became the Blettsworthy I am to-day.

From the first moment of our acquaintance he was the most real and reassuring thing in life for me. It was like awakening on a bright morning merely to see him. Everything in my life before his appearance had been vague, minatory and yet unconvincing; I felt I was wrong and unsafe, that I was surrounded by shadowy and yet destructive powers and driven by impulses that could be as disastrous as they were uncontrollable. Daily life was the mask of a tornado. But now that effect of a daylight dream which might at any time become a nightmare, which was already creeping into my life in childhood in spite of a sort of stoical resistance I offered its invasion, was banished for many years from my mind. " Things have got a little wrong with you," he said in effect in that Cheltenham parlour, " but, as a matter of fact and fundamentally, they are *all right*."

And so long as he lived, either they were fundamentally all right or by some essential personal magic he made them seem so. Even now I cannot tell which of these things it was.

I do not remember my Aunt Dorcas as vividly as I do my uncle. Indeed, I do not remember her as fully as I do old Blackwell or the cook. This is odd, because she must have had a lot to do with me. But she was a busy self-effacing woman, who effected her ministrations so efficiently that they seemed to be not her acts but part of the routine of the universe. I believe she had always desired children of her own, and at first she had been a little distressed to realise that her sole family was to be one half alien nephew, a doubtful scrutinising being already past babyhood, eking out a limited English vocabulary with dubious scraps of Portuguese. Perhaps there remained a certain estrangement of spirit always. She never betrayed any want of affection ; she did her duty by me completely, but it is clear as I look back upon these things that there was no motherhood, no sonship between us. The realities of her life were turned away from me altogether. All the more did my heart go out to my uncle, who seemed to diffuse kindliness as a hayfield in good weather diffuses scent, and who presided, in my childish imagination, not only over the house and the church and all the souls of Harrow Hoeward, but over the wide bare downland and the very sunshine. It is extraordinary how extensively he has effaced my father from my mind.

My idea of God is still all mixed up with him. In Madeira I had heard much of Dios by way of expletive and invocation, a subtropical passionate Dios, hot and thundery; but I never connected the two divinities until I reached years of comparison. God began afresh with me in England as the confederated shadow of my uncle, a dear English gentleman of a God, a super-Blettsworthy in control, a God of dew and bright frosty mornings, helpful and unresentful, whose peculiar festivals were Easter and Christmas and the Harvest Thanksgiving. He was the God of a world that was right way up, stern only to smile again, and even through the solemnity and restraint of Good Friday peeped out my uncle's assurance that the young gentleman would come back safe and sound on Sunday. A serious time, of course, occasion for grave reflections, but meanwhile we had our hot cross buns.

There were crosses in my uncle's church but no crucifix, no crown of thorns, no nails.

My uncle shook back his surplice from his shapely hands, leant over the pulpit and talked to us pleasantly of this pleasant supreme power who ruled the world, for twenty minutes at the most, since God must not be made tiresome to the weaker brethren. He needed explanation at times, this God of the Blettsworthys, his ways had to be justified to man, but not tediously. My uncle loved particularly to talk in his sermons of the rainbow and the ark and God's certain covenants. He was awfully decent, was God, as my uncle displayed him, and he and my uncle made me want to be decent too. In a world of " All right " and " Right O " and " Right you are, Sir." I lived in it and was safe in it all those years. Was it no more than a dream ?

Evil was very far away and hell forgotten. " You don't do that sort of thing," said my uncle, and you didn't. " Play up," said my uncle, and you did. " Fair doos," said my uncle ; " you mustn't be *hard* on people." And patience with the poor performer ; " How do you *know* the fellow isn't trying ? " Even the gipsies who drifted through that tranquil Downland and sometimes had to confer with my uncle in his secular might upon the bench, about minor issues of conduct, were deeply Anglicised gipsies ; if they pinched a trifle now and again they were neither robbers nor violent. Dear England! Shall I never see you again as I saw you in those safe and happy days? Languedoc and Provence they say are gentle regions also, and Saxony; and here and there in Scandinavia you will find whole countrysides of kindliness, needing only the simplest explanations. I do not know about these places. It is to the English Downland that my heart returns.

My uncle shook back the sleeves of his surplice and leant smiling and persuasive over his pulpit, making everything clear and mild like English air, and I felt that if I were given a vision sufficiently penetrating I should see high above the blue ether another such kindly Father, instructing His fortunate world. Under Him in pews as it were and looking up to Him, were princes, potentates and powers all to be credited with the best intentions until there was positive proof to the contrary. Queen Victoria, simple and good and wise and rather the shape of a cottage loaf with a crown upon it, sat highest of all, not, I felt, so much a Queen and Empress as a sort of Vice Deity in the earth. On Sundays she occupied the big imperial pew right under God's pulpit and no doubt took Him home to lunch. To dusky potentates who happened to know and respect her better than they knew God, she presented copies of the Authorised Version of the English Bible and referred them up magnanimously to her friend and ruler. No doubt she wrote Him earnest letters, with her particular wishes underlined, just as she wrote to Lord Beaconsfield and the German Emperor, upon what her fine instinct, a little instructed by Baron Stockmar, told her was best for the Realm, His World and her Family connexions. Beneath her was a system of hierarchic kindliness. Our local magnate was Sir Willoughby Denby, a great man for the irrigation of subtropical lands and the growing of cotton for the mills of Manchester and the needs of all mankind. A ruddy handsome man, inclined to be fat, and riding through the village on a stout cob. Farther towards Devizes spread the dominion and influence of Lord Penhartingdon, banker and archæologist, and Blettsworthy on the mother's side. Actually Blettsworthys held their ancestral lands from Downton to Shaftesbury and again towards Wincanton.

In this benevolent world which my uncle's God and his own goodness had made upon the Wiltshire uplands, I grew from childhood to adolescence, and the dark stain of my mother's blood, sorrowful and errant, flowed unsuspected in my veins and gave no sign. Perhaps for a Blettsworthy I was a trifle garrulous and quick with languages. First I had a governess, a Miss Duffield from Boars Hill near Oxford, the daughter of a friend of my uncle's, blindly adoring him and very successful with my French and German, and then I went as a weekly boarder to the excellent school at Imfield that Sir Willoughby Denby under God and the Ecclesiastical Commissioners had done so much to revive and re-endow. It was tremendously modern for those days and we had classes in carpentry and did experimental biology with plants and frog spawn, and learnt Babylonian and Greek history instead of learning Greek grammar. My uncle was a governor of this school and came at times and talked to us.

They were unpremeditated talks of perhaps five or ten minutes that sprang up in his mind when he came down to us, not so much attempts to put anything over us as, in response to our youth and activity and fresh expectation a kindly word to clear difficulties away.

" Civilisation," he would say to us. " Grow sound and strong here and go out to civilise the earth."

That was what Imfield School was for. " Civilisation " was his word; I think I must have heard it from him six times as often as " Christianity." Theology was a mental play for him, and rather idle play. He was all for the Reunion of Christendom in the interests of civilisation, and had great hopes of the holy men who lived in the Troitzko-Sergiyevskaya Lavra near Moscow and never put their feet to earth. He wanted an interchange of Orthodox and Anglican orders. His power of imagining resemblances was far greater than his power of recognising differences. He could imagine the mentality of a gentle curate beneath the long hair and beard of a Russian priest. He thought Russian country gentlemen could presently become like English country gentlemen with a parliament in St. Petersburg just the same. He corresponded with several of the Cadets. And that point between the creeds of Latin and Greek about Filioque, that most vital point, seemed, I fear to him, no better than a quibble.

" At bottom we are all the same thing," he said to me, preparing me for confirmation. " Never get excited about forms of formulæ. There is only one truth in the world and all good men have got it."

" Darwin and Huxley ? " I reflected.

" Sound Christians both," said he, " in the proper sense of the word. Honest men that is. No belief is healthy unless it takes air and exercise and turns itself round and about and stands upon its head for a bit."

Huxley was a great loss to the bench of bishops, he assured me, an athlete of the spirit and respectable to the bone. Everyone would take his word before that of many a bishop. Because science and religion were two sides of the medal of truth, it did not follow that they were in opposition, and to be unconsciously a Christian was perhaps the very essence of sound Christianity.

" Let him who thinketh he stand," quoted my uncle, " take heed lest he fall."

All men meant the same thing really and everyone was fundamentally good. But sometimes people forgot themselves. Or didn't quite understand how things ought to be explained. If the Origin of Evil troubled my uncle but little, he was sometimes perplexed I think by the moral inadvertence of our fellow creatures. He would talk over his newspaper at breakfast to his wife and Miss Duffield and me, or with our frequent guests at lunch or dinner, about crimes, about the disconcerting behaviour of pitiful ungracious individuals, murderers, swindlers and the like.

" Tut, tut," he would say at breakfast. " Now that's really too disgraceful."

" What have they done now ? " asked my Aunt Dorcas.

" It's the wicked foolishness of it," he would say.

Miss Duffield would sit back and admire him and wait, but my aunt would go on with her breakfast.

" Here's a poor silly muddle-witted fellow must poison his wife. Insures her for quite a lot of money—which is what attracted attention to the whole thing—and then gives her poison. Three nice little children too. When they tell in court the way the woman suffered and how she made a remark about its being hard on her, the poor wretch chokes and weeps. Silly poor idiot ! Tut, tut ! He never knew which way to turn for money. . . . Pitiful."

" But she was murdered," said my Aunt Dorcas.

" They lose all sense of proportion when they get into that state of worry. I've seen it so often before me when I've been upon the bench. No confidence in life and then comes a sort of moral stampede. Very probably to begin with he wanted money because he couldn't bear to see that poor woman living in such poverty. And then the craving for money became overpowering. At any cost he must have money. Forgot everything else in that."

Miss Duffield nodded her head very fast in token of intelligent edification, but my Aunt Dorcas still hung undecided.

" But what would you do with him, dearest ? " said my Aunt Dorcas. " You wouldn't let him out to poison someone else."

" You don't *know* he would," said my uncle.

" Christ would have forgiven him," Miss Duffield said softly and with some obscure difficulty.

" I suppose he ought to be hanged," said my uncle, dealing firmly with my aunt's question ; " Yes, I suppose he ought to be hanged. (These are excellent kippers. The best we have had for some time.) "

He viewed all sides of the question. " I would forgive him—his sin if not his punishment. No. For the sake of the weaker brethren under temptation, I grant you he ought to be hanged. Yes. He ought to be hanged." He sighed deeply. " But in a civilised spirit. You see— Someone ought to go to him and make it clear to him that it is to be a hanging without malice, that we realise we are all poor sinful tempted things not a bit better than he is, not a bit better, sinners all, but that it is just because of that, that he has to die. We have to be helped by the certainty of punishment, so that though he has now to go through with this disagreeable experience, he dies for the good of the world just as much as any soldier on the battle-field. . . . I wish it wasn't a case of a hangman. The hangman is barbaric. A bowl of hemlock would be far more civilised, a bowl of hemlock, a sober witness or so, sitting at hand, and a friendly voice to comfort and console.

" We shall come to that," said my uncle. " Cases of this sort get rarer—exactly as people become more tolerant and better arrangements are made. The more we civilise the less there is of this fretting and vexation and hopelessness—and meanness, out of which such crises arise. And such punishments as we award them. Things get better. When you are my age, Arnold, you will be able to realise that steadily things get better."

He shook his head sadly at his newspaper and seemed to hesitate whether he would read it again.

No, he had had enough newspaper for the day. He got up absent-mindedly, found the sideboard attractive, and helped himself to a second kipper. . . .

It was his favourite contention that he had never in the whole course of his experience as a magistrate tried a really bad man or woman, but only ignorant creatures, morally dense and hopelessly muddled. I realise now his utter inconsistency. All his professional theology was based upon the doctrine of a fall, and daily he denied it. What was sin ? Sin shrank before civilisation. There may have been real wicked sins in the past, but such weeds had been kept under so long that now they were very rare, very rare indeed. All his practical and informal teaching was permeated by the idea not of sin but of inadvertent error. He did not preach therefore. It was so much better to explain.

He taught me not to be afraid of life. To walk fearlessly and even carelessly round the darkest corner. To tell the truth and shame the devil. To pay the sum demanded without haggling or asking questions. One might be cheated now and then or meet here and there with brutality, but on the whole if one trusted people, if one trusted oneself to people, one was not betrayed. Just as one couldn't be bitten by a dog or kicked by a horse unless one threatened or startled it. Or betrayed a provocative distrust and an inviting fear. So long as your movements explain themselves even a dog will not bite you. If you had argued that there were not only dogs in the world but tigers and wolves, he would have answered that in a civilised world one so rarely met the latter that they could be ignored. We lived in a civilised world that grew in civilisation daily. For all practical purposes things ignored were things exterminated. Accidents happen in life and there may be moral as well as material accidents, but there were enough honest people about and enough simple goodwill for us to disregard these adverse chances and walk about unarmed. He thought a man who carried weapons upon him either a bully or a coward. He disliked precautions of every sort against one's fellow creatures. So he hated Cash Registers. And every sort of spying upon people. And he hated hiding things from people and all misleading tricks. He thought every secret a darkening of life and any lie a sin.

Human beings are good unless they are pressed or vexed or deluded or starved or startled or scared. Men really are brothers. Getting this explained and believed, and above all believing and acting upon it oneself, was what my dear uncle meant by civilisation. When at last all the world was civilised everyone would be happy.

And thanks to his teaching and his candid confident example, I became, what I hope I still am, in spite of the frightful adventures that have happened to me and the dark streaks of fear and baseness that have been revealed in my composition, an essentially civilised man.

Little did I hear of the wars and social conflicts that loomed over us, in these golden Victorian days among the Wiltshire hills. The latest great war had been the Franco-German war, of which the animosities, my uncle said, were dying down year by year. That Germany and England should ever be at war was dead against the laws of consanguinity. A man may not marry his grandmother and still less may he fight her, and our Queen was grandmother to the world in general and their Emperor William in particular.

Revolutions were even remoter than wars. Socialism my uncle taught me was a most wholesome corrective to a certain hardness, a certain arithmetical prepossession on the part of manufacturers and business men. Due mainly to their social inexperience. So that they did the sort of things that really are not done. He gave me Ruskin's " Unto this Last " to read and afterwards " News from Nowhere " by William Morris. I agreed enthusiastically with the spirit of these books, and I looked forward with a quiet assurance to a time when everyone would understand and agree.

§ 3

THE RECTOR IS ILL AND DIES

THERE was hardly more evil in my school life than in my uncle's home. I have heard much since of the peculiar vileness of schoolboys and of the sinks of systematic vice public schools in Britain could be.   Much of this talk I am convinced is exaggerated stuff and anyhow there was little or no viciousness at Imfield. We had the curiosities natural to our years and satisfied them unobtrusively, and like all boys we evoked a certain facetiousness from things that lurk coyly and provocatively beneath our social conventions. The Deity in his inscrutable wisdom has seen fit to make certain aspects of life a running commentary upon human dignity, and the youthful mind has to pass through a phase of shocked astonishment and healing laughter in its effort to grasp the universe.

Save for a few such explicable kinks and crumplings of the mind I grew up simple and clean and healthy. I acquired and hid away a fair knowledge of three languages and some science, and I attained considerable skill at cricket, learning to bat with style and vigour and to bowl balls less straight-forward than they seemed. I rode a little and played the primitive tennis of those days.. I grew long in the limb and fairer. Had you met me in my flannels on the way to the practice nets in Sir Willoughby Denby's park you would no more have suspected that my mother was Portuguese and Syrian with a dash of Madeira than that the remoter ancestors of the Blettsworthys had hair and tails. So completely had the assimilative power of our Blettsworthy countryside worked upon me and civilised me.

I grew to manhood clean, confident and trustful, and if I did not look disagreeable facts in the face that was largely because in that green and tranquil part of Wiltshire there were no disagreeable facts sufficiently obtrusive to invite it. And when presently I went up to Oxford, to Lattmeer, I met with no great shock either there or on my way thither. It was my Aunt Constance who paid for me to go to Oxford and presently died and left me all her little property, subject only to a life annuity that absorbed most of the income for her Companion. From a dismayed apprehension of me, both these ladies had passed over to a real and confessed liking as I opened out in the sunshine of my uncle's care. The will was made when my father was killed in Bechuanaland and I was left a penniless orphan. He was killed in a rather intricate and never completely documented affair in which the Boer War, his disputed marriage to the daughter of a Bechuanaland notable and the mineral rights under certain lands claimed by his possible father-in-law, were involved. He failed to explain his presence within the Boer lines upon some mission connected with his always complicated but never I believe dishonourable private life and his complex inexplicable search for gold. But at the time, we believed him to have been killed for King and Country in the normal course of warfare.

That Boer War left no scars upon my boyish mind. It was certainly the most civilised war in all history, fought with restraint and frequent chivalry, a white man's war, which ended in mutual respect and a general shaking of hands. Most of us must be orphaned sooner or later, and to have had a father one had long forgotten dying, as we supposed, a hero's death in a fair fight, was as satisfactory a way of realising that customary bereavement as I can imagine.

Nor did the passing of the great Queen Victoria throw any permanent shadow upon my mind. It had the effect of a stupendous epoch and I was a little surprised to find *Punch* and the Established Church still going on after it. But they did go on ; gradually one realised that most things were going on, with a widowed air indeed but not hopelessly widowed ; King Edward reigned in her stead, reformed but still amiable, and one's sense of the stability of things was if anything strengthened by her demise.

My life at Lattmeer confirmed my faith in the civilisation of the universe. I felt I was not only safe but privileged. I took to the water and rowed number four in the college boat. I swam with distinction. I anointed my hair and parted it in the middle. I adorned my person gaily. I had a knitted waistcoat of purple with lines of primrose yellow that few excelled. I learnt to distinguish one wine from another. I formed friendships and one or two were confidential and exalted ; I fell in love with the daughter of a tobacconist, a widow who kept a shop in the street that leads from the back lane of Lattmeer towards Johns. I even acquired the small amount of classical learning needed for a special degree. And I shared without pre-eminence in the activities of the O.U.D.S.

I had every reason to be happy in those days and I look back to them now as a prisoner for life might look back upon a summer's holiday in his free unchallenged past. The bequest of my aunt's small but by no means contemptible fortune relieved me of those worldly forebodings that oppress the dawn of manhood for the majority of young men. I sustained the death of her former Companion, which presently released the entire income for my use, with a manly fortitude, and prepared to take my place in the scheme of God's indulgences with an easy confidence in their continuation. I had no suspicion that all this happiness and hope was destined to be only a bright foil for the series of dark experiences that was now descending upon me.

The first great shadow that fell upon my young life was the deaths in rapid succession of my aunt and uncle. My uncle was the first to be evidently ailing and the last of the two to die. The exact nature of his disease I do not know nor was it I think ever clearly known. The professional training and organisation of English doctors conduce rather to their dignity, comfort and orderly behaviour than to any great skill in diagnosis, and the appendix, kidneys, liver, spleen, stomach, sympathetic system, musculature and obscure internal infections were mentioned without any compromising exactitude by the medical man in attendance as being among other possible causes of his discomfort and disease. The ultimate certificate alleged cardiac failure following a cold. No specialists were summoned, perhaps because too many would have been involved and their aggregate mileage beyond my uncle's means. Treatment at that distance from London was largely determined by the doctor's memory, such as it was, of his own and other treatment in apparently similar cases, and by the current resources of the local pharmacy.

My uncle supported considerable suffering with courage and a sustaining hopefulness. He was greatly touched by the fact that on one occasion when he was in pain the doctor responded to a call in the small hours, getting up from a warm bed and coming no less than two miles through the rain, and he was sincerely apologetic for the obscurity of his malady, and the bad hours it kept. I think he felt that he was being a little disingenuous and putting an honest friend in a difficult position not to have one simple definable daytime complaint. " You doctors," he said, " are the salt of the earth. What should we do without you ? "

My aunt died of pneumonia following upon a chill that she neglected while nursing him, and he lay for two or three days unaware of his loss.

He believed he would pull through almost to the end. " I'm a Tough Old Bird," he repeated ; and so he never gave me any last instructions about the world, and after he had realised, if ever he did fully realise the death of his wife, a kind of silence fell upon him. " Gone," he echoed dully to their tactful answer to his question where she was, and sighed : " Gone. Dorcas *gone*," and said no more about her. He seemed to retire within himself and think. He died three nights later under the ministrations of the village nurse.

Towards the end he forgot whatever pain he felt in a light delirium. He seemed to be wandering about in his world with the God he had always served, having things made plainer than ever to him.

" The wonder of the flowers, the wonder of the stars," he whispered.
" the wonder of the heart of man. Why should I doubt for a moment
that all things work together for good ? Why should I doubt ? "

And he said suddenly, apropos of nothing : " All my life I have gone
about and never marvelled how beautiful crystals and precious stones
could be. Blind ingratitude. All that taken for granted. The good
things taken for granted and every little necessary trial—a burthen."

A long time before he spoke again. Then he had forgotten his jewels
and crystals. He was debating something with himself—with a manifest
bias. " Never a burthen one cannot bear. If it seems heavy at times.
. . . No *real* injustice."

His voice died away, but later I heard him whispering.

My last memory of him alive is of his voice in the stillness of his
lamp-lit room when suddenly he mentioned my name. He must have
become aware of me standing in the doorway. The windows of his
bedroom were as wide open as they could be, but still he wanted more
air. " Fresh air," he repeated, " plenty of fresh air. Bring them all
into the fresh air ; everything into the fresh air. Then everything will
be well."

" Keep your windows open. Always keep your windows open.
As wide—as wide . . ."

" And don't be afraid of things, because God is behind them all,
however strange."

" Behind them all. . . ."

His expression grew strained. Presently his eyelids drooped and he
no longer regarded me, and his breathing became laboured and slower
and dry and audible.

For a long time that noisy breathing went on. Never shall I forget
it. It hesitated, resumed, ceased. The strained look passed. His
eyes opened slowly and regarded the world calmly, but very fixedly.

I stared, waiting for him to speak, but he did not speak. Awe came
upon me.

" *Uncle !* " I whispered.

The village nurse plucked at my sleeve.

In the morning when they called me to him his face was already a
serene mask, with the eyes closed upon the world for ever, still kindly,
but preoccupied now with things unspeakable. That ancestral marble
in the nave at Salisbury is the very man. Even to the folded hands.

I had a great desire to speak to him and say much I had wanted to
say, but I saw now that nothing could pass between us again any more
for ever.

Never was anything more saturated with absence as his presence on that sunlit morning. I sat by the bedside and looked for a long time at that dear mask that had been so familiar and was already so strange, and I thought ten thousand things up and down the scale of life. I was grieved at my loss and also, I remember among other things, I was meanly glad to be alive.

But slowly an unfamiliar coldness about my heart, too still and deep to be fear, began to dominate all other impressions. I tried to escape from it. I went to the window, and the sunlight on the downland turf seemed to have lost some magic gladness it had hitherto possessed. There were the familiar outhouse roofs, the grey stone wall of the yard, the paddock and the superannuated pony, the hedge and the steep rise of the hill. There they were, and they were not the same.

The coldness I had felt at the sight of my uncle's face was not less but greater, when I looked out upon that wonted scene; it was not, I perceive, a physical sensation; it was a chill not of the heart but of the soul, it was a new feeling altogether, the feeling of being alone and unsupported in a world that might prove to be something quite other than it seemed.

I turned back to my uncle with a vague sense of appealing against that change.

Again I was moved to speak to him and found I had nothing to say.

§ 4

LOVE AND OLIVE SLAUGHTER

FOR a time I went on without any fundamental change in the life I was leading. The first intimations of loneliness that had come to me at my uncle's death-bed hung about me and developed rather than faded, but I struggled to keep them out of my consciousness as he would have had me do.

I had already, after my graduation, taken modestly comfortable lodgings in the hamlet of Carew Fossetts, towards Boars Hill, on the outskirts of Oxford, and there I remained. A number of friends and acquaintances in and about the University made a social world for me, and there seemed no better place anywhere for me to go. I promised myself Long Vacations in the Alps, in Scandinavia, in Africa and the Near East, and perhaps some sort of footing in the graver but heavier world of London, and I counted the artistic stir of Paris among my happy possibilities. There I considered, after the fashion of the time, I could meet America and Russia in a diluted but sufficiently appreciable state. So on Russia itself I turned my back, it was a wilderness with a perverted alphabet and an unspeakable language, and I dismissed the bristling glories of New York, its exhilaration and its luminous exaltations, as disagreeable but avoidable fact. If people chose to go over there and be Americans and make a world of their own, I did not see why I should be interested.

I was conscious of a certain liveliness of mind and some ability, though I was never clear what sort of ability it might be, and I was very anxious to do well with my life. I was sensible of being fortunate in my lot and privileged, and I believed it was my duty to make an adequate return. This I thought I might do most agreeably by practising art in some form, and I played with such ideas as giving the world a trilogy of novels—in those days no novelist was respected who did not produce triplets—studying the art galleries of Europe after the fashion of Ruskin and recording my impressions, organising an artistic printing press to produce choice editions of meritorious works, or of turning my experience in the O.U.D.S. to account in the writing of plays. I also contemplated poetry, having some sort of epic in mind, but I found the technical ingenuities required hampered my creative impulse. I was not unmindful of the social issues of the time, and determined that a strain of moral and humanitarian purposiveness should underlie the perfect artistic expression of whatever I decided to do.

Moreover I had also been persuaded to take up the affairs of a moribund archery club as honorary secretary, with considerable success.

I discussed this question of the general disposition of my life with almost anyone who made no objection to my doing so, but particularly I talked it over with my friend Lyulph Graves, in whose company I was in the habit of taking long walks, and with Olive Slaughter, the lovely girl I have mentioned already, for whom my undergraduate admiration and friendship was fast deepening into a great ideal love. How bright she was and fair and fine-featured ! Even to-day I could recall a thousand lovely effects, did I care to pain myself by doing so. She was golden fair. She shone through the interstices of the packets of tobacco and cigarettes in the shop window like the sun through leaves. Even in my undergraduate days she would come to the door and smile at me as I hovered past whenever my various occasions took me in that direction—and it is wonderful how few of my various occasions failed to take me in that direction. She smiled with her brows and her eyes as well, and her mouth was this much short of perfect symmetry that the left side of her upper lip lifted a little more when her smile came and showed a gleam of teeth.

Opportunities recurred for brief surreptitious conversations, and in my third year they seemed to multiply. One early-closing day we met upon our bicycles near Abingdon and spent a very delightful afternoon together. We got tea in a cottage and afterwards, in an orchard which went down to the river, we kissed, atremble with the magic of forces greater than ourselves. I kissed her, I kissed the corner of her mouth where the little teeth were betrayed, and then I took her in my arms and drew her close and kissed her fine and slender neck, while her soft hair caressed my cheek. And after that we rode back together as far as we dared towards Oxford before we parted, and all the way back we said scarcely a word to each other. It seemed to me, and I thought it must seem to her, that the greatest thing in life had happened to us both.

The sunset was warm and soft and golden, and she was warm and soft and golden, and each was more wonderful than the other, and my soul was a mote in a sunbeam that shone like a star.

After that we both developed a great taste for kissing and, since I had been well brought up, I seasoned our embraces with gracious and noble interpretations. I talked between our kisses of the high aims to which our passions were to be consecrated, and all my thoughts surrounded her with protective possessiveness, as though I was a church dedicated to her and she was the holy altar therein. And so to kissing again. She kissed with such eagerness and caressed me so tenderly that only my sense of her perfect innocence restrained the ardour of my responses. And I was extremely happy.

Since my mind was filled to overflowing with her after our first sacramental act of intimacy, she became, almost in spite of my disposition to reserve, a constant presence in my talks to Lyulph Graves. He and I, after much debating of our destinies, had developed a very hopeful plan for a new sort of bookselling enterprise which was to be not only of very great educational value to the country but a source of wealth and influence to ourselves. In those days there was a considerable amount of discussion in England about the defects and enormities of the bookseller, and Blettsworthy & Graves was to be our response to these complaints. We were to appear in several towns, and ultimately in a great number of towns, as a series of shops, all coloured and decorated uniformly in an excessively recognisable art blue, and all communicating and economising and interlocking with one another. We were to do for bookselling what Boots the Cash Chemist was doing for chemists' shops. Our shops would be furnished like homes, with easy chairs and reading lamps, and our customers were to be talked to improvingly and tempted to read rather than pressed to buy. Directly it began to rain a sign would be put out : " Come in and Read until the Rain is over." And we contemplated many other such agreeable improvements on the bookshop of the time.

On our walks we would explain to each other—waiting impatiently until the other had done—how great were the advantages of our enterprise to ourselves and to mankind. We would buy in greater and greater quantities until we dominated the publishers, and we would win the respect and affection of the whole intellectual world. " We will," said Lyulph Graves, " *organise* the public mind." We would protect and stimulate good young publishing firms, and discourage and reform bad ones. I cherished the idea of an increasing critical and selective influence, embodied in a literary review, which was to have a cover of the same arresting blue as distinguished—in our forecasts—the façades of our shops. It would be a coveted honour, I decided, to contribute to this review. We gave a whole happy afternoon's walk to telling each other the people we would *not* let contribute.

We formed a company duly. We had a capital of four thousand pounds, of which each supplied half. As Graves had no money of his own, I lent him the necessary two thousand pounds at a considerate rate of interest. I was for taking no interest at all, but Graves, who was the soul of honour in money matters, overruled me. We appointed ourselves managing directors with a salary each of five hundred pounds a year, so that I found my private income increased rather than diminished by these commitments. We decided to open our first shop in Oxford. We secured a long lease of decaying, ramshackle but commodious premises between a butcher's shop and an undertaker, upon advantageous terms, and we had the whole house practically reconstructed with an office behind, filled with the most convenient and expensive desks and files, and extremely attractive apartments over the shop in which Graves proposed to take up his quarters so as to have everything under his eye. He insisted he must have everything under his eye ; night and day he would devote himself to our great enterprise.

We had the shop front repainted three times before we were satisfied that the tone of blue we had chosen spelt success—and certainly I have rarely seen a brighter shop. Our decorator unhappily appreciated our taste so highly that he overstocked the paint we required and, in order, he said, to use it up, persuaded a tea and bun shop in the same street to adopt what we had hoped would be a strictly distinctive hue. This brought us a few inquiries for China tea and buttered scones, but no doubt it also diverted the petty cash of a few potential readers into the path of mere physical refreshment. We took Counsel's opinion on the question of copyright in colour, but we found the legal position too uncertain for litigation.

Apart from this minor vexation, our enterprise opened out bravely. I recall that phase of my life as one of its happiest. It has always been a Blettsworthy tradition to ennoble rather than disdain business operations, and I saw Blettsworthy's Bookshops (Blettsworthy & Graves) spreading over the land and discharging as useful and honourable a task of exchange and stimulation in the mental world as Blettsworthy's Bank and its branches had discharged in the west of England. I saw myself guiding and inspiring without being too completely involved in the operations of a harder, compacter and perhaps more energetic partner. My life would be irradiated by the glowing presence of my Olive, and my ample and increasing leisure—as the business became more and more of a machine—would be devoted to the cultivation of my undoubted æsthetic and intellectual gifts so soon as their nature could be more precisely ascertained.

I am telling here of the secret thoughts of a young man, the high and comprehensive propositions with which youth faces life. Outwardly I bore myself with a seemly modesty, always conceding superiority and advantage to others, giving way politely, never disputing the pretensions of those who might seem to compete with me. But my heart was full of self-assurance. I felt myself to be unique and distinguished and that all about me had a quality of distinction because it was about me. I felt that a path of high responsibility lay before me. Graves, too, was a wonderful associate, amazingly capable, though all the finer concepts of our enterprise came from my own brain. And glowing topaz, fire opal, with her pale lips and amethystine eyes, was my Olive Slaughter, chastely passionate, honestly mysterious, a being of profound and outstanding loveliness, who would be remembered some day in con- nexion with me, though after a more legitimate fashion, as la Giaconda is linked with Leonardo, a star down the ages.

I have no portrait of myself as I was in that last phase of my content- ment. I doubt if my self-satisfaction and my immense ambitions betrayed themselves in my bearing. I dare say I seemed just one pleasant specimen of all the pleasantly youthful youths who went about the land in those days. At any rate, if I thought well of myself and mine, I also thought well of the whole world. And the bladder of my self- complacency was pricked soon enough and cruelly enough to avenge all who might otherwise be offended by my happiness.

I had run up to London for a few days to deal with various small matters of business. My solicitors, an old-fashioned firm I had inherited from my uncle, had gone rather beyond their professional rights in the criticism of my new enterprise and I wanted to reassure them about Graves. Moreover I had a fancy for giving Olive a necklace of green jade set in gold, that I wanted to see made exactly as I wished it. And one of the Sussex Blettsworthys was being married, and I felt I had to attend his wedding. I had engaged myself for four days altogether, but after I had seen my cousin married on the third of them, it occurred to me that I would dash back to Oxford a day earlier and delight Olive by my unexpected appearance in the morning. We were now formally engaged ; her mother indeed had accepted and kissed me with great appreciation ; I could now give Olive presents without concealment, and so I took down a very beautiful bunch of flowers to enhance my little surprise.

I went down in the evening, dining in the train, and I repaired to the new shop, of which I had a latch-key, to get my bicycle. There was no light in Graves' sitting-room above, and I concluded he was out. I entered, I suppose, noiselessly, and instead of taking my machine at once, remained hovering for some minutes, regarding the admirable and unparalleled appointments of the place. Few shops had arm-chairs and a big table set with books like a table in a club library. Then I perceived there was a green-shaded light in the office behind ; Graves, I thought, must have forgotten it, and I went in to extinguish it.

The office was empty, but upon the writing slope of the large bureau consecrated to Graves lay an unfinished letter of several sheets. I glanced at it and saw : " My dear Arnold." Why on earth had he been writing a letter to me ? When he saw me every day. I saw no harm in sitting down on his rotating arm-chair and reading it.

I began to read it carelessly, but soon I was reading with strained attention.

" There are some things best explained in a letter," it opened ; " and particularly questions involving figures. You are always a little impatient of figures. . . ."

What was coming ?

I had spent a very disagreeable two hours in Lincoln's Inn the day before, repelling what I regarded as old-fashioned detractions of the finance of our new company. Old Ferndyke (Ferndyke, Pantoufle, Hobson, Stark, Ferndyke & Ferndyke), who had been my uncle's school-fellow and had Blettsworthy blood on his mother's side, had suggested points of view about Graves that moved me to reply : " But, sir, that amounts to an insinuation ! " And old Ferndyke had answered : " Not at all ! Not at all ! Still, it is customary to ask such questions."

" Needless in the case of Graves," said I, and the old gentleman had shrugged his shoulders.

Oddly enough, I had repeated that conversation to myself several times during the night, being unusually wakeful, and it had been in my mind again after dinner in the train. Now it jumped into present reality as I read the next sentence of my partner's letter.

" My dear Arnold," it went on, " we are up against it."

The gist of the letter was that we had been planning our business on too bold a scale. He wanted to put that plainly before me. In the end that might not be a bad thing, but the immediate result was embarrassment. " You remember I told you at first that it was a ten-thousand-pound job," he had written. " It is."

In decoration, furnishing, preliminary expenses, office stationery and directors' salaries we had expended practically all of our available resources. We had hardly begun to buy stock. " In addition I have got an overdraft," he wrote, " up to the limit you guaranteed." I reflected—I had guaranteed a thousand, in an extremely tortuous and windy document. We were already paying wages to two assistants, a light porter and a stenographer for Lyulph's correspondence, and so far we had not formally opened for sale. We took down our shutters indeed and served casual customers, but we meant to reserve the éclat of opening in style until Term had begun. Then we had to make a splash, and a splash meant more expenditure. Most of the stock we contemplated had still to be bought, and we would have to carry on some months. In Oxford particularly there is a lot of inevitable credit business to be done. The callow undergraduate buys like a duckling feeding, but not for cash. " There is nothing for it," wrote Graves, " but to bring in fresh capital and go ahead. We can't go back now."

And here the writing trailed off. He would seem to have been interrupted.

I held the letter in my hand and stared into the brown shadows of my new bureau. More capital ? I had it, but I was getting near what Ferndyke called my safety line. Hitherto I had risked nothing but retrenchment ; this might mean a loss of the independence I found so pleasant. And the face of old Ferndyke became very vivid in the shadows, and his inquiry : " Isn't your friend just a little wanting in, what shall I say ?—ballast, as well as experience ? "

I looked round that very solid and impressive office. It had been very amusing to furnish it, but what if it did prove to be rather too big and heavy for the business to carry ?

And was Graves, my quick-minded and inventive friend, possibly by ever so little, less solidly weighted than, for example, this wonderful letter file of ours, capable of holding forty thousand letters ?

Upon these thoughts there presently crept a consciousness of various

creaks and stirrings over my head. Gradually they shaped themselves
into a realisation that Graves must be up there in his bedroom. I
might talk all this over with him. I *would* talk it all over with him now.
The flat had a private entrance on the street, and I went across to the
door that led from the shop into the passage and staircase. Shop and
staircase were carpeted with excellent but expensive blue Axminster,
the right blue, and I was in the unlit front room before Graves knew I
was there. The bedroom door was a little ajar and the gas was lit.

I was just about to speak when I was arrested by the sound of a kiss,
an access of creaking and a loud sigh.

Then, amazing, incredible, came the voice of Olive Slaughter in tones
that I recognised only too surely. " *Well !* " she sighed in tones of deep
contentment, " if you ain't the Champion Kisser ! "

Then Graves whispering and some sort of struggling readjustment.

" Stop it ! " said Olive Slaughter without conviction, and then more
more sharply : " *Stop* it, I tell you."

At that my memory halts for a time. I do not know through what
black eternities I lived in the next few seconds. The picture that follows
I see from the door of the bedroom, which I have flung open. Both
Graves and Olive lie upon the bed, staring at me. Graves has raised
himself upon his elbow. He is in boating flannels and a silk shirt which
is unbuttoned in front. Olive is prone and looks over her shoulder at
me, her blouse much disarranged, more of her lovely torso betrayed
than I had ever seen before, and her bare arm lying across his bare chest.
Each is flushed and dishevelled. Both of these faces gaze stupidly and
then very gradually become intelligent and alert. Slowly, moving with
extreme slowness and keeping their eyes on me, the two of them come
into a sitting position.

I seem to remember a phase in which I was asking myself what it
became me to do, and then more distinctly a provisional decision that
I had to be extremely violent.

Graves had considerable taste and, at the charge of our company,
he had decorated the mantelshelf of his room with two slender old
Chianti flasks. They were heavier than I expected because he had
filled them with water to steady them. One I hurled at his head and it
struck it, burst with a gulp and fell about him in water and fragments.
The second I threw to miss him and it poured out its water on the bed.
Then casting about for further material for violent demonstration I
think I must have turned to the washhand stand because I recall the
bursting of the full ewer against the bedpost and how disconcerting it
was to find the basin in my hand too light and flimsy for any effective use.
There seems to be another gap at that point. I found Graves standing

close to me with a thin red streak across his forehead that had not yet begun to bleed. His face was white and seemed luminous and his expression was an enquiring observant one. I replaced the basin almost carefully, I remember, before laying hands on him. He was no match for me in weight and muscle and I had spun him out of the bedroom and through the sitting-room and out upon the stairs in no time. And then I went back to Olive.

The divinity of my former life had vanished. In her place was a common young woman with tangled hair the colour of ripe corn, whom I had greatly desired and who was still inordinately exciting. She was struggling to replace a brooch that fastened her blouse at the neck. Her hands trembled so much she could not do it. Her expression was one of scared anger.

" You two dirty cads have put this on me," she said. " You and your partner. Think I don't see it ? You and your engagement ! Filthy sneaks ! "

I stood, not heeding what she was saying—though I recalled it clearly afterwards—wondering with what marvel of frightfulness I could strike her down. I cannot trace the storm of impulses that tore at me. But this I know that suddenly I laid hold of her and began to tear the clothes off her. She fought fiercely and then became almost passive in my hands with her eyes on mine. I stripped her body until she was next to naked and flung her on the bed. I met her eyes. I was aghast. Her hostility had gone ! God knows what abysses I hung over in that moment. Then in an instant my tornado had spun round into a new quarter. " Out you go ! " I said, and picked her up and bundled her after Graves.

For a moment I was in a panic at the thing that had come so near to me. I despised myself both for my desire and for my retreat from my desire.

I was at a loss what to do further and filled up the interval by striding about and shouting : " My God ! My God ! "

Then I remember the scared but still collected face of Graves in the doorway—he was bleeding now rather badly—saying : " Let her have her clothes, you silly fool. Everyone will say we did this together."

That was reasonable. That was very reasonable. In spite of a strong resistance reason was returning to me. But I still had to act amazingly. I thought for a moment, then scrabbled her torn and crumpled things into an armful and flung them suddenly upon Graves. " Both of you ! " I cried.

His head emerged from her dress. He gathered her clothes to him and turned about.

I heard him stumbling downstairs. " You can't go out in the street like that," I heard him saying.

Neither bedroom nor sitting-room seemed any longer the place for me. ˙I remembered my bicycle was in the shop. With an effort at dignity I went down to the door that opened into the shop and closed it behind me. I was now very calm and methodical. I felt my way to the bicycle, struck a match and lit the lamp. I thought of the letter from Graves I had been reading. It had vanished and I felt I could not go upstairs again to look for it. My bunch of flowers was lying on the counter near my bicycle handles. I had forgotten those flowers. I picked them up, smelled them, and put them down. I let myself out by the front door of the shop, mounted my bicycle and set off through the lit streets, over the bridge and out upon the silent high road that leads to Carew Fossetts.

I went to bed at once and slept well for the greater part of the night, and about dawn I was wide awake all of a sudden and asking myself what had happened to me.

I was annoyed when presently some birds began singing. They prevented my thinking clearly.

§ 5

INTERLUDE WITH MRS. SLAUGHTER

I FEEL that it is important to my story that I should tell all I can of the phases through which I passed in the days following my discovery. But it is not very easy to do. My memories are extraordinarily irregular ; now clear and detailed and as sharp as though they came from yesterday instead of a third of a life-time ago ; now foggy, distorted and uncertain, and now interrupted by gaps of the completest obliteration. I can find no sense nor system in this selective action of my brain. I cannot explain why I should recall my awakening that morning in the utmost detail and, if this is not being too subtle, it is in my memory of that morning that my memory of the overnight events is embedded. It is not as if I remembered directly throwing a glass flask at Graves, but as if I remembered, remembering doing so and wondering why I had done so.

Perhaps those wakeful hours are so impressed upon me because they were the first of a great series of similar states of mind. It was as if the whole universe, and I with it, had become something different, as if the self I had known hitherto had been a dream in a dream world, and this now was reality. The dawn came but it was the dawn of a new sort of day that was joyless ; the rising sun poured its warm light into my room and that light had no soul. The birds sang, and presently a cart creaked in the lane and a boy whistled, but I knew that the birds were but singing-machines and the cart going on a bootless errand and the boy, for all his unawareness, dead and damned.

I bent my mind to the insoluble problem of why I had linked all the motives of my waking life to this witless and vulgar demi-vierge and to a partner who would have been a knave had he not been, before his knavery had a chance with him, a vain and self-indulgent fool. And still more was I perplexed by the problem of disentangling the living threads of my heedless self from these two casually chosen associates.

But utterly incompatible with the main stream of my thoughts was something narrower and more powerful. Irrelevant and indifferent to the other memories was the figure of Olive Slaughter, half stripped as I had flung her on the bed, and the extraordinary expression on her face, staring at me, as her struggles died away. I despised her and in a way I hated her, but this vision had associated with it such an intensity of desire as I had never known before. What a fool I had been to break off and come away ! How can I convey the relationship of these different streams of thought that were going on simultaneously and very actively in my mind ? · It was as if I, a young savage, sat and brooded in silence while an old gentleman discoursed of Space and Time and Predestination and Free Will.

One part of my brain was scheming and planning how I would go back to Oxford and catch Olive Slaughter tripping—and beyond that it was utterly careless of consequences—while most of the rest of me was still demanding, in forms I cannot recall, what had happened to my soul and why my world was damned. Of Graves I thought little and with contemptuous hatred. I did not think so much that he had betrayed me with Olive Slaughter as that Olive Slaughter had betrayed me with him. And not clear but very present in my mind was a profounder reproach that in some way I was the betrayer, that with both of them—I could not determine whether it was before my discovery or after—I had betrayed myself.

But what self ?

Queer fluctuations occurred. I got up and flung her framed portrait which stood upon my chest of drawers into the fender. The glass cracked but did not break. Then I picked it up again and put it back. " You wait, my lady," I said, and told her in the foulest language what I meant to do to her.

After that comes the memory of cycling down through a warm morning to Oxford. I suppose I had breakfast and talked to my landlady and got through the intervening time until half-past ten or eleven, but all that detail is effaced. I suppose too that I had some idea of what I meant to do in Oxford, but my only clear recollection is that I observed that the leaves upon the trees were beginning to show a little red and yellow, and wondered whether that was premature autumn or only the effect of a spell of dry weather.

Graves had packed and gone. Our charwoman had found him gone when she arrived in the morning. She was puzzled, especially by the broken glass and crockery, the wet bed, which had not been slept in, and three hairpins she had found on the floor. I affected a not too extravagant interest. These things lay between her and Graves. " No doubt Mr. Graves will explain it all," I said, " when he comes back."

Then I seem to have made the errand-boy put up the shop shutters again, for our employees had assembled according to routine, and I paid off the staff. What stands out most distinctly among these incidents is that the flowers I had left in the shop had been put in a large ornamental bowl on the table in the centre of the book-lounge. I wondered transitorily who had done that. Paying off the staff in this way, seems to show that I had already decided to abandon the bookshops scheme completely. I suppose they departed marvelling. At this length of time I cannot remember either their faces or their names. I must have carried myself with the sort of gloomy majesty that repels enquiry or conversation. But at last they were all cleared out and, leaving the flowers in the bowl to rot, I went to the entrance and halted for a moment watching passers-by in the sunlit street before slamming the door behind me. My bicycle stood supported by its pedal against the kerb.

Suddenly I became aware of Mrs. Slaughter far down the street, hurrying towards me with gestures to arrest my attention.

I can still feel the twinge of disgust that the sight of her brought me. Disgust with a touch of dismay. I had forgotten Mrs. Slaughter.

There was my bicycle at hand but flight would have been undignified.

" Just a word with you, Mr. Blettsworthy, just a word with you," she said confronting me.

She was shorter than Olive and with an entirely different complexion. Olive's gold became ginger in her hair and the skin was ruddy and freckled in the extremest contrast with Olive's warm ivory. She had small brown eyes for Olive's blue, and she was flushed and a little out of breath. She was wearing her black shop dress and she had, as the expression went in those days, " thrown on a bonnet " with only approximate accuracy. Possibly one of my released assistants in passing had told her of my presence. Possibly she had called earlier in the day before my return.

I considered her for a moment without speaking and then made way for her silently into the darkened shop.

She had some sort of speech prepared. She adopted a tone of friendly and reasonable remonstrance. " What's all this 'as come between you and Olive ? " she asked. " What's this talk about breaking off her engagement and never seeing each other any more ? What 'ave you two young people been quarrelling about ? Not a word can I get from her, except that you're angry with her and lifted your 'and against her. Lifted your 'and you did. And she's crying 'er eyes out ! Crying 'er 'eart out ! Why, I didn't even know she was round 'ere last night. She slipped in like a mouse and upstairs. And when I went up in the morning, there she was in bed—sobbing ! She's been crying all the night."

In such phrases did Mrs. Slaughter open her maternal solicitudes upon me.

I spoke for the first time. " I said nothing," I remarked, " of breaking off our engagement."

" She said it was all over between you," replied Mrs. Slaughter with the gesture of one who is hopelessly baffled.

I leaned against the counter with my eyes on the innocent extravagance of my flowers, which seemed now like flowers laid on the coffin of my dead imaginations. " I don't think," I said slowly, " that it *is* all over between us."

" Now that's better ! " said Mrs. Slaughter warmly, and I turned my eyes upon her foolish face, discovering for the first time the infinite obtuseness of which mothers of daughters are capable.

" Then we needn't say anything about Actions for Breach of Promise or anything like that," she went on, crumpling up a long premeditated discussion that she had occasion for no longer, and hurling it at me in one sentence. I had thought even less of an action for Breach of Promise than I had thought of Mrs. Slaughter. I regarded the two of them together and they seemed to go very well together. " No," I agreed, " we needn't say anything about that."

" Then what's all the trouble about ? " asked Mrs. Slaughter.

" That," I answered, " lies between Olive and myself."

Mrs. Slaughter regarded me fixedly for some seconds and her face assumed a combative expression. She folded her arms and bridled her head. " Hoity toity ! " cried Mrs. Slaughter. " None of my business, I suppose ? "

" None, that I can see."

" And so the happiness of my daughter is no business of mine, isn't it ? I'm to keep off the grass, eh ? While you break her heart ? Not it, young man, not it ! "

Mrs. Slaughter paused for a reply, and I made none. I refrained from pointing out that the happiness of her daughter was not what I had in mind. My silence disconcerted her, I think, because her debating strength lay largely in repartee.

The interval lengthened. I remained polite and patient. Mrs. Slaughter modified her personality by a few swift alterations and came closer.

" Now look here, Arnold," she said with a rich motherliness that made me happy to be an orphan. " Don't you and Olive go flying off at nothing and make a couple of young fools of yourselves. You know you love her. You know you do. You know she thinks of nobody in the world but you. I don't know what it's all about, but I'm pretty well sure it's all about nothing. Some jealousy or something. Don't I know ? Haven't I been through it all with Slaughter years ago ? Wipe it out. Don't think of it. There she is crying herself ill ! Come back to her. Give her a kiss and tell her it's all right, and in ten minutes you'll be kissing each other again like the two pretty love-birds you are. Stop sulking. I can't abear a sulk. Come right back and settle it, I say, and 'ave done with it. It's getting near lunch and I've got a bit of mutton on the boil. Never 'ave you honoured my 'umble 'ome yet, by staying to a meal. Honour it now and 'ave done with all this 'uffy high and mightiness. Kiss and be friends and stay the afternoon. Take her out somewhere. That's my remedy, Arnold. I can't say fairer than that."

She paused, and anxiety peeped through her geniality.

I came near the crowning insult of calling her " my good woman." I spoke as one who has pondered. " Mrs. Slaughter," I said, " I can only repeat that the present trouble is between me and Olive. I want to go through it with her—alone."

Mrs. Slaughter was about to interrupt, but I raised my voice. " And not to-day. Not to-day. Sometimes things have to cool off, and sometimes they have to—ripen."

Her face fell. She was repulsed. She became aware of something she had not hitherto observed. " Why is the shop all shut up again ? "

" It is shut up," I said, " for business reasons. But that again is a matter I am quite unable to discuss now."

" And Mr. Graves ? "

" Isn't here."

That at any rate was the gist of our talk. She said some more things of no great moment, went through long passages *da capo*, and at last

departed to the call of the boiling mutton. For a long time I seem to
have stayed in the shop doing nothing.

Then I remember myself with one foot on the pavement and a leg
over the saddle of my bicycle ready to mount. I am asking myself :
" And now where the devil am I to go ? "

§ 6

COLLISION IN THE DARK

I SAT at tea in the dark and shining dining-room of the " Spread Eagle "
at Thame, which in spite of its minuteness is in the list of the Hundred
Wonderful Inns. The landlord, who was wearing a bottle green suit
with brass buttons, honoured me by talking to me.

" Did you ever lose yourself ? " I asked him.

" And find somebody else ? "

" I'm looking for a certain Arnold Blettsworthy who vanished about
sixteen hours ago."

" We all play hide and seek with ourselves. Was Arnold Blettsworthy
a young man full of hopes and ambitions ? "

I nodded.

" They go very suddenly."

" Do they ever come back ? "

" In the end. Sometimes. Sooner sometimes. And sometimes not
at all."

He sighed, looked out of the long low window and suddenly perceived
something that needed his attention. He left me with an indistinct
apology. He did not return, and after awhile I paid the maid and went
off upon my bicycle towards Amersham. Shyness prevented my waiting
overlong for him. I was sorry he had not resumed our conversation
because the quality of his voice and his manner had attracted me and he
seemed to understand my trouble. But if he had come back to me I
should probably have talked of other things.

I rode on into a great loneliness.

I rode aimlessly through the warm evening of a late summer day,
turning myself eastward to keep the sunset out of my eyes. I was
pursuing some recondite problem about my own identity. Was Arnold
Blettsworthy no better than the name and shell of a conflicting mass of
selves ? I knew the Blettsworthy standards of honour and goodwill

by which I ought to be steering my course through my present perplexities. I knew them perfectly. What astonished me was the stormy
whirl of lust, brute lust, mingled with anger and masquerading as the
justice of self-vindication, which was thrusting aside all these standards
and disciplines as though they meant nothing. Who was this Angry
and Lustful Egoist who struggled to take control of my will, whose one
supreme image was Olive, stripped, dismayed and unresisting? Not I.
Surely not I. In the old days they called him the Devil—or a devil.
An interloper in possession. Does it alter him so very much to call
him in the modern fashion a secondary self? But was I Arnold Blettsworthy or this other? By the side of this great complex of passion that
sought to tear the direction of my acts out of my possession, another
alien spirit of shame and contempt, the Cynical Observer, thrust himself
into the confusion—with evil advice. " Fool you have been," he urged,
" and fool you are. Fool and weakling. Why all this indignant pos-
turing? If you want the girl, take her, and if you hate her get square
with her. But set about her so that you come to no harm. You can
make it her own act and not yours. Her eyes told you your power
over her. Ruin her and get away. Though why she should enslave
your will like this and drag you towards shame and danger is more than
I can say. That first glimpse of a warm and supple body was too much
for you, my boy. This comes of being an excitable virgin. Was it
so very marvellous? Are there no others in the world? I ask you, are
there no others in the world? "

Not along country lanes but through that turmoil of motives did I
steer my way that afternoon. Among other forces I remember a strong
craving to get myself once more into communication with the spirit
of my uncle. If only I could recall his presence and his voice these evil
forces would be robbed of half their power. Maybe something of him
lingered still among the Wiltshire hills. But when I turned my face
westward, the sunset levelled its spears of gold and thrust them into
my eyes and beat me back.

Did I pray, you ask? Did I find any help in the religion of my
world? Never for a moment. I realised as I had never done before
that it was my uncle I believed in and not in that kindly God the light
of his goodness had projected upon the indifferent sky. I never gave
the God of my professions a thought in all my trouble. I could as soon
have addressed myself to Sirius.

It was dark at last and my headlamp was still unlit. I came round a
corner and discovered within a yard of me the back of a tradesman's
van, dimly lustrous in the twilight. I thought it was moving on and
made to pass it, and then its back panels foreshortened as rapidly as a

conjuring trick and I realised it was turning round too late to avoid a crash.   I can see now my bicycle handles moving swiftly to their impact against the big wooden wheels and feel my loss of balance and my belated impulse to turn.

To that point I remember simply and clearly, and then I vanish completely out of my own memory.   Probably I went over and was hit by the van.   There is no record.   Certainly I was stunned.   But it is queer I do not remember anything up to the instant of being stunned. The light goes out, so to speak, while I am still only just coming into touch with the wheels and side of the van.

§ 7

MR. BLETTSWORTHY FORGETS HIMSELF

ALTOGETHER

MY explicit personal narrative must give place here to a vague and circumstantial one.   Of the events of six weeks there is nothing but blankness in my record.   I have never been able to find out what became of my bicycle nor how I reached Oxford.   I did get back to my lodgings in Carew Fossetts late that night, in a cab and with my head bound up and properly dressed.

I seem to have loitered about Oxford for a week or even longer.   I attended very incompetently to my business affairs.   I learnt that Graves had availed himself of his guaranteed overdraft to the utmost and had accepted a post with a trading company on the Gold Coast.   I think he wrote me a letter promising reparation and repayment and expressing some regret.   Probably he did, but I doubt if the document survives. I do not seem to have let Mr. Ferndyke know of my business betrayals and distresses.   I suppose it would have been too great a come-down for me after my recent posturings of assurance.   Instead I took a shabby little Oxford solicitor, chiefly concerned with the affairs of the betting touts who lie in wait for undergraduate sportsmen and forbidden minors, into my confidence, and made some very rash and disadvantageous dispositions of the assets of our company.   All this has been quite effaced from my mind.   I seem to have made two and perhaps more efforts to see Olive Slaughter alone, but she may have told her mother she was afraid of me, and anyhow these tentatives came to nothing. A formidable bandage over one eye may have detracted from the natural innocence of my appearance. I think somehow that I gave way to violent fits of rage, but I doubt if I did that in the presence of other people. There is the shadow of a memory to that effect. There was never any action for Breach of Promise.

Nobody knew exactly how and when I left Oxford. I went my lone way and was only missed by my landlady. My debt for my apartment was settled up afterwards by Mr. Ferndyke and he collected my effects. My movements for three weeks are untraceable. At the end of that time I was found wandering along a back street in the outskirts of Norwich. I was found at three o'clock in the morning by a policeman. I was mud-stained, hatless and penniless and in a high fever. I gather I had been drinking hard and taking drugs and I had evidently been in low company. I smelt strongly of ether. I had completely forgotten my name and who I was, and there were no papers on me to establish my identity. From the police station they sent me to the workhouse infirmary, and there an intelligent nurse, noting that my clothes were tailor made, looked in the inner pocket and found the Oxford tailor's label with my name and college on it, and through that narrow channel reopened communications with my lost and forgotten circumstances. Meanwhile I remained in bed, not answering to my name, suffering from an illness and too apathetic to make an easy recovery.

A new consciousness gathered itself together slowly but surely. There is no definite movement of its beginning. I have a vague impression of being removed to a paying ward and made more comfortable, and of being pleased to hear that Mr. Ferndyke was to come and see me there. I remembered his name as of an amiable person while my own still eluded me. My first intimation of returning vitality was a wave of aversion from my particular nurse, a chattering creature, with meagre flaxen hair, very hostile to two men whose names she reiterated endlessly in an exasperating refrain, " Hall Dane " and " Hall Caine," as she went about her business. Hall Caine was, I realised, the great romancer, and one of his heroines, Gloria Storm, had given her umbrage by being represented as a passion-torn nurse ; Hall Dane emerged with greater difficulty as Lord Haldane, who had made some changes in the status of the army nurse. I lay and hated her, and suddenly recalled a visit of Lord Haldane to the Union. And that brought back some phrases of a speech by Lyulph Graves, Lyulph Graves rising up from the seat next to mine.

I was Arnold Blettsworthy of Lattmeer ! The memories returned like a reassembling school. They got into their places, nodding, shouting out names, and calling to one another. . . .

Came old Ferndyke a day later, rosy and spectacled and solicitous.

His face, round and clean-shaven, enlarges in my recollections, becomes more than life-size, more than individual.

It is as though I saw him through a big lens. A face as kindly as my uncle's, but with a worldliness my uncle's never betrayed. A fold above one eyelid droops a little and makes his rimless glasses seem a trifle askew. His hair just touched with grey over one ear is as smooth and neat as the fur of a cat. He watches me as he talks, like one accustomed to difficult dealings with men.

"Neurasthenia," he says assuringly. "A run of mischances. It might happen to anyone. You just went down. There's nothing to regret or be ashamed of."

He seemed to consult his pink left hand. "I could tell you things about my own start in life," he intimated with the effect of a daring confidence. "But it just happened that luck didn't conspire against me. 'The ample proposition that hope makes' . . . In some form, my dear Mr. Blettsworthy, we all go through it. But usually—less violently. You were taken by surprise. Nothing for us that I can see but to pull ourselves together and go on living according to our best traditions and our true selves."

"I want that," I said.

"I'd like your instructions. What are we going to do about it all ? "

"If you'd advise, sir," I submitted.

"Precisely," he accepted. "Now, first, don't bother about the mess at Oxford. Leave us to clear up all that. That can all be settled. Mr. Graves and the overdraft *gone*. Write that off. The particular bad end he will come to is for God to decide. The other entanglement—well, the mother is not unreasonable, particularly now she thinks you are insolvent. Don't worry about these things. But for the present you are cut off from your roots. You are very much in the air. You will feel that life is very empty and aimless if you let yourself drift back to Oxford or London. *Ergo*, don't drift back to Oxford or London. Get clean away and come back to England with new perspectives. Travel. I come to it, you see—*travel*. A voyage round the world. Not in great passenger liners nor in hotels de luxe, but rather more humanly. In trading steamers and on muleback. I believe that can be very beneficial—very beneficial. See how many sorts of transport you can use between here and California, starting East. That would be interesting. And, possibly, you might even write about it."

"Like Conrad," I said.

"Why not ? " asked Mr. Ferndyke, betraying no elation that I nibbled at his hook, and making no cavil about the probability of my writing like Conrad. "It will be a healthy life. Your nerves will recover. You will get over your little illness. And I think most of the preliminary arrangements could be saved you. Romer, of Romer & Godden, the shipowners, is your cousin once removed. You met him at some wedding, and he liked you. Their ships go here, there and everywhere, and they can put you aboard any of them, though few carry passengers, as their clerk or purser or supercargo, or what-not. They can send you to all the ends of the earth—which are endless. You can see work, you can see trade, adventure, *real* adventure, something of the Empire, much of the world. You have known the Upper Thames long enough— a rivulet for boys to splash in. Go down now to the Lower Thames which is the estuary of the whole world. Start there again. You have lost your youth and that is gone for ever. Granted ! What of it, Mr. Blettsworthy ? Go out and find the man."

Mr. Ferndyke stopped short and coughed and blushed. He had been betrayed into rhetoric. His eyes watered slightly, or he imagined they did. He took off his glasses, wiped them, and replaced them askew exactly as they had been before.

" In short, Mr. Blettsworthy," he resumed briskly, " I advise a good long sea voyage to begin with. Your affairs are disordered, but there will be quite enough still to keep you independent. Everything can be arranged."

CHAPTER THE SECOND

Tells how Mr. Blettsworthy put out to Sea and of his Voyage and how he was Shipwrecked and left on a Derelict Ship and how Savages appeared and captured him.

CONTENTS OF CHAPTER THE SECOND

CHAPTER THE SECOND

MR. BLETTSWORTHY CHOOSES A SHIP

In the presence of Mr. Ferndyke I could be almost the Blettsworthy I had been before my disillusionment, but when after a second interview in London in which his suggestion was more fully developed and accepted, I went out from his office across the pleasant spaces of Lincoln's Inn into the busy gully of Chancery Lane, I felt a very insecure and uncertain being indeed, with a desolating need of reassurance. The echoes of hard laughter and foul memories clung to me from my days of anonymous vice, and I had learnt something of the meanness of trusted fellow-creatures, and something also of the vile cellars in my own foundations. Mr. Ferndyke, on this second occasion, had given me exactly twenty minutes of his time, glanced up at his clock and bowed me out. He was very helpful, but he was a transitory helper. I wanted a Friend. I wanted a Friend who would listen unendingly and with comforting interpretations to my personal exposition of my perplexities.

"The sea! The round world! Mankind!" Fine words they were, but I wished I had made a better response, wished I had been able to make a better response.

For example I might have said; "Right you are, sir. Trust a Blettsworthy to make good."

Queer how one can think of saying to a man things one could never possibly say to him.

I liked young Romer, who was not a dozen years my senior, and he too gave me all the help he could in the time at his disposal. In his case that was nearly half a day. He talked of ships that were going here and there, and their reputations and merits. Should he give me letters of introduction to people at the ports of call? Mostly they would be business correspondents, but some I might find pleasant. He fingered a list. Would I like to go to Manaos right up the Amazons? That I could do quite soon. An interesting line would be the Canaries, and then across to Brazil and down to Rio. Or—yes—we could skip the Canaries. Or I could go East. A big consignment of stoppered bottles and cheap sewing machines, celluloid dolls, brass images, paraffin lamps and cotton thread, patent medicines, infant food and German clocks were going to Burmah. What of Burmah? Would I like to look at an Atlas in his anteroom for a bit, with his list before me?

It was heartening, it gave me a fine sense of mastery to take the whole world and peruse it like a bill of fare.

In the end we settled on the *Golden Lion*, bound in the first instance for Pernambuco and Rio.

§ 2

MR. BLETTSWORTHY PUTS OUT TO SEA

How many thousands of men must have shared with me the delusion of enlargement I experienced as I stood on the quivering deck of the *Golden Lion* and watched the shores of Kent and Essex gliding past me and reefing themselves up towards the London I had left behind! It seemed to me that evening that I was passing out from a little life to freedom and adventure, and that the man I was going to find was bound to be all the better for the taste of salt in the search.

The vast, low, crowded realms of the docks on either hand, where houses, inns and churches appear to float on the water amongst ships and barges, had gone; where Tilbury's ferry-boat pants across to Gravesend, little yellow lights popped out one by one and soon multiplied abundantly, and now the great city itself was no more than a fuliginous smear beneath the afterglow, and the flats of Canvey Island were streaming by on one hand and the low soft hills of Kent upon the other. The blues of twilight deepened towards darkness and Southend's glittering sea-front was in line with us, and the long pier pointed at us and then turned its aim towards London. The Kentish watering-places, mere stains of illumination upon the selvage of the night, drifted by and passed away. Vivid eyes of light, yellow and red, that winked out and returned and winked out again in significant rhythm, and sweeping beams of whiteness, guided our outward course, closed in behind us and receded and sank, and at last, save for a remote uncommunicative musing ship or so, lit without regard to us, lit egotistically for its own protection, we were alone and at sea.

And I felt that night that I had come out into something vast, whereas indeed I was for the first time in my life a prisoner.

The literature of the world, and particularly the literature of us who read English, is full of the assumption that to go to sea in a ship is to go out into the " open." But there is in truth no " open " in the world but the roads and paths in a land of kindly people. The lights and multitude are left behind, the ample space in which one can move, the events and the changing scene. Nothing remains at last but night—blank night. You go below, come up again, pace the restricted deck, feeling that you savour immensity. You turn in and sleep. The creaking dawn seeps into your darkness and makes the swinging oil-lamp smoky yellow.

You stare about you before you realise your new circumstances. You recognise your things still half unpacked. Everything is engaged in mysteriously pivoted motions and slowly changing its level towards you. The sky outside and the horizon have joined in that slow unending dance. You get up and dress staggeringly, and blunder up the gangway to the deck and clutch the rail. Water. An immeasurable quantity and extent of water about you and below, and wet and windy air above ; these are the enormous and invisible walls of your still unrealised incarceration. Every prison on land has at least a door upon the world, even though that door is locked, but this prison needs no locks to enforce your complete captivity.

Mr. Ferndyke had meant well in sending me to sea. I think he had judged me very acutely, but he had no judgment about the sea. He believed by habit and tradition that to go to sea, and particularly in a ship not adapted to passengers, is in itself a lovely and exalting experience. So my uncle would have thought also. Britannia our land rules and is ruled by the waves, and the wounded soul of the Briton in trouble returns to them as a child to its mother. The sea winds search our island from end to end, and it is the peculiar blessedness of England never to be a hundred miles from the redeeming waters. All of us Blettsworthys, it is understood, revert to the sea by instinct. Directly we get our sea legs we are happy and at home. I did my best to feel happy and at home, but that morning my sea legs had still to mature. Yet I clung to the rail and waved my head from side to side like a sea dog, and hummed the refrain of a nautical song—the only nautical song I knew. I can still recall the words, because suddenly I became aware of their peculiar incongruity to my circumstances, and broke off in mid-refrain.

> " See there she stands and waves her hands to Jack at sea,
> And every day while I'm away she'll watch for me.
> A sailor's lass, a sailor's star should be.
> Ye ho, my lads, heave ho ! "

I was crooning that extremely inappropriate song to keep my doubts off. Already there were doubts. I must be in the key of my shipmates whom I knew from every writer in our language, were specially, distinctively and even extravagantly, *men* ; salted men ; hard and tough upon the exterior no doubt, but tender and delicate beyond description at the core. A certain ungraciousness in the captain's overnight reception of me, a certain vileness and violence in his diction—he had interfered to contradict the mate as the ship had manœuvred down the river, were merely the superficial roughness on the rind of this precious human fruit.

Our wake trailed away like an ineffective story and lost itself behind, and our smoke streamed far to leeward. Someone was partly visible at the wheel in the little house upon the bridge, and there was a remote head and back forward ; otherwise I could see no shipmates at all. Swaying and tumbling water, a greyish-blue sky and nothing but ourselves.

This, with a few variations of sky and wave, was, I reflected, the appearance of three-quarters of the globe. This was the normal scenery of the planet Earth. Landscape was the exception. It was well to remember that. The poor crowded souls ashore were turning their backs on three-quarters of our world. I felt a moral disapproval of such behaviour.

I did my best to appreciate the honest manliness of the five fellow-creatures who shared this detached fragment of man's world with me. For five souls was now for an indefinite time the full tale of my kind. Of the rest of the population of the ship, with the exception of Vett, our deft little steward, I saw hardly anything before our landing at Pernambuco.

A glimpse of a stoker taking the air or of three or four men engaged upon some incomprehensible job under the direction of the second officer, or the sound of a concertina laboriously acquiring and never achieving a music-hall tune and suffering sudden and apparently violent extinctions, and small knots of men forward sitting about on a fine evening or so, gossiping and sewing and the like, were all the reminders I had of the lower classes in our little sample of human society. Between them and ourselves a great gulf was fixed. Their motives, it was understood, were not our motives, nor their thoughts our thoughts. We six were of a finer clay and led a higher life. We spoke to them sparingly and distantly. It was as if some intense quarrel was insecurely battened down and might at any time flare up again should that tension be relaxed. As I went about amidships, I could feel that the black entrance of the forecastle was watching me and judging me shrewdly, and I was not in the vein just then to like being watched and judged.

No doubt my peculiar state of mind made me a hypercritical and difficult companion for these five on whom my company had been imposed. Upon my sanguine youth and inexperience, which had rushed out upon the world with the most generous interpretations, had fallen quenching disappointment and disillusionment. I had bruised and crippled my capacity for accepting my fellow-creatures. I had lost confidence with them now, I was distrustful and a little afraid of them. I tried not to quail or retreat within myself, but I was not at my ease with them, and so my first attempts at cordiality and fellowship had a real and manifest artificiality. And from the first, no doubt because of faults in my bearing and accent and conduct, and, possibly also through some grievance about having me thrust upon him, the Old Man took a grudge against me.

He was a sturdy, square-faced, ginger-haired individual, with sandy eyelashes and a bitter mouth. His little grey-green eyes regarded me poisonously.

" Third time I've had a bastard passenger on this blasted supercargo stunt," he said, when Midborough, the second officer to whose care young Romer had committed me at the dock, introduced me to him. And he turned away and took no further notice of me.

His second attention was also indirect. " Vett," I heard him bawling, just as my thoughts were turning to coffee—Vett was the steward. " Have you called our extra super-*gentleman* ? "

More than a little disconcerted by these preliminaries, I set myself to the job of developing my new relationships as pleasantly as possible. Everything plainly turned on the captain. The engineer, by all rights and traditions, ought to have been a Scotsman, but instead he was a huge, dark, curly-headed, strongly Semitic type, with a dropping lower lip and an accent he seemed to have baled up from the lower Thames. The first officer was a thin, small, preoccupied, greyish individual, with a gift for setting sententious remarks in wide stretches of silence. He picked his teeth a great deal, and agreed with the captain in everything, even before the captain had finished saying it. Midborough, the second officer, had a Nordic fairness, boninness and pallor, and bore himself discreetly towards the captain, a discretion that verged on panic in the case of Rudge, the youthful third officer. Seeing how dominant the captain was, I made the mistake of addressing myself too frequently and too exclusively to him, for, like royalty, a captain is not supposed to be led to his topics, but to choose them. And sheer dread of my own terror may have deprived my manner of deference. I should have waited to see how the others spoke to him and imitated them.

Moreover, since I was a very young man with little knowledge of the world beyond Wiltshire and Oxford, for my unfortunate lapse into vicious living was already banished from my mind, I had, if I was to talk at all, to talk about myself and Oxford affairs or the little I knew of books and sports and plays. Or about the Blettsworthys. My idea was to make myself known to my companions and to provoke similar confidences, but I quite see now that much that I said may have struck them as limited and egotistical.

" Have you ever gone in for archery, Captain ? " I asked.

The captain paused in his eating for a moment and then made a sound that was partly a short, sharp bite and partly the word " *What ?* "

" Archery," I said.

The captain put down his knife and fork, and regarded me very earnestly. That pause, which I began to feel was in some obscure way interrogative, lengthened.

The mate broke the spell. " It does actually occur," he said. " Toxoffery, they call it. I've seen 'em at it at Folkestone. Missing great targets like the behind of an out-size wash-basket. You'd wonder how they could do it."

" It's great fun," I said, " with a green lawn and a sunny day."

" If you've nothing else to do, possibly," said the engineer.

" Brings back Robin Hood and his merry men," I elaborated, " Old England and the golden age. The grey goose-shaft, and all that." I changed to reminiscence. " One or two of the dons' wives shoot uncommonly well."

No one had anything further to say about archery, and another long pause ensued. I was about to ask the captain whether he had ever gone in for amateur theatricals when he himself broke the silence by putting some highly technical question about the cargo to the mate. I listened attentively in the hope of making some contribution, but if the topic had been chosen specially to exclude me it could not have silenced me more effectively.

" What," I asked at one point, " are these bulkheads you speak of ? "

Nobody answered me.

I struggled for some days to make my poor conversational stuff acceptable and to work my way to a reasonable intimacy, but gradually my heart failed me. These five men did not want me on any terms I could make ; they did not want me at all. My first clumsy tentatives faded and died out. I became a more and more passive listener to the sagacities of the captain, the sentiments of the mate, the conversation of the engineer, and the acquiescences of the two junior officers. But they had conceived now so profound a contempt for me and such a distaste for my company that they would not let me efface myself, but set themselves to devise little sarcasms, allusions and annoyances that would hurt and embarrass me. The engineer invented a brilliant insult. At first he had called me " Mister," now by imperceptible degrees he dropped the second syllable and at last addressed me plainly as " Miss." The captain, in his more genial moments, and generally these came towards the end of a meal, developed a strain of lewdness in his talk that was honestly relished and echoed by the engineer and deferentially applauded by the younger men. The mate became wood and gave no sign of either approval or disapproval. " I'm afraid we shock you, Miss Blettsworthy," said the engineer as a refrain to every " good one."

I scored a point by an effort.

" Not at all," said I to the hundredth repetition of the engineer's refrain. " I used to know a dirty old man in a pot-house at Oxford who could have given the captain points and a beating."

That got a round of silence. " Don't you believe it," said the mate belatedly, and as though taking soundings.

" This old fellow had a rare stock of limericks," I said. " And they *were* limericks."

I had heard a few things in my time and I trotted out one or two of the fouler samples. No one dared laugh, and the captain glared at me over his serviette.

" I didn't think it of you, Miss," said the engineer reproachfully.

Then the captain struck to crush.

" If you can't keep a clean mouth at table, Miss Blettsworthy, you'll have to take your meals in your cabin," he said, and I found no retort that seemed adequate. " Thought you liked such verses," I said, and added for the first time the respectful " sir " used by my companions.

The captain grunted dreadfully.

But after that his discourse sweetened considerably, and the engineer's fear of shocking me vanished from our talk. Nevertheless, I felt that my presence carried with it a miasma of hostility and distrust, and perhaps even more social embarrassment than before. Between meals I was forced to sulk alone or sleep. Did I drift towards a shipmate, he edged away. The days in that spell of good weather and steady steaming seemed measureless and made their slow retreat through labyrinths of twilight into interminable nights. The clock fell asleep and did not stir. The junior officers played some game of cards which elated or depressed them alternately. The engineer read endlessly, and the mate gave himself up to lethargy. The captain was usually invisible.

I borrowed a book or so from the engineer, who lent them reluctantly, volume by volume, and with stringent stipulations for their proper treatment and return. He lent me a very worn volume of Helmholtz' "History of the World," dealing with the Tatar dynasties and China, a book on "How to Ski," and Stanley's account of the rescue of Livingstone. He was engaged himself chiefly with Kirke's "Text-Book of Physiology," trying to master the structure of the brain from the descriptions and plates, and becoming perplexed and cross about it. I did my best to get some talk going with him apropos of these books, but I had nothing to offer but comments, and he wanted nothing but facts.

He bought all his books, he told me, second-hand, from barrows in the London street markets and he never gave more than a shilling for one. He liked a *big* book about actual things. He contemned fiction as deceptive. He read with his loose mouth open and generally scratched his cheek as he read. What he read seemed to pass deeply into him, none remained upon the surface and he resented any probing questions. He would stare in a startled way when questioned and answer defensively or evasively. He insisted that I should finish each book he lent me before I began another. The Tatars ended me. I promised myself that at Pernambuco I would buy every novel in English or French that I could discover.

More and more did I long for Pernambuco. The slow days followed one another with minor variations. Sometimes the waves increased and sometimes they diminished under the variable wind, there were several days of greasy swell with no wind at all, the engines pounded, the ship quivered and creaked, everything was slightly querulous, the deck seemed always seeking a satisfactory angle with the horizon and perpetually failing in the attempt, the man with the concertina forward made his desperate efforts to get through the tune that was always suppressed, and never for a moment could I efface my consciousness of that same endless, inhuman wilderness of water that pent us in.

The stars I found more companionable than anything else in my restricted world, and I waited for them to appear as one waits for the return of a friend. They grew brighter, they seemed to glow larger as we slanted southward into the tropics. The Milky Way became a more

and more lively smear of glittering powder. I was glad I knew some of
the stars by name. Orion and Sirius I was sure of, Canopus (which
ascended upon me), Arcturus and Rigel in the corner of Orion I guessed
at with some confidence. Friends of mine and I nodded to them. The
Great Bear followed the Pole Star down and down ; I began to look out
for the Southern Cross, and was disappointed and incredulous when I
found it. Presently a crescent moon crept out of the sunset night after
night and became arrogant as it grew and spread a luminous blue over
its conquests and banished all but the brightest stars out of the invaded
heaven. I would stay on deck far into the night, sky-gazing, and sleep
far into the day, for the night was less tedious and lonely and perplexing.

Gradually over the raw distresses of my mind spread a defensive
surface of Byronic scorn that for a time protected me greatly. I was a
scorner of filth, a friend of the best stars. I held on to rails and stanchions
less and folded my arms more. For a nervous readiness to respect I
substituted a cold taciturnity. I brooded over my disappointments and
my vices and found a sombre consolation now in both. Little they knew
who called me *Miss* Blettsworthy ! But, oh God ! The length of those
days and the hopes I had of Pernambuco !

§ 3

LANDFALL AT PERNAMBUCO

As we came in to Recife, which is the real name of the place people call
Pernambuco, as we came into the outer harbour, I had that same delusion
of imminent emancipation I had felt when I steamed down the Thames
from London. The town seemed to open itself out to me in a wide and
various invitation. We had emerged from the lonely wilderness and
every quay and street and building spread like a limitless offer of escape
from this vibrating shuttle of salted and rusting iron in which we had
crossed the Atlantic. The forecastle deck was a bunch of expectant
figures and their postures expressed the same surmise of release. I tell
of these things now with understanding, but at the time I was quite
carried away by the general illusion. I felt so glad, I could have been
gay with the captain had his bearing invited gaiety. I forgave the
engineer with all my heart, in my heart. It was difficult to keep my arms
folded and remain even outwardly Byronic.

But those who give themselves into captivity to the sea do not get away from it again so easily. Each one of that smiling multitude of houses which seems to offer itself to the incoming voyager is in reality furnished with locks and bars against him. Such doors as stand open upon the quays are traps for his thirsty and lusting and lonely soul. The custom house will scrutinize his poor luggage and seem to motion him onward to the amplitude of the new land, but behind the customs and the port authorities there is drawn a cordon of those who prey upon his immediate needs and weaknesses. He is offered transparently false love, false fellowship and stale and meretricious fun. Should he by a great effort of restraint disentangle himself from these, he will wander on to streets of shops displaying things it is useless for him to buy and among people with habits, ways of thought and language altogether different from his own. Tramways and omnibuses invite him to come aboard and visit suburbs and quarters with unheard-of names, that, when he reaches them, do not want him to the ultimate degree.

Hope dies only with life, for life and hope are the same, and so the sailorman goes on his way through the town still looking for his share in the ease and freedom of human intercourse that seems to flow so naturally and yet so inaccessibly about him. To be paid off is only an intensification of his essential homelessness on shore, for now there is not even the return to the ship at the back of his mind. When I saw my shipmates ready to go ashore for the night and all more or less togged-up for the adventure, it seemed to me highly improbable that we should ever reassemble again. But we reassembled surely enough. The captain changed into a genteel person with a high-low felt hat and a pinch of handkerchief conscientiously displayed at his breast pocket ; the engineer was wonderful in ginger cloth and a tie of a promiscuous splendour. Midborough and Rudge became incredibly common in dark blue suits and bowlers and departed like twins ; the men were similarly trans-figured. " See how nice we are ! " cried these earnest efforts at personal decoration. " Have you no welcome here for such gentlemen ? " So one after the other, sons of hope, we turned our backs on the *Golden Lion* and went ashore, and the chief officer left in charge of the ship watched us go. Pernambuco showed no excessive dismay nor pleasure at our invasion.

Would any lucky one of us penetrate those intricate defences and at last get through to humanity ? The town lit up as we went ashore, but it did so indifferently with no air of reception and with still less endorse-ment of our expectation.

I have seen other ports and harbours but that going ashore at Pernam-buco still sticks in my memory as the quintessence of my impression of the sea. The sea is part of the great outside and it is a cant that would incorporate its vast desolation with the human world. We detach our floating packages and thrust them across the watery wilderness and upon them these marginal men are obliged to go, because they have lost their foothold on the dry land.

Perhaps my memories are coloured by the mood of disillusionment which was creeping up to an absolute empire over me, perhaps the obvious delight of nearly everyone on the *Golden Lion* to get away from the rest has become exaggerated and generalized since I first observed it. I admit the steady deepening of the pessimistic hues of my mind in those days. Nevertheless, even now I find myself still thinking of the sailor as a man trying perpetually and most desperately to recover his terrestrial rooting, staying ashore whenever he gets a chance, sticking there until hunger and his inadaptability to any other sort of earning push him back with no excessive gentleness towards the sea again. There he must live once more a crowded prisoner at the end—fore or aft, according to his degree—of one of these pounding and floundering, water-washed iron cases loaded with goods he will never consume, and commodities the very use of which is for the most part unknown to him. And each time he draws near to land again, his hopes of getting back to the main of human life revive.

I went off into the town alone.

Young Romer had given me a letter to a business correspondent with whom the firm cultivated friendly relations. He was a Dane but he was understood to talk English. That night he had left his office and gone home and the place was locked-up so that I put up at an hotel without advice and was thrown back upon my own resources for amusement. I found very little. I dined in a restaurant kept by a Swiss from Ticino, who talked some English and helped me to order my food and afterwards I went back to wandering in the streets. They were either wide and well-lit or murderously dark and narrow. I tried to go into a theatre, but I suppose I was too late and anyhow, for some reason, they would not let me in. I could not understand their explanations. I would have gone with one of the prostitutes who solicited me for the mere sake of human company, could I have found one who had more than a few gross words of English. As I stood at last, tired and defeated, on the entrance of my hotel before turning in, I saw Midborough and Rudge pass by, their faces were flushed and eager and they were in the company of a huge negro who discoursed as he went. So they at least had found a guide and were going somewhere. I was disposed to follow them but I did not do so.

I remember I sat on my bed for a long time before I undressed. " Am

I a lost soul ? " I asked myself and " Do I hate mankind ? What is wrong
with my world or me that amidst a quarter of a million human beings
I am sitting here, solitary in body and soul ? "

§ 4

VILLA ELSENEUR

MR. ANDERSEN, to whom I presented my letter next day, did little to
help me in my perplexity, though he showed the most hospitable will
imaginable. His English was abundant and enthusiastic rather than
good—he had acquired it mainly by reading—and unless one was to
interrupt him constantly, one had to let very much of it go past one.
Since he was evidently disconcerted by the want of comprehension I was
obliged to betray ever and again, I had to pretend to a slight deafness.
But that brought to light that he had begun life as a medical student in
Copenhagen and was still an eager amateur doctor. We spent nearly
half an hour over an examination of my ears. His verdict was that my
ears in themselves were structurally perfect but that I suffered from
soul deafness due to the egotistical preoccupations of youth. He then,
still talking rapidly, took me out to lunch at the same Swiss restaurant
at which I had dined over night. It was a particularly good restaurant
he said and no foreigners ever discovered it. "

He warmed himself with some excellent Brazilian wine, a distinctly
generous red wine of which I have forgotten the name, and as his tem-
perature rose, his English became more definitely Danish with fragments
of French and other Latin ingredients that I suppose were Portuguese.
But it went slower and on the whole I understood it better. He explained
the country to me with the animosity of an alien of dissimilar race and
religion whose chief business was to cheapen local products and ship
them abroad, and to sell foreign commodities to the reluctant native
buyer. Yet he had married a Brazilian wife. He retailed frightful
anecdotes of unpunctuality, jobbing and dishonesty and gave me an
impression of a population which spent its infrequent working hours in
the production of sugar and its saint's days, and other leisure in dancing,
horse-racing, gambling, intoxication, adultery, homicide and the las-
situdes, anxieties and conflicts arising out of such pursuits. And finally
he invited me to lunch at his home outside the town, on the following

day, which was Sunday, and to play tennis with his family.

His daughters, he boasted, knew English, but they knew it only to avoid it and I conversed with them and their mother in simplified yet conventional French. The mother was handsome and dark and frankly and stoutly middle-aged ; the daughters were tall and handsome with flaxen hair and tawny skins and very fine dark grey eyes. They competed for me pleasantly until two young Brazilians drifted in with a flavour of proprietorship and a joyless attitude towards me. Conversation became Portuguese and rapid. The racket of one of the young Brazilians had been lent to me and I gathered he objected to the way in which I used it to pick up balls, but I considered it more comfortable not to understand what was said and went on with my scooping—but now with greater care. Everyone played tennis as badly as I did, the court was a dust court and very loose in patches and the game was full of surprises. When both the young Brazilians had lost their tempers completely, we had tea.

Mr. Andersen, who had gone away to sleep, reappeared refreshed and talked syncopated English faster than ever while Mrs. Andersen purred to me in French. The young gentlemen refused to talk or attend to anything but Portuguese and the young ladies struck out wildly so that you never knew from moment to moment whether they were really talking Portuguese or only giving a peculiar quality to French. I talked English and French about half-half. In this way we compared our views about Wagner, Nice, the Corniche road (for some time I supposed we were discussing the Cornish coast, but that did just as well), the Monroe Doctrine, the morals of Edward the Seventh, the peculiar charm of Paris and its many resemblances to Recife, the richness of vegetation in the tropics, moths, wasps, snakes, and the newly-introduced game of bridge. At least that is my conception of what we were talking about. They may have had a different version. I was agreeable to exercise my mind again so freely after the pent-up concentration of the *Golden Lion*, but after a time I experienced a certain fatigue. My hosts, I think, experienced a similar fatigue. But fearing this fatigue might be observed and interpreted unfavourably, we all of us redoubled our conversational efforts, except for the young men who presently withdrew towards the tennis court and made signs and noises, supposed conventionally to be inappreciable by me, indicative of a desire for the company of the two daughters.

To cover their defection, Mrs. Andersen launched into a vividly interesting but nearly interminable description of something which was either the brilliancy of the South American humming birds or the splendour of the indigenous flowers or the glorious colouring of dying fish caught from tropical seas or the splendour of the Carnival decorations and costumes, or all, or any, or none of these things. But it was a very beautiful description and her gestures and intonations were charming. " Mais oui," said I, " Mais oui."

When at last I went, the Andersen family still battling nobly with their baser impulses, heaped invitations upon me for the next day, for the day after that, for any day, invitations I accepted with effusion in the same spirit. But the more taciturn of the two daughters injected quite a new factor into the talk by remarking quietly at the last moment and with her eyes far away : " We are yost by our selfs in the wik-days."

I perceived it would be ungracious not to call again.

I called again several times.

When I think of those odd visits to the Villa Elseneur, it is as if I thought of myself peering through curtains of dark gauze in the hope of discovering a fellow-creature who might or might not be there. The younger Andersen, by a mere intonation of her voice, had conveyed to me that mystical promise of feminine fellowship for which the soul of man hungers and thirsts perpetually. It was a promise she never redeemed, never even repeated, which probably she had never intended to convey. But it kept me alive in Recife. I called ostensibly to make a fourth at tennis with the two girls and the mother, for in the weekdays their betrothed Brazilians were about their commercial activities in the town. Andersen was by way of being an Anglomaniac and very progressive and his girls had a freedom which was still unusual in Brazil in those pre-war days. They even went about upon bicycles in the safer parts of the district, their skirts showed their ankles and their collars revealed their necks. And they conjugated a wonderful English word " flirt." With regard to the younger sister, there arose a convention that I was " son flirt "—and surely nothing could be more English than that !

I never got beyond that. I never penetrated those gauzes. On one occasion in the garden when we were alone together, it seemed to me just possible that she might have wished to be kissed but the opportunity passed before I could put her intentions to the test. She may have thought me unenterprising and unworthy of further chances. I cannot now recall with any precision what it was put that idea and that hesitation into my head. And it was hard to see what sort of triangle I should have made with her fiancè if that kiss had been given and returned. I bought her and her sister chocolates and her mother immense bunches of flowers. We whacked the tennis balls about and talked French that was at once abortive and decaying and fell back on tennis to escape the strain. We did not talk to convey anything to each other, we talked to conceal the fact that we had nothing on earth to convey. That phantom promise faded away to nothing and when the *Golden Lion* had finished its un-loading and loading and was ready to put to sea, I was as prepared to go as any other of the crew.

Something I had not perceived before, something almost like an attenuated friendliness, pervaded the steamer as the sunset swallowed up the town. It was a beautiful serene evening; our luck with the weather was holding out. I asked the second officer if he had had a good time and he said he had had a damned sight too much work and responsibility and only three nights ashore, grumbling to me quite amiably about the apathy of the mate and the uselessness of the third officer, and when I showed the engineer the books I had bought, he expressed his disapproval of such trash without any personal hostility. The mate agreed with me that Recife was the centre of a growing railway network and the third officer passed me the salt unsolicited. But the captain remained implacable.

This irritated me. He made noises with his soup at dinner and suddenly it occurred to me to make exactly similar noises with my soup. Everyone else looked startled and the captain regarded me over his soup spoon with a malignant interest that was manifestly brightly revived.

I made a prolonged, tumultuous finale to my soup. Then very calmly I put down my spoon and waited patiently and with an expression of quiet interest for the captain to finish his. He did so in a subdued manner and he was very red in the face. The mate and the engineer threw up a conversational sound screen for him and the mate also helped with a cough. Midborough was aghast, but respect mingled with the terror in the eyes that met mine.

At the time I felt I had had a brilliant inspiration, but in the doubtful hours of the night I did not feel so pleased with myself.

I had done an entirely undignified and offensive thing and I was ashamed. I hated and I despised the captain in order not to fear him and now I had brought myself down to his level. And I feared him still. I was no Blettsworthy.

§ 5

PASSAGE TO RIO

I HAVE told of these opening experiences of my voyage round the world with some particularity because I want to convey, as well as I can, the background and conditions against which my mental trouble was slowly developing. For in truth, the story I have to tell is at its core a mental case.

After the first breakdown of my will and memory, I had supposed that I had nothing more than an adverse accident to deal with and to recover from. I had accepted the view that I had merely to break with a particular set of associations in Oxford and London and begin again and all would be well, but now my doubting mind in the interminable small hours presented me with much more intricate and far-reaching interpretations of my distress.

It added much to my uneasiness that after Pernambuco the weather ceased to be uniformly benign and an increasing bodily discomfort gave an undertow of physical apprehension to the upheaval of my ideas. Blind matter joined now with humanity in the work of undermining my confidence and courage. Was I becoming sea-sick? Amidst these scoffing enemies. It was an intolerable thought. But I struggled against it in vain. I tried an amateurish Christian Science to subdue the treason of my diaphragm. Anticipating Coué I kept repeating : " I am not sea-sick. I am not sea-sick." At dinner that night I decided that I was and left the slanting table suddenly and ingloriously.

That night the storm increased and my cabin, which had been heaving and swaying and creaking more and more, seemed to lose all sense of its ancient association with the sober, solid land. It leapt and bounded, it rushed up and up, and when one was wholly reconciled to the idea of a continual uprush, then it stood on its head, reflected and went down abysmally. It lay over suddenly on its side. It pretended to be a cork-screw twisting into the waters. It pretended to be a swing-boat at a fair. It altered its mind ; it was an elevator—that had broken and was falling down an endless shaft. And now it was a switchback railway coyly leading its passengers to the sickening, screaming dip. Then discomfort changed to alarm. Frightful concussions made the whole ship dance and quiver. Frothy water came into the cabin like a lost dog in search of its master, rushed about, wetted abundantly, and went out again. Everything loose in my cabin leapt hither and thither ; a pair of boots departed in the custody of a wave and never returned ; I twisted my wrist horribly and bruised a knee. My water bottle got free, lived dangerously and broke and left its splinters chasing madly from side to side in search of a hand or foot. Five days I had of that sort of incident. After a time I ate, though still the sickness returned in fits. I drank hot coffee with increasing comfort and wolfed the bread that Vett brought me.

The four or five days I spent in my cabin during that storm with no one to heed me but Vett, the very intermittent steward, and one limited visit from the second officer and a few unanswerable interrogations from the engineer, have become the setting in my mind for a whole tornado of vague and cloudy perplexities that did in reality oppress me both before and after that period. I did not so much think these riddles as toss and roll and heave while they grimaced and whirled about me. I was both hungry and sick under their reiteration. Only by putting the issues disjointedly and amorphously can I convey anything of their actual values.

The broadest fact, the foundation fact so to speak, of the situation, was this, that I had started out in life with the completest confidence in myself, mankind and nature, and all that confidence was gone. I had lost all assurance in my personal character ; I had become alien to and afraid of my fellow creatures and now my body was in hideous discord with the entirely inhospitable world into which it had come. Never had I dreamt of the feebleness of its powers of adjustment and self-protection when matter and chance in their incomprehensible preoccupations saw fit to turn against it. And this ill-omened, lonely and limitless voyage upon which I was going was the supreme folly of a nature essentially and hopelessly foolish. Why, why had I turned my back on my proper world ? Why had I let old Ferndyke pack me off ? I had been happy, or at least if I had not been exactly happy, I had fitted in.

The astonishing thing to think in that wet, heaving misery, riding my buck-jumping berth with difficulty and dodging the sacrilegious blows of my own luggage and furniture was that I had once been happy and stable. I had walked the resounding earth with firm and confident paces and laughed like a friend at the stars. I recalled the sunlit downs of Wiltshire and the evening streets of Oxford as an experience of incredible beauty, static beauty. Had it ever been real ? To that world, to the life of comfortable, prosperous people in the centre and broad south of England I was adapted. I could understand their conventions, trust them, live honestly, conduct myself easily and surely among them. By merely taking a step out of that world socially my troubles had begun. And now I was going farther and farther away from it !

Yes, but was I not abnormal in my excessive inadaptability ?

I remember a swinging rhythm running through my brain, " abnormal, normal, normal, abnormal, normal ? "

For instance, I was the sea-sickest thing abroad. Had any of the others qualms, uneasinesses ? Had they in the past suffered like this ? Did they possibly suffer now ? I watched Vett narrowly. Was he really comfortable ? He staggered a lot. He looked pale and wet. But he stuck to his work and brought me coffee. And while I was wallowing in this black conviction of my complete unfitness to live, were all these others or some of these others just not giving way to similar depressing forces ?

Tougher perhaps.

Then this friendlessness ; what was it ? Had I an abnormal inability to mix ? Or was I merely hyper-sensitive to a universal failing ? Did any of them mix ? Or were they all in truth just as utterly lonely as I— without in some way knowing it ? Did they not note how little they communicated ? But if they were all going about the world alone, what became of the delusion of human society ? About Oxford one said " How do ? " and " Hello ! " and had a feeling of limitless possible responses. Had that been so ? Or had one simply imagined it was so ? Had there ever been these possible responses ? If I went back now, now that I had lost my youth, should I find Oxford and Wiltshire and friendship again ?

After all, friendship in the chosen person of Lyulph Graves had turned itself round and displayed itself as hollow as love. And if all that dear world was no more than a dream, if this hideous pitch and toss amidst the seething waters was waking up from such dreams, to what was I awakening ?

For some days I think I had a fever and talked ramblingly to Vett. Then with an effect of rapidity the wind abated, a blazing sun set itself to dry the decks of our little cast-iron world, the creaking and groaning of the ship resumed a more familiar rhythm, the ponderous caperings of the waves became a regular and dignified dance and wearied slowly towards a heavy swell. I found myself hungry and in courage. Vett helped me to restore a sort of order in my cabin and I shaved a stubbly beard off very painfully, got some dried underclothes, attended to my tie and collar and went to eat.

" Come back to life again," said the engineer with something like friendship and his mouth full. " You know a bit more than you did of what the sea can do."

" You get worse than that round the Horn," said the mate. " Any time."

" Beans," Vett offered. Preserved baked beans out of a can. " Rather ! " How good and filling they were !

" I had a book once," said the engineer, " that told about the force in the tides and the waves. It's something terrific. There were calculations in that book. They went a little beyond me but they were something striking. You could build a big tower and run all the trains in Europe and light almost everywhere with the force that wastes itself in one bit of a blow like that. All gone to waste. Wonderful, eh ? "

" Don't you believe it," said the mate.

" You can't go against mathematics," said the engineer.

" We live on the surface of things," I said, but nobody could find a handle on that remark.

" I've seen a place near Newhaven where they tried to make use of the tides," said the third officer with an effort.

" A failure ? " said the mate.

" All broken up again, sir."

" I thought so," said the mate. " What did they think they could use the tides for ? "

" I don't know, sir."

" Nor them either," said the mate, with profound contempt.

The captain said nothing to that. He sat looking before him at unknown things. His face seemed whiter, harder and more viciously intent than ever. His white eyelashes masked his eyes. What, I wondered, was he thinking ? " Rio," he said suddenly and with extraordinary bitterness in his voice. " *Rio.*" No one answered—and indeed what could one answer ?—and he said no more. For a moment the mate regarded his colleague with an eye slightly cocked to one side and then turned his attention back to his meal.

" You'll find plenty of better men at Rio," said the engineer, suddenly reading the captain's thoughts.

§ 6

ENGINES OUT OF TUNE

WE went into Rio and Rio pushed me and my shipmates back into the sea with no more ado than Pernambuco, and after that the *Golden Lion* smelt strongly of coffee and a mixture of rum and vegetable decay, and steamed into ill-luck and evil acts.

I was greatly depressed at our departure from Rio. There I had been even more lonely and difficult with myself than at Recife. I had not even an introduction to any people like the Andersens and so I put up alone in a second-rate hotel and entertained myself as well as I could and that was not at all well. I was astonished at the size and vigour of the place, the tropical vegetation and sunshine, the handsomeness of the great avenue—I forget its name—which is the Champs Elysées of the town, and at the endless resorts and pleasant beaches on the sea-front.

It was astonishing to discover that these South Americans had watering places far jollier than Brighton or Bournemouth. They had opened a new Art Museum full of good modern pictures and I spent hours in it, and the cinema theatres, the large, good cinema theatres, were a great help to me. Those were the days when Charlie Chaplin was shown freely and abundantly without any fuss, the good old days of the cinema. The population struck me as far more prosperous and happy than our people at home. I could have been quite amused there with any congenial companion, but I was now reduced to such a condition of social ineptitude that I could scrape acquaintance with no one. I had a meretricious encounter or so of which the less said the better. How excellent and merciful a profession the courtesan's could be, were she but sustained by human respect and did she but know how to touch and console the hearts of the lonely souls who resort to her ! But I could buy nothing but harsh laughter and the clumsiest assuagements of desire. I tried to drink but my Norwich adventures had left me with a vague distaste for drink. And my whole being now was crying out for friendship and intimacy. I prowled through the city's prosperity asking if this multitude which seemed so pleased and gay could really be human and not realise my desolate need for humanity. Or was all this place no more than a collection of animated masks that looked like a friendly community ? Such fancies were growing upon me.

For one thing I could not speak Portuguese. Surely there are enough barriers between man and man without these complex estrangements of language ! But often I heard English spoken and twice I saw such pleasant-looking compatriots going about, a family of five people in one case and a couple of tourists whom I guessed to be newly married, that I followed them until manifestly I attracted their attention and aroused their suspicions. I followed them stupidly without inventing any way of accosting them and attaching their interest. My isolation was becoming a paralysing obsession.

And after all, I asked myself, what had I to give them ? Was I, too, anything more than a mask ? I had yet to find humanity not only in the world about me but within. Suppose these good-looking people had suddenly turned a glow of geniality upon me, asked me to sit down at lunch with them or go upon some excursion in their company and got me talking, what had I to tell them ? What could I have done to entertain them or co-operate with them ?

So presently the ship's company assembled again. We were pushed back to the seas, as the Monday morning worker goes back to his factory and the miner to his seam, because there is nowhere else to go and nothing else to do. Back we came to our clanking prison and worked our seaward way athwart the mighty harbour.

That evening " clanking prison " seemed to describe the *Golden Lion* very exactly.

" Mr. Midborough," I ventured to say to the second officer whom I found standing beside me ; " this old clock has changed its tick."

He replied. " You ! " he said. " You notice it too."

I went further. " Did anything happen in that storm ? I fancied we were a bit out of tune even before Rio. There was a sort of catch in the beat, though nothing as bad as this."

He came a step nearer. He addressed the Brazilian hills in a low meditative voice, speaking between his teeth. " The old man is as obstinate as a bloody mule. If He says the engines will last out to Buenos Aires, it doesn't matter what the engineer says—not a bit."

" It doesn't seem to matter what the engines say," I remarked.

We both turned our backs upon Brazil and listened to the ugly melody.

" Falling to pieces. Every bump may be her last. That one ? No. On she goes. That's the bent part. Hear that one ! The bearings swim in oil, but oil isn't everything. And the engineer sits and reads."

I awaited further confidences.

" There were cables sent to London," he said. " The captain said one thing and the engineer another. Buenos Aires is where we have the overhaul. The captain insists. And if the weather holds, why not ? "

Mr. Midborough regarded the open sea with a speculative eye. Manifestly he lacked confidence in the weather.

" There's a sort of man," he reflected, " who never learns he isn't God. Never. What he says *is*. And when what he says turns out not to be so, it's Hell and Tommy for all the world. But he keeps on being God all the same and looking for someone to vent his holy wrath upon."

§ 7

THE ENGINEER'S REVOLVER

I HAD been vaguely aware that there was trouble between the captain and the men before we went into Rio. But my intense and morbid self-preoccupation had veiled my observation. There was some sort of dispute at Rio about discipline and pay which involved a visit to the

British Consulate. There was shouting in the street and a police agent
was invoked. " It was pretty tough of the Old Man," Rudge had said
to Midborough coming aboard ; " but " but perhaps now we shall be
happier."

No good asking questions about a remark it was not my business to
overhear.

Midborough had said something about too many Dagoes.

I gave some attention to the crew and noted one or two new faces and
missed a man or so. That concertina had gone ashore at Rio and never
returned.

I speculated a little about the connexion between this trouble with the
forecastle and the sense of tension at the dinner table. I suspect that it
was the captain's established habit of mind to be at war with his men.
He was a man who found life obdurate and the only sensitive part of
this obdurate system upon which he could relieve his feelings were the
men. Perhaps there is a flavour of class-war between the ends of every
tramp steamer and the class-war cuts both ways. But only after Rio did
I get any intimation of the grim possibilities beneath those scowls and
moody silences that had nipped my early endeavours at sociability so
fatally.

I went to return a book on Co-operative Dairies in Denmark, with
Statistical Charts and Diagrams, which the engineer had recommended
for light reading, and I found him with a newly-cleaned revolver in his
brawny paw and a neat row of cartridges for reloading, on the bunk
beside him.

" That's heavy for a toy," I said.

" It isn't a toy," said the engineer.

" What do you want it loaded for here ?—with two hundred miles of
sea to anywhere or anything ? "

" That's just it," said the engineer, and seemed to weigh the wisdom
of further confidences. He decided against me.

" Have you read that book *through* ? " he asked after a pause. " I
doubt it. You skim over life, young man. You skip everything. You've
what I should call the mind of a butterfly."

He paused, and seeing I was still looking at the squat blue-black
weapon in his hands, he made his remark more general.

" That Oxford of yours," he said, " to my mind, turns out nothing
in the world except butterflies and clothes moths. Flitting and nibbling
and making little mean holes in things. No grasp to it. The place is
just an insect incubatorium."

" I've read the book through."

His grunt called me a liar. " All I've got to lend you now is Robinson,

Functional Diseases of the Lower Bowel. You've got a Lower Bowel of your own, but will that make you read it ? No ! "

" Have you tried my novels ? "

" Dustyovsky wasn't so bad. The rest muck. But Dustyovsky's interesting in a way. I've figured out the roubles and kopeks in Dustyovsky in shillings and pence. Some of the stuff was twice as dear as in London and some of it not half."

He slipped in his last cartridge, shut that enigmatical revolver with a satisfied click, listened for a few seconds to the stuttering noise of the engines and turned with an air of escape to his little cupboard full of second-hand books.

§ 8

THE CRY IN THE DARKNESS

I DO not know what happened in the darkness and I reproach myself because I do not know. I ought to have pushed myself into that affair. I have said, I think, that I suffered increasingly from insomnia and that I had a habit of prowling the deck during the night. But on this particular night I wakened out of a sleep and I had an impression that I had heard a shot. But perhaps I had merely had a dream suggested by the engineer's revolver. A flapping cord could have given the necessary sound. But I was uneasy. I sat up and listened for a time and then pulled on some clothes and went on deck.

We thrust our heaving way through an oily swell that broke to a faint phosphorescence against the side ; the sky was covered with thin uneven clouds through which the waning moon shone fitfully. I went forward. For a moment everything seemed quiet. High above me a dim man on the pale moonlit deckhouse stood at the wheel as indifferent as God. On the forward deck a dark figure looking ahead, was as rigid under a swinging light. Then I became aware of something astir in the darkness amidst the deck hamper near the forward hatches. I felt rather than saw a group of people clustering about some sort of tussle and perceived, at the same time, that one or two watchers were standing quite still in the shadow about the unlit entrance to the forecastle. Then suddenly a sharp cry, almost a scream, and a voice, a youthful voice that gasped as if in agony ; " Oh ! Oh, for God's sake ! "

The captain's voice came hard on that. " Will you do your work to-morrow—properly ? "

" Yes.   Yes, if I can.   Oh !   Oh, for God's sake !   I will.   I can."

Came a silence that seemed long to me.

" Let him go," I heard the mate's voice.   " He's had enough."

" Go ! " the captain answered.   " Could a shirking swine like that ever get enough ? "

The mate's voice sank a little lower.   " It's not only him I'm thinking of."

The captain responded forcibly.   " Let 'em *all* come," he snarled.

" I'm with the mate," said the engineer, and the captain cursed again.

There was a sound as though a heap of rope knots had been flung on the deck and then a whimpering in the darkness like the whimpering of a hurt and frightened child.   I was stirred to go across and intervene and I was afraid.   I stood rigid in the moonlight.   Silence fell again. The mate said something I did not catch.

" He's shamming," said the captain, and then : " Lend a hand there some of you and put him in his berth."

Then the thud of a kick.

A light appeared in the forecastle and I had a glimpse of figures moving.   Muttered talk.   " I'll have what I say attended to," came the captain's voice.   " While I'm at sea I'm the master of this ship. . . . British Consul be damned ! "   Some inert object was carried forward and swallowed up in the forecastle.   The figures of the captain, mate and engineer came out against the pink illumination, standing quite still with their backs to me, looking forward.   The engineer spoke in a low tone, a tone, as I fancied, of remonstrance.

" Damn it ! " cried the captain wrathfully ; " don't I know my own business ? "

They moved towards me.

" Hul-*lo* ! " cried the engineer, discovering me.

" Well, Mr. Snooper," said the captain, peering into my moonlit face.   " Keeping an eye on us, eh ? "

I made no reply, I had nothing to say, and the three men went on past me aft.

Forward a raucous voice began talking interminably out of the depths. Other voices injected a word now and then.   The men seemed all awake.

Above me the man at the wheel still steered as if in a dream.   The lookout man had gone back to his place on the forward deck if ever he had left it.   The staggering engines still beat us onward.   But the moon in its thin halo and its drifting rags of cloud, and the silently heaving sea lazily reflecting the slow flitting moon-glow had become now in their smooth acquiescence like conspirators in some terrifying deed. What had happened? In that outcry there had been an intensity of agony.

" Manhandled," the word came into my head, an evil word.

I went back with a hushed mind to my solitary cabin and lay awake until dawn.

Was there no way of doing the world's affairs without the brutalising of men?

§ 9

BURIAL AT SEA

NEXT morning Vett remarked that one of the men had overstrained himself and was thought to be dying, and after our midday meal, which was even more than usually sullen and constrained, Rudge told me the man was dead. The engineer was invisible; he was down below amidst his complaining machinery. Or else I would have asked him some questions. Rudge professed entire ignorance of the cause of the man's death. Was I to know nothing?

I saw something long and white lying on a hatch forward, and approaching discovered it a stiff unmistakable outline wrapped in a blanket. I stood for a time regarding it and the four or five men who were standing and sitting about it stopped their talk and watched me in an enigmatical silence. I thought of questioning them and did not do so for fear of what they might tell me and the fires my questions might release.

I felt myself challenged in some manner for which I was unprepared. I looked up and the captain was leaning on the rail of the bridge watching me with a wary hostility. I went to the side and put my face between my hands and considered. Should I go and question these men? Dared I go and question these men? I told myself I would first talk to Vett.

But Vett was pinned to the vague word " Overstrain."

The next day the weather, which had been dull and warm, began to change. The swell increased and the ship rolled more and more. The screw, which had been going slow, stopped, went on again and stopped again.

In the afternoon the dead man was committed to the sea. Nearly everyone aboard, except the stokers, the engineer and the three hands working with him and ever and again hammering with a vast clangour below, appeared at the ceremony—so far as it was a ceremony. The body had been sewn up in rough packing canvas and was laid, feet straight to a port, on two greased boards under a dirty red ensign. But contrary to established practice, it was not the captain but the chief officer who read the service. The captain had inverted their rôles and remained in charge of the ship overhead. The mate hovered for a time, inspected the position of the body and then quite suddenly produced a prayer book, stared for a moment at the ominous sky as though he thought it had said something, and set himself to read the burial service, reading in a detached querulous manner. He seemed to protest against the whole business. I had placed myself beside Midborough at the rail and held my hat in my hand. Almost everyone was uncovered. The captain kept to the bridge, hunched and immobile, watching like an owl from its tree, and the men stood or squatted about in sullen groups, saying very little. Two of them stood ready to tilt the body overboard.

I was preoccupied at first with the tense humanity of the scene so that I paid little heed to a strangeness in the atmosphere. For a while I forgot the weather. I perceived that in the bearing of everyone was a quality of uneasy foreboding, as if they felt that something impended, and to me, the most obvious connexion was with the secret undertow of this melancholy event. Everyone I thought must be bursting with things that remained unsaid. Accusations seemed to smoulder in every face ; threats bided their time. Beyond this present autocracy of our grim-faced captain the land awaited us and law and its doubtful, tedious essays at justice. Ahead there were surely denunciations, assertions, witness and false witness, the doubtful verdict. What would the mate there, hurrying now through the service, have to testify ? What would the engineer have to tell ? Would they lie to save the captain and themselves ? Would the reality of the darkness remain in darkness for ever ? What had the men seen ? What did they know and what did they guess at ? Would they combine upon a common story ? What was the truth about that bitter passion in the darkness, or was there any truth ? If I were called upon, what exactly had I to relate ? How would my story survive a cross-examination ?

The mate read on. Dimly then I became aware of the gathering physical storm that enveloped this mental one. As he read, reading badly and with little regard for punctuation, the swelling sea behind him would rise slowly but steadily until it seemed far above his head and then sink again and pass out of sight, leaving him as it were outstanding against the sky.

But that sky, I apprehended suddenly, was of an unusual brightness and yet almost white. Its customary blue had become shrill! And forthwith my consciousness was pervaded by the swift onset of a storm. I stared up at the great hemisphere at whose centre we rolled and wallowed. Behold! half of it was sweeping ascendant blue-black cloud, with ragged swirling edges. Even as I looked up those edges became a clutching claw and seized upon the sun, and all the watery world about us was suffused with a dark coppery glow. The deck passed into a chilly shadow and every figure and shape upon it was touched with an inky quality. The leeward sky by contrast became still clearer and brighter and whiter than before.

Every face it seemed had shifted its regard from the dead body on its planks to this black canopy that furies were dragging over us all. The mate looked up, turned a page, and began to gabble very fast and skip what he was reading, and I heard the captain's message clang to the engine-room. After a brief interval the broken throbbing of the machinery, which had been stilled for a time, resumed.

" Ow, get *on* with it," whispered Midborough.

Then came a noise like the noise of ten thousand little kettle drums and I saw the mate, prayer-book in hand, gesticulate windily to the two men who stood beside the corpse. The words of the service had become inaudible. The deck slanted down towards a mounting whale-back of ghastly glaucous-green water, and the poor cocoon that had so recently been a living man, shot forth and smote and cleft the glassy expanse, just as the bulwarks rose again to hide it from my eyes. The mate, ascending slowly heavenward, went on reading the final prayer, but everyone else had turned about with a sense of imminent practical obligation.

Like the sting of a whip came the hail. I made for the nearest gangway, and as I did so, the thunder burst like a pistol at my ear.

I had a glimpse of the mate, bareheaded, his prayer-book still open in his hand, staggering about like a drunken man, and then involuntarily I went down the ladder and found myself climbing rather than walking the alleyway.

§ 10

THE STORM

But now I was to some extent weathered to the extravagances of the ocean, and my experiences, though disagreeable enough, were not accompanied by the same prostration of spirit as my former ones. My sickness was more bodily than mental and I can recall many incidents in their proper order.

And through all my memories rages the captain in an ever more deadly fury.

It is strange, but now for the first time and when he was at his maddest, I began to understand the man. Or at least that is how I remember it, though in fact my understanding may have come later. But at first I had seen nothing in this creature but a repellent ungraciousness. His desperate and exasperated struggle against an obdurate universe for the assertion of his own imperfectly apprehended will, became manifest only as he battered himself towards ultimate defeat. Just like myself he had come into life an open expectation, a vast if vacuous desire, the would-be recipient of a magnificence that was perpetually denied. What satisfactions, what predominances had he not promised himself in youth ! What secret resolutions to succeed had he not made ! And inexorably he had been thrust to this minor service of the sea, to be the irritated commander of a crew of equally thwarted and even more relentlessly constrained fellow-creatures, and the master of an old steamship of which he was ashamed. For manifestly he hated his ship ; he lusted to kick it out of the water. He hated his owners for employing him and still more would he have hated them if they had not employed him. And he hated his task of taking clocks and sewing machines and ready-made clothes to Brazil, and coffee and sugar and cigarettes and cotton to the Argentine, and thence on with a residue of still unloaded British goods and whatever else was to be picked up, to the antipodes, Except for distance and danger he was little more than a vanboy, and meanwhile other men went about the land, prevailing and ruling, consuming and enjoying. And even this low task of his he did with difficulty and with a desperate effort to maintain a sort of dignity. At least in this temporary little dominion he would be king. And the men would not obey him. A fleering young man of no use aboard, derided him at his meals ! The machinery would not respect him. The weather mocked his forecasts. To hell with them all ! Oh ! to hell with them !

The weather mocked him. He had counted upon getting to Buenos Aires before the weather broke. He had damned the engineer for a fool and brought his ship out of safety at Rio. And here, two days at least from Buenos Aires, was the break of the weather.

For the captain's life had become unendurable, and he lived those days of his culminating disappointment in a frenzy of hate like a wildcat in a net.

Down the middle passage-way he came disputing with the engineer. "I told you I wouldn't answer for it," said the engineer. "The thing should have been done at Rio."

The captain burst in emulation of the storm outside. He screamed as he swore and swung his clenched fists to heaven. The engineer answered with a shrug and a grimace.

I tried to stand aside and a lurch of the ship flung me into his path. His face lit to fiendish anger and he struck at me and hurled me against a teak door. I was amazed and helpless. Such is the majesty of a ship's master that I did not attempt to strike him back, and when they had gone through a door under the break of the poop I struggled on to my cabin.

And now the ship began again to plunge and rear and ram herself into the ever-mounting seas, and after a little time or a long time—I do not know which—came a metallic concussion, a grinding and smashing, that told that the engine was done. It hardly came as a shock. So far as I know there was no excitement, only a stoical acceptance of a thing foredoomed. The whole crew had realised the approach of this disaster ; the wonderful thing had been its delay. The wonderful thing had been that even for a little while we had been able to fight our way and steer through this elemental chaos into which the ocean had dissolved.

I had a glimpse of the engineer with a wet and exhausted yet still expressionless face, making his way from one handhold to another back to his cabin. His work was done. Indeed all work was done, except to pump and hold back and bar the pitiless invasion of water. The character of our motion had changed instantly with the death of the engines. We rolled and danced far more but with less effort and vibration. We came round sideways to the waves. We had the temporary respite of a garrison that has surrendered and awaits a massacre. The ship had become a helpless floating thing at the mercy of the waters. Little mercy was there in them. They seemed resolved to turn her over sideways if not longways. We made no resistance now. We looked the waves in the face no longer. They beat against her and rolled over her until it was like night under the smother. We were tamed. They shoved her up and out into the daylight again and then, brawling and shouting, sent her headlong down vast declivities.

Was she taking water? The next morning I ventured from my cabin to see if peradventure there was food to be got, and met Rudge bound upon the same errand and shouted a few words with him. Was she taking water? Little, it seemed, except for the frothing waves that swept athwart her and came pouring in cascades down the gangways.

That much water we could deal with, he said, if the plates of her skin held.

There was nothing for it but to stick it out. Those were the days before wireless became general and we had no means of calling help in our plight. We were derelict unless and until some ship chanced upon us and came to our assistance. Or until the weather had done with us and cast us ashore. Or until we sank. And if no help came we should drive while the storm held and drift when it diminished. So Rudge.

The cook in some marvellous way had got his fire alight and had made a sort of soup of stock and meat-extract and bread and so forth, very savoury and heartening. It chanted with onions. Men had fought their way through the waves that were leaping over us for a share of this savouriness, and most of us drank out of a common cup, staggered against each other, said " Who-ah ! " and " Steady, there ! " and respected no etiquette. But when suddenly the captain appeared in streaming oilskins, with his white eyelashes grey with salt and his face as he clawed at the door-jambs a rigid mask of fury, everyone stood aside, two of the men went out of the galley to struggle back to their own quarters and Vett found him a cup for himself.

No one addressed him, and he muttered and swore to himself. I was holding on near to him, gnawing a chunk of hard biscuit, and I heard a few words. " We go into Buenos Aires," he said. " We go into Buenos Aires. Or by Almighty God—— ! "

" Almighty God has it," said the engineer's inaudible lips.

" Nothing for these swine to do, eh ? " the captain snarled to himself, his wicked little eyes peering through his eyelashes at us. " Just you wait till the wind falls ! "

But for four or five days—I do not know how many, because, for a very good reason, I lost count—the wind did not fall. We went on living shut up in our cabins, or clambering about the passages, or making desperate rushes from point to point on slippery planks, knee-deep and waist-deep in waves and foam. We were flung hither and thither, and battered and bruised. At one time I fancied I had some ribs stove in, and spent half an hour perhaps feeling my side and taking experimental deep breaths. Intermittently the cook repeated his miracle of warmth, but chiefly with coffee. In between we lived on hope. We made desperate expeditions into depths of seething water to reconnoitre the cook's galley. Often I would start and never get there. I would survey a stretch of perhaps thirty feet of wave-washed deck vanishing ever and again beneath swirling foam-marbled water, I would note the scanty handholds, weigh the risk and return. I secured a small tin of biscuits for my cabin, but I suffered a good deal from thirst. The salt seemed to get on my lips because of my breathing. It got upon my imagination also and made me retch. Everyone, I suppose, was more or less starved, drenched, eviscerated, bruised and tormented during that clinging life while the waves hunted for us and the very ship seemed trying to fling us out. I saw one man throw himself down on the tilting deck as in despair, but another clutched at his coat collar, holding on to a stanchion, hung on to him for a time and then tumbled him into shelter as the ship swung down.

And I saw one thing no one will believe. I saw a great shark come aboard. A wave, tall and pointed like the Jungfrau, towered up over the side, hung hissing with hate, an olive-green mountain with the wind blowing out a streaming mane, and then with all its strength and substance beat itself down upon the deck. I was clinging on up by the bridge and a little sheltered. It seemed impossible that this would not break the ship asunder or drive us down and down into the deeps. The water swished over my ankles and up my legs with something of the manner of an aggressively friendly terrier. Everything forward was hidden under a dither of broken water except the fore deck and the shut entrance to the forecastle, and then slowly the main deck came up again, covered with wild-rushing fleecy foam, and there, rolling across the deck leeward, bending itself into a bow and flashing out straight again and snapping like an angry square-mouthed handbag, was this great white-bellied fish. It was enormously bigger than a man. It lashed and flung itself about, trailing threads of slime after it that blew straight out in the wind. It was bloody under its belly. The ship seemed for a moment to survey our new shipmate with amazement, and then with a resolute effort rolled it and the swirling foam it came with, over the starboard rail as though there were some things that even a disabled ocean tramp would not endure.

That I surely saw with my own eyes.

§ 11

MUTINY AND MURDER

THROUGH all that storm I did not change a single wet garment, though I spent many hours wrapped up in a sort of bale of my blankets and a rug.

And I do not remember the slightest diminution of the storm. So far as I was concerned, it never diminished; it stopped abruptly. I awoke out of something between sleep and complete unconsciousness to find that the storm was over. But how long my insensibility had lasted I do not know.

When I tried to sit up I found something inexplicable had happened to my berth. It was no longer swaying and dipping about the horizontal; it and the partition of my cabin had become a V-shaped trough in which I was lying. I was very weak and sick and thirsty and helpless, but I felt called upon to understand this rearrangement of my co-ordinates. Holding the bracket of my oil lamp, which was also hanging crooked, I looked out of my port and saw that the sea, a calm blue sea, was askew. Or if it was not, then everything else was. My cabin was steadily and permanently aslant.

I was astonished. After I had been so beaten upon and overwhelmed by the storm, it may seem strange that I could still be astonished, but I suppose my poor brain was so fatigued that it was quite unable to suggest a reason for this motionless general slant of everything in my apartment. I got out of my berth and opened my door to see if the alleyway was also slanting. It was. Vaguely wandering, I came out on deck and found the whole ship aslant. It was only then that my dulled and attenuated wits realised what had happened. The blue horizon I saw now was all right and at an honest horizontal. But the ship was down by the head and all the stern part was uphill. She must have shipped water forward and filled as far as the forward bulkhead. Probably some cargo had shifted, because there was a distinct list to port. I put my hand to my head as I meditated these things, and found it sore and bruised. In some way I had had a knock on the head, but how that happened I never learnt. Probably I had been thrown about in my cabin. I may have lain stunned or in the deep sleep of exhaustion for quite a long time.

Three or four gulls were circling above us. One was much larger than the others and seemed able to soar for ever without moving its wings. It went to and fro as if it were an expectant legatee. One or two had settled down on the raised deck aft. I did not remember seeing gulls aboard before, and I had a curious anticipation that perhaps the ship was deserted. Then I became aware of a busy hammering forward and was reassured. I went in search of the hammerer.

I came out upon what I thought at first was the whole ship's company grouped in the most extraordinary fashion on the main deck before the bridge. The men were nearly all in two close groups to the left of me. Shaving had gone out of fashion and they looked an evil lot.

One had his forearm wrapped in a bloody rag. One or two were eating, the rest crouched or lounged, looking alertly repressed. To the right one of the ship's boats lay on the deck bottom upward, and the carpenter was meekly busy with her bottom planking. A boy assisted him. Sitting astride the boat's keel was the engineer with his pistol in his hand, and behind him Rudge leant against the boat's rump. The mate with another pistol, and Midborough trying to hold a hatchet as though it wasn't anything in particular, were standing with their backs to me, and turned sharply at my apparition. Everyone regarded me like a forgotten thing that has been suddenly recalled.

" God ! " exclaimed the engineer. " *You've* turned up again ! "

I could make no reply. I took a step forward, caught at an iron rail, slipped, and sat down on the deck. Simply I felt—queer. " I'm weak," I said.

" Ow !—Give him some grub," said Midborough. " Don't you see he's nearly done ? "

There was a restrained movement among the men. Someone put a chunk of hard biscuit and pressed-beef in my hand. That, I thought, was probably partly the clue to my weakness. I took a mouthful and felt that that was so. I ate up my portion and drank some coffee. My strength crept back to me and I began to look about me.

A voice came from overhead.

" He goes with the men."

I looked up and saw the captain directly over me, for, because of the slant of the ship, the bridge overhung us. The captain, too, I realised, clutched a ready revolver. He was none the prettier for four or five days' growth of ginger stubble.

" No fear," said the tall dark man I supposed to be the boatswain. " That's for *your* boat."

" He's no use to us," the captain said.

" Well, you'll have to keep him. What's the good of argument ? "

" He's our passenger," said the engineer in a resigned tone, and the mate beside me nodded.

" I don't understand all this," I said at large.

" The boats are all stove in, except the one they've got afloat over the side there," said Midborough. " The men took it into their heads to go off in her, out on the wide, wide sea. When we saw land to starboard there was no holding them. See ? Only the Old Man spotted what they were up to and asked them to stop. And here they are stopping. What should we do without them ? The carpenter, bless his eyes, has kindly consented to put this little boat right for us before he goes. Just a friendly afterthought. And that's how things stand."

I understood the significance of those three revolvers.

" The first man who tries to go over that side starts the shooting," said the engineer, speaking to me and at the men.

" And the carpenter goes in *our* boat," said the mate, " to show he trusts his own work."

" That point we haven't settled," said the tall dark man.

" *We* have," said the engineer.

" Over there we may want the carpenter."

" Carpentering's a damned useful trade," said the engineer, not disputing that point. " You'd hardly imagine all the joints a carpenter has to know. There's books about it."

The men grunted, and a little knot began whispering and muttering among themselves.

" Where's this land ? " I said to the second officer. " I don't see it."

Midborough stared at the horizon. " This ship," he said, " keeps turning round. Let's see, where's the sun ? It's westward under the sun."

" It's there all right," said the cook. " Though when the hell we shall start for it, I don't know. Hurry up, Jimmy."

" Damn you," swore the carpenter. " Do you think I'm playing about here ? "

" The sun's setting."

" That's not my business—anyhow."

Slowly, slowly, with the rotation of the ship, the western sky unrolled itself like a panorama behind the heads of the men. It was clear and golden above the leaden water, and before the blaze of the sun came round to blind me, I saw the pale grey-mauve silhouette of a coastline, faint and clear, with mountains and what seemed to me a smoking peak. Then in an instant the golden-red fire of the sun itself poured into my eyes and everything else melted in the glow.

" 'Ow are we going to make that coast in the darkness ? " said a voice.

" Go west, young man, go west," quoted the bookish engineer. He used his revolver to point to his left. " You've got all Patagonia there like a wall. You can't miss it. Hundreds and hundreds of miles of it. Take what you like."

" We could have been half-way there by now," said the voice.

" Selfish swine," said the engineer.

" Half an hour more," sung out the carpenter, " and my job'll be done. I want this boat turned over. How'yr going to set about it ? "

" Mr. Gibbs," said the captain to the mate. " Tell Mr. Midborough to take off Mr. Blettsworthy and bring out our stores from the galley. We four will watch the men. Two of you chaps—and not more than two of you, mind, help the carpenter. Dutchy for one, he's hefty and harmless. I'm watching you all, remember."

He thought of something else. " We'll want some lamps, Mr. Midborough, before the light goes. We want this deck to be lit. Get some lamps. We don't want things to happen in the dark here."

The man with the bandaged arm spat and swore bitterly. " We do *not*," he said.

" No fear," said a friend, and produced an unreal laugh.

After we had put all the accumulation in the galley at the side where the boat would be launched, I went with Midborough to the ship's stores, which had already been looted in a careless fashion by the men. " Better more than less," said Midborough, piling my arms with biscuits. As we went about this business, the sun sank and the blue twilight deepened into night. The men became black figures under the two lanterns Midborough rigged up over their heads. The captain was lost in mystery overhead. " There you are," said the carpenter, and stood out of his job. " Stow your dunnage."

" Stop ! " cried the captain like the crack of a whip as a man stood up on the port bulwark.

" You old swine," cried a shrill voice ; " if it comes to blows——! "

The threat remained unspoken and unheeded.

" We want the carpenter," the voice of the boatswain declared.

" Dead or alive ? " asked the engineer politely.

The men growled.

" Get our boat overside," the captain said, " and chuck in the stuff."

There was a struggle and a flat splash as the smaller boat took the water and a sound of boxes and tins and packages being dropped into it. I did my share until the deck was clear. Rudge packed. " Damned little room left," cried Rudge.

Came a smack, a crash, and a tingle of falling glass. Both the lanterns that had kept the men in sight had been smashed simultaneously. " Come along, Jimmy ! " cried a voice to the carpenter. " This way ! "

" No, you don't ! " I heard the engineer, and he fired across the deck into the brown—I think without hitting anyone. The men went bundling down into their boat.

" Blettsworthy ! " came astonishingly from above. " Is Blettsworthy there ? "

I obeyed the call and went back to the ladder that led up to the deck-house. The captain came down swift and silent like a big cat, and before

I realised his hostile intention he had collared me and flung me backward through the open door into Vett's little pantry. I was too amazed
at the moment to resist. I heard him fumble at the key of the door and
leapt forward too late. He hit me in the face with his revolver and as I
went down again I heard him repeat in tones of the bitterest hatred :
" Eat your Soup ! *Eat* ya soup ! "

Then the door slammed and I was locked in.

The blow had dazed me. I gathered myself together slowly, feeling
over my face for the source of the trickling blood I tasted. I heard the
captain's voice answering someone : " He's all right. He's in the big
boat ! " I felt over the door in the darkness as though I might find some
way of unlocking it. I did not think to knock or cry out until it was too
late. Even then I might not have been heard. For something happened,
I know not what, that must have gripped the attention of everyone. It
is my belief that the captain fired at the men's boat. He may have done
that out of sheer hatred for the men or to drown any protest from me.
Or the shots may have been provoked. The engineer may have fired
those shots and not the captain. At any rate I heard three shots and
shouts and a splashing. Then came the regular swish and thud of oars
and the whole tumult receded. Possibly the men were pulling out of
range of the captain's fury.

Silence healed again like curtains quietly drawn together. I remained
listening for some time and at last there was nothing but the rippling of
water forward against the ship's side.

§ 12

DERELICT

I DID not get out of that little cabin until dawn.

The forcing of either door or window in the dark was too much for
me. But in the morning I found a little drawer in which Vett kept some
tools, and with a chisel and a hammer—there was no screw-driver—I
managed to release the lock. I had spent most of the night in futile rage
against the captain and now it was as if everything I did was done against
him. I had to live in order to defeat and denounce him. As I had
ransacked Vett's pantry for a lever against the door, I had found among
other things, his bottle of brandy, some water, a collection of things

called sparklets, with a specially constructed bottle which could be used for making sodawater, tins of cheese, biscuits, tins of sardines, some boxes of dates and figs for dessert and suchlike accessory provisions, and there was a store of matches, a trimmed lamp and so forth, all carefully stowed against breakage. The captain, I reflected, might have pitched me into an uglier corner than this. As soon as I had got the door open and felt free, I ate and went out with a handful of dates to devour while I reconnoitred my position.

I hoped to find I was drifting ashore so that I could follow on the track of my enemy forthwith, though what I expected to do with him and his party if I found them together on a Patagonian beach, I cannot imagine. I made for the bridge. The deck seemed a little steeper than it did before, heeling more to port, but so far as I could judge I was no nearer sinking. I went up to the deck-house behind the impotent wheel and the tilted compass—a sacred place which had hitherto been forbidden ground to me, and found various charts and diagrams of the ship and a brass instrument or so clustering in the lowest corner. My first solicitude was to see the land. It had gone. I stood with my back to the sunrise and scrutinised the long, hard, dark blue line of the westward sea, and the coastline that had been so clear overnight was invisible. I clambered to the roof of the deck-house to get a still wider circle. There was no sign of land and no speck that might be a boat. I had to persuade myself that mist or some trick of the atmosphere was hiding land from me, but indeed the horizon was as hard and positive as one of Euclid's propositions. Perhaps the *Golden Lion* was drifting parallel to the coast and yesterday we had passed some projecting land areas. Now maybe some great bight had carried the shore line down below the curve of the world. It would return. Surely it would return.

But though I comforted myself this way, this shoreless circle of the sea disappointed and depressed me acutely, brought with it a sudden sense of helplessness. My idea of getting to land forthwith upon some lightly improvised raft was manifestly knocked on the head. I was incapable of making or propelling a raft for anything but the briefest of transits.

I dismissed my idea of a pursuit hot upon the heels of the captain. He had understood the situation as I was now only beginning to understand it. I might have to stay in this wreck for an indefinite time. In a graver mood I set myself to explore as much of the ship as remained above water. I was speedily satisfied that I need feel no anxiety about food ; the food supply would last as long as the ship, and the ship, I assured myself, was good until the weather broke and might-even stand a certain amount of heavy weather. After all, whatever the leakage was, it was forward and the bulkhead held. There was fuel in the galley and I might even cook. I had raw potatoes, a residue of green vegetables, dried onions and tinned meat. In my exploration I came to the captain's cabin. I went in to think out what I had next to do and adjusted myself on his cushions in his wicker chair, to decide how I might get even with him.

I should either drift ashore or be picked up. Still there were other and less agreeable possibilities, and perhaps it might be well to write a statement of my case and commit it to a bottle. Or perhaps even write several statements for several bottles. That was an affair that could be put in hand at once. I looked round the cabin for paper and ink and became interested in the lights his abandoned possessions threw upon this man's character. Evidently he read little, but poor, craving devil ! he had got a little accumulation of pornographic photographs, and pages and whole numbers of French and Spanish coloured illustrated papers of an indecent type. Over some of these he must have brooded intently, for he had made forceful marks on them with a pencil. In my under-graduate days this find would have disgusted me utterly, but I had learnt since then what monstrous storms the body can brew, and this revelation of festering and tormenting desire in my enemy did on the whole rather mitigate my resentment for the ugly treachery of which I was the victim. If the man was half insane through these things his madness was anyhow kindred to the normal stresses of our sanity. He had detested me from the very first. Why had he detested me ? Had I in any degree justified his detestation ? Had I possibly resembled someone, recalled some disagreeable experience ? I gave up the riddle. I stowed his art gallery back in its drawer. I sat down to write. " I am Arnold Blettsworthy "—and I gave the brief data for my identification. I stated when I had left London and the dates and other particulars of my voyage. " Some days out of Rio our engines broke down and the ship became unmanageable and sprung a leak forward." So far good. And now for the gist of the story : " A certain animosity towards me on the part of the captain had developed into a mutual hostility," I wrote and then stopped writing for a time, recalling the circumstances of my desertion and many particulars of my companions. How dirty my hands were ! I noted with a start.

I went back to my own cabin and on the way visited those of my former companions. The engineer had had a secret store of cigars and I found one very satisfactory. In his cabin there was amidst a queer miscellany of old, stained and sometimes coverless books, an orderly accumulation of printed matter of various dates, offering the ninth edition of the Encyclopædia Britannica on various subscription schemes. Against the prices the engineer had made various computations in pencil, and evidently he had contemplated ballasting the ship and myself with all this store of knowledge. The mate's hole revealed a more pedestrian spirit. There was a Bible, some boxes of paper collars, several very unattractive framed portraits and the photograph of some house property on which was written " last instalment to be paid " with a date. Rudge had cleared out his photographs and his most remarkable properties were a number of gay toys, bought I should imagine as presents for some child at home. Midborough seemed to have been preoccupied with the sanitary dangers of seaports. It dawned upon me that I was prying and I went on to my own cabin.

There I washed my hands and my dirty, bloody face, and encouraged by the refreshment of cleanliness, shaved myself and changed into clean, folded, shore-going clothes. I felt more like Arnold Blettsworthy and less of a dirty rag of suffering than I had done for many days. There was even a certain elation at finding myself in effect master of the ship and able to do exactly what I pleased on it. I went back to the captain's cabin to finish writing my statement and I began a fair copy. But after a time, I felt the flavour of the captain too strongly there ; moreover, I perceived that I was in fact very tired and sleepy and I left my writing unfinished and went to find some corner for a sleep. I had a desire also, after so many days of wetness, to sun myself. I dragged some bedding from one of the cabins on to the upper deck abaft the funnel and laid myself out in the light. The sun, because of the circular motion of the ship, seemed to be clambering in a flat spiral course up the sky, and this deck, I decided, was the place where I could be most continuously hot. The shadow of the funnel moved over me with a scarcely perceptible motion as I lay and presently I fell into a deep sleep.

I awakened with a start and with a queer impression that the captain was in a boat close at hand directing the sinking of the ship. Also mixed up with that was a realisation that the birds had gone again and that I was increasing my distance from the land. I suppose I had been dreaming. The sun was low in the sky. I stood up and stretched. This deck rose highest above the water and I decided that I would get some more blankets and pass the night upon it.

I went upon the bridge and then down to the forward deck to see how the ship was floating. I remember staying forward for a long time, resisting disagreeable conclusions. She certainly seemed more down in the water than I had at first observed and now she was rocking slightly. The water was right across the deck so that to reach the forecastle, had I wished to do it, I should have had to wade. Either I had not observed that before or it had not been so at first. As she rocked, the water swilled into the hatchway and then swilled out again, lazily as though it was at home there. I went down the companion-way amidships and found things dark and lonely below. I peered into the engine-room aft and there was water shining darkly in the deeps. It was already twilight before I thought of getting Vett's lantern and matches for the night. When the night grew cold under the stars, I found the lantern useful in a hunt for more blankets. But that thin sheet of water across the forward deck troubled my mind, I could not sleep very well and I lay with the lantern alight beside me, staring at the stars.

§ 13

MEDITATIONS OF A CASTAWAY

IT was only in the night that the full desperation of my case began to dawn upon me.

I had not been refusing to see the completeness of my isolation hitherto. I had simply been unable to think it. Too many habits and associations had clung about me for me to perceive that now I was altogether bare. I had behaved so far as a man, a little delayed and obstructed indeed, who had a case to bring against another who had attempted to murder him. Everything about me in the daylight had seemed to point to that. Now the realisation was creeping in upon me that I was already, for all practical purposes, murdered and that I should never bring that case.

What were my chances of getting back into the world of men? I surveyed them with a lucid dismay. I was living, breathing, fed and physically more comfortable than I had been for many days, but that did not in the least affect the extremity of my detachment. In reality I was already as far from the general play of life as though I had fallen right off this planet. My exact position I did not know, but I was far away south of Bahia Blanca, the last Argentine port with any traffic. The chances of a coastwise vessel happening upon me were infinitesimal. And for shipping that would be going round the Horn I was certainly much too far to the west. It would be a miracle if I were picked up before bad weather came to end me. And end me it surely would. There was no need of further leak or breach of bulkhead, for a mere ordinary rough sea could swamp the middle section of the ship now, so low was she in the water.

In the interest of my situation, my enemy the captain ceased for a time to dominate my thoughts. I accepted the fact that I was now isolated from all my kind, in an isolation that could only end in my death—as a fact. Nevertheless, I perceived that I did not *realise* this fact. I was thinking out my situation exactly as if I was preparing to tell someone about it. Perhaps the human mind is not made to register complete isolation. Perhaps it is true, as people begin to say nowadays, that one cannot think without a slight if imperceptible motion of mouth and vocal cords, nor talk except to at least a phantom outside oneself. Solitary thought can exist, no doubt, but it cannot be posed as solitary thought.

I began to talk to myself with a curious feeling I could not eliminate of a distinction and a difference between the personalities of the talker and the hearer.

" Now what," said I, speaking aloud, " is this thing called life ? Which begins so obscurely in the warmth and in the dark, and comes to such ends as this ! It seems to me extraordinary that I should be adrift here on my way to drowning ; but why do I think it extraordinary ? I do not see why I should judge it to be extraordinary, seeing I have no outer standards by which to judge it at all. I suppose it seems extraordinary because I was led to expect that life would be something quite different from what it is. But I had not the slightest reason for expecting it to be different from what it is. To keep us quiet when we are children, and to make us nice and good and confident, we are given all sorts of assurances about life for which there are no justifications, and by the time we have found them out we are already too far off from human things to expose the deception. I was led to expect that if I was reasonably honest and active and helpful, I should be fairly paid in amusement, happiness, safety and a continuing, expanding and enduring contentment with the scheme of things. And here I am ! Against such expectations I look like the victim of a practical joke. And now that I am in the sun and fed and restful, albeit for the last time, I can even laugh at the joke that has been played upon me."

Some such speech I made to my hearer, but my hearer made no reply.

" A joke ? " I said, and reflected.

" And if it is not a joke, what on earth is it ? What is all this affair about ? If there is not even Somebody or Something laughing at this tremendous Sell ? "

My brain lay fallow for a time, and then I found myself reaping the conclusions of a new point of view.

"But the Sell," I argued, "is of our own making. The Sell is in ourselves. The Nature of Things has neither promised nor cheated. It is just that we have misunderstood it. This death-bed on a sinking ship is merely the end of over-confidence. Destiny has always been harder and sterner than we have seen fit to recognise. Life is a sillier, softer child than its parentage justifies. It falls down heedlessly. What right has it to complain that it squalls unheeded?"

Ten thousand pollen grains blow to waste for one that reaches a pistil; why should man be an exception to the common way of life?

That was as far as my philosophy took me that night. I seem to remember squatting up meditating profoundly on my brotherhood with the pollen grain. Scattered all over the earth are the waste pollen grains, silent, becoming drearily aware of their fate, realising it too late to proclaim it. The world that has flung them aside haphazard, goes on to its destinies. I have either forgotten the rest of that meditation, or I lay down to be more comfortable and dropped off to sleep.

§ 14

THE PATIENT COMPANION

THE next morning my mind had come down from philosophy to the captain again. I woke up in a decidedly bad temper, which was not improved by the extreme difficulty I found in making coffee. The captain, I swore, should pay for all this. After coffee I became extremely industrious; got my statement written out in triplicate, found wine or vinegar bottles with sound corks—I distrusted the endurance of stoppered beer bottles—and sealed up my denunciations. Then I went to the side and threw them well away, one after the other, clear of the ship. Each in its turn dived, came up and floated, bobbing nearly erect. And stayed where it was! I remember that I felt a slight chagrin that these messengers did not start off at once, at a good pace, northward towards civilisation. I had certainly imagined something of the sort. But there they stayed, and for all the rest of my time these bottles drifted with me, coming very slowly in until they were close alongside.

I did not like that, and another thing that presently expanded in my imagination was a glimpse I had of a dark line of shining back, slightly curved, with a fin along it, that became visible for a moment after the third splash. Something, I felt only too surely it was a shark, had come to see what it was had fallen into the water.

Now my mind was quite reconciled to the idea that presently, not yet but presently, I should go down into the water and drown, but I had thought of myself drowning with dignity. The possibility of going down into the water for a hopeless scuffle with a shark was altogether less acceptable. Indeed I found it detestable. For a time it made me reject the fate of drowning altogether and renew my waning conviction that in some manner finally I should be picked up. And meanwhile I watched the water nervously and persistently for some further sign of a shark.

It became evident to me that I had an idiosyncrasy about sharks. Just as some people have about cats. Once I had realised the neighbourhood of one or more of them, I could not keep my mind off them. I must have worried quite a lot about them, because in the afternoon I sacrificed a whole cabbage to reassure myself that I had been mistaken. I thought I saw something dark and lurking in the water aft and I got this cabbage —it was one of those round red ones people pickle, and flung it as far as I could towards the shadow. I must have gone below to get that cabbage and come back with it, though I do not remember doing so.

The shadow stirred at the splash, went down out of sight and reappeared, turning over spirally. It showed a shining white belly as it took my cabbage. There was no mistaking the shark's inverted snatch.

My test had been at once conclusive and very unsatisfactory.

§ 15

THE UNCHRISTIAN STARS

IN order to keep my mind off sharks, I brought it back to the captain and how at last I would confront him. I dramatised a variety of encounters, in towns, in law courts, on desert islands and inhospitable coasts. " So here at length we meet again ! " And when that ceased to hold my mind because of my underlying sense of its extreme improbability, I forced myself into long philosophical and religious arguments, sitting and thinking about them steadfastly and calling myself to order whenever the fact that the chamber in which this discussion was held was papered, so to speak, with a wall-paper of sharks and captains, distracted my attention.

I continued to analyse the justice of my fate. I generalised so that I questioned the righteousness not merely of my own fate but of the common fate of my kind. I associated the large expectations that had sustained my adolescence not only with the assumptions natural to youth, but with the whole system of religious hopes and beliefs by which mankind had been persuaded to face its destinies. During my under-graduate days, some chance allusion during an argument in a man's room had made me read Winwood Reade's " Martyrdom of Man," and now I found the broad outline of that sombre history very present in my thoughts. I saw the priests unfolding religion after religion like veils before the harsh reality of things ; I saw the trade in hope perpetually failing and perpetually renewed. I thought of my long chain of ancestors, innumerable through the ages, struggling upward to this strange finale above the waiting waters under the scorching sun and the cold circling stars, and now I saw it only as an anticipatory symbol of the whole destiny of our species. Well, I at least should die disillusioned.

I tried to recall the beliefs of my childhood and wondered if they had ever seemed valid. What had been far stronger was the tacit confidence of youth. The universal natural religion of mankind, indeed of all the animal world, is embodied in the simple creed : " It's all right," until some shock, some series of shocks, comes to destroy it. And then, I asked myself, what is there left ?

So far as the species is concerned there need be nothing left. Life can always begin again. Birth and death are the warp and woof of its process ; it is like a fraudulent tradesman who can only keep going by destroying his accounts. I was just a discarded obligation, a bilked creditor, a repudiated debt.

I thought of the meteoric career of Christianity, the last of our western veils upon reality, so comprehensive and infinite in its assurances, so recent in human history and so dominant over the world of my up-bringing ; I weighed its value as a creed of comfort. Surely it had comforted. Surely it had fortified assurance. It must have built up habits of assurance in millions of souls. But how far had it held out against wasting disease and the vast tragedies of life that destroy human beings by the myriad and leave none but lucky survivors to tell the tale of destruction ? The lucky survivor naturally tells the bright side of the tragedy. He was mercifully spared. The pollen grain that fell on stony soil tells no tales. Were the ages of faith indeed ages of courage ? At Oxford I had heard a bold blasphemer call Christianity an anæsthetic.

Could we even answer, I questioned now, for the anæsthesia of those who die defeated ? And was Christianity so specially a comforting and sustaining creed ? What of the other faiths, more proud and more heroic, that came before the Cross ? What of the Stoic and his soul ? And while I searched my ill-stored mind for some measure of value in this vague arraignment of my uncle's teaching, a queer idea hit my mind and set it glancing off in a new direction. It was an idea at once extraordinary and startling. It flashed into my thoughts with such an effect of discovery, that I still remember it clearly and distinctly. Perhaps it is the most original observation I have ever made.

I had been staring at my disappointing Southern Cross as it passed slowly with the rotation of the ship across my field of vision. " They might," I grumbled, " have found a better cross than that." And then my astonishing discovery came to me. I sat up and stared about me at the vast dome of stars. The Southern Cross ! It was the one poor little constellation that had been left for Christianity out of all the glories of the sky. Christianity was so recent that the stars of heaven still paid allegiance to the gods of the pagan and the Persian. Christianity had never conquered the sky, nor for that matter the days of the week, nor the months of the year. There, serene and unassailed, ruled the ancient gods. But how wonderful it was that there had never been a Christian conquest of the skies ! The Wounds, the Nails were there ; the Sacred Stream, the Pleiades like a Crown of Thorns and Orion the very Son of Man coming again in Glory. The planets were like shining witnesses and saints and the Pole Star was the Word on which all things were turning. I sat up marvelling that Christianity had never had the pause and the peace needed for that celestial rechristening.

I fell so much in love with this odd notion that I forgot my utter loss of faith and spent the best part of a night on the conversion of the constellations to Christianity. I was still at it, when one by one they melted into the returning day. There was no sudden extinction. They faded out. I looked round to verify some recent observation and the star I sought had vanished into the day. It was rather like putting out one's hand for a stair rail that has suddenly ceased to exist.

" So," thought I, with a sudden recoil from my pious task, " so also does the faith in Christian doctrine dissolve and pass away. With the passing of my generation. Never now will Orion become the Son of Man coming again in Glory, and Jupiter and Saturn will still rule above there when the transitory tangles of our Trinities are altogether forgotten.

Such were the thoughts that came to me, adrift, deserted and despairing upon the Southern Main.

§ 16

SHARKS AND NIGHTMARES

BUT as the days of my solitude wore on I found it increasingly difficult
to defend my mind from horrible anticipations and lurid dreams. My
dreams were worse than my waking thoughts and there came a time when
I would try to keep myself awake, because of the frightful suggestions
that haunted the borderland of slumber. My feeling that the ship was
sinking beneath me grew constantly more oppressive. At first I had put
off the sinking of the ship as a definite fact in the future ; now I felt it
was sinking all the time. I dreamt repeatedly of the ship's hold, only it
was immensely dark and noisome, and so vividly of water weeping
through the bulkheads that even when I was awake I believed I must
have seen this. A dozen times a day I set marks to the level of the water
on the forward deck. I would forget when I had made the marks and
alternate between panic and reassurance as I tried to remember which
of two of them was the earlier made. The fear grew upon me that the
ship would go down while I was slumbering. As I dropped off to sleep
it would seem to me that the whole ship was swaying downward and I
would start up into a painful wakefulness.

One dream did at least give me the idea of a way in which that final
encounter with a shark might be avoided. It is still brighter in my
memory than all but a few real experiences.

It took the form of a long dispute with a shark and after the inscrutable
way of dreams, the shark was not only a shark, but the captain. In this
dream I sat nearly waist-deep in water all the time, but that was certainly
caused by the fact that my heap of blankets had been drawn away from
my legs and that these lay exposed to the chilly starlight. The shark
came, wearing an immense white waistcoat and a crimson fob, and asked
me when I proposed to meet him at dinner. " But which will be host,"
said I, " and which will be guest ? " The shark had no conventional
graces at all and put the facts offensively. " I shall eat you before you
are drowned. I've got a one-way throat and there's no getting out of
it again." I told the shark I doubted if he had ever met my uncle, the
Rev. Rupert Blettsworthy, the vicar of Harrow Hoeward, or he would
know it was possible to discharge the most disagreeable duties urbanely.
" But after all," said the shark, " why criticise before you know ? A
certain bluntness often goes with a good heart. It may not be so bad.
The swallowing will distract you from the drowning and the drowning

from the swallowing and as I shall probably snap too, your attention may be so confused in the rush of these various excitements that you will hardly grasp for a moment that you are even beginning to suffer."

I told him that I would rather hear nothing of these technical points. No doubt he had considerable advantages in the present situation, but there was a certain dunning urgency in his insistence upon his final claim that I found excessively underbred. I had long since learnt from my uncle that it was possible to eat and be master of one's own world with tact and courtesy.

But this shark was not to be rebuked. That sort of thing, he said, would not do for the sea, and after all, the sea was the centre of life. Nobody knew anything of life who hadn't lived in the sea. It was not for the land to teach the sea how to live. A certain number of creatures had crept out upon the land, but that, he declared, was merely a retreat from active living. One got glimpses of them at times looking back regretfully. They crawled upon the land. There was no real buoyancy in the air. They were no better than crabs and sea lice and things that hid among the rocks. But in the sea, life at its best was bold and free and frank and fundamental, and one saw it for what it was. I squatted on my deck, parting reluctantly from my airy illusions one by one, saying a long good-bye to the flimsy flopping life of the land, but he, thank God, had neither lungs nor illusions. What price hope and fear, the desire of the human heart, its dreams of sacrifice and glory after two minutes in the gullet of Reality? For he was Real! "Come into the sea for two minutes," said the shark, "and learn what reality is." "Come up here," I retorted, "and I'll have shark steak for supper."

"This game ends my way," snapped the shark. For it irritated this eater even to think of being eaten.

And then it was I had my dream inspiration.

"Not a bit of it!" said I. "You've forgotten one thing. You poor old snapping bag of guts, you never learnt to build a ship and you have the vaguest ideas about cabins, and as soon as this old steamer begins its last dive, into my cabin I go and lock myself in. Eh? And down I go past you, in all my human dignity! And you nosing against the planks and turning yourself over for the meal that escapes you! Down I go—down to the deeps into which you, poor bathymetric captive! can no more dive than you can soar up into the air."

"Oh, but this is—*shabby*!" cried the shark. "And what good will it do you? The waste of it!"

"If one doesn't like sharks——" I said.

At which he lost his temper and made a sort of backward leap at me, much as I had seen that other shark leap upon the forward deck. I clutched him and we had a violent struggle from which I awoke to find myself in a mortal grapple with my mattress.

But when I had emerged from that, it was quite clear in my mind that henceforth I must sleep only in my cabin and be ready to bolt thither directly the ship seemed nearing the moment for its plunge. I laughed with triumph over the shark at my idea, even when I was fully awake.

That was one of my pleasanter—and if one can use such a word for dreaming—one of my saner dreams.

There were other dreams, I know, upon which the controls of my memory have since turned, to expunge them from this record. And from such dreams, under the steady continuing pressure of fear, I passed on very speedily to the waking dreams of delirium. But over that too, for the most part, veils have been drawn so that all these later recollections are uncertain and indistinct.

But once I recall, hurrying from side to side of the ship with a hatchet in my hand, if haply I could catch a glimpse of the giant octopus with a face like the captain, which was slowly and steadily spreading its almost invisible tentacles over the vessel, confirming its grip and preparing to drag me down into the deeps. Once when I came upon a tentacle and hacked it to pieces, it seemed afterwards to be merely a frayed-out rope. And also, in the night, it seemed to me that the funnel was really the captain, who had stayed aboard in that disguise to make sure the ship went down. A passion of fear and hatred for the funnel seized me and I attacked it with my hatchet furiously and repeatedly in order to cast it overboard and free the ship, already water-logged and overburthened from its tilting weight.

§ 17

RAMPOLE ISLAND COMES ABOARD

My recollection of the savages coming aboard is very obscure. It may have happened while I was insensible.

I was lying on the after deck and I found two of them standing over me and regarding me. They were naked men of a dusky buff colour ; they had extraordinarily hard faces, unpleasantly tattooed, and their black hair was drawn harshly back. They leant upon tall spears and they stared at me with inexpressive eyes. Both were chewing slowly and steadily with their heavy jaws.

For some seconds I stared back at them blinking, and then rubbed my eyes, thinking they were the dregs of some nightmare that would presently vanish. Then perceiving they were real, I snatched at the chipped hatchet that was lying close at hand and leapt to my feet to defend myself.

But one of them gripped my wrist and the two overpowered me with the utmost ease.

CHAPTER THE THIRD

Tells how Mr. Blettsworthy found himself among the Savages of Rampole Island and of his early impressions of their Manners and Customs. How he saw the Megatherium, the Giant Ground Sloth, still surviving, and of its extraordinary natural history. What he learnt of the Religion of the Rampole Islanders, their marriages and their laws. How he talked to them of the Realities of Civilisation and how War came to Rampole Island.

CONTENTS OF CHAPTER THE THIRD

CHAPTER THE THIRD

§ 1

THE SINISTER LANDING

I AM anxious to tell the story of my adventures upon Rampole Island in the order in which they happened to me, as they unfold themselves now in my consciousness and as my mind recalls them. But I am sorry to say that because of the confusion that came to my brain there must be here and there a certain obscurity and disconnectedness. There may even be a disarrangement of the order of these events in time. I warn the reader plainly. I was in a delirium when the savages seized me, and for some time my mental disturbance must have been very considerable. By their standards I was plainly mad.

In a way, that was fortunate for me, for those savages, confirmed and impenitent cannibals as they are, living on each other persistently and ruthlessly, have a superstition that the flesh of madmen is taboo and deadly to the eater. Moreover in common with unenlightened people the whole world over, they have an awe of the mad. Insanity they think is a peculiar distinction conferred by their Great Goddess. So that I was given food and shelter by these eaters of men, and an amount of liberty that might have been denied me in a more highly developed community.

Since my memories have to be told in fragments, given like peeps into a book opened here and there, the reader may even be a little incredulous of some of the things I have to tell. He would prefer, but then I equally would prefer, a story continuous in every detail and going on consecutively from Monday morning to Saturday night. He would no doubt skip a good deal of so full and explicit a narrative, but he would have the satisfaction of feeling that it was there. As it is, it is I who have to do the skipping. And I must admit that I never did feel even at the time that it was all there. Even in the early days of my captivity I had my doubts.

I am vividly convinced of the reality of these two savages with whom I grappled, and I can even remember the smell of the rancid oil with which their extremely hard bodies were anointed, and still more vividly do I remember my impact upon the ribs of the long canoe into which I was dropped. It gives me a bruised feeling in my back even now. I was thrown down among a lot of recently caught fish, most of which were still wrigglingly alive and flapped under me and about me, so that I was speckled with silvery scales. There were nets festooned along the side. And I have a precise memory of being stepped upon and walked over by the savages as they came back into the canoe with such plunder as the ship afforded them. My mind is patterned, I might say, with feet and shins and knees and buff bodies, seen in perspective from below. They were a people essentially unhygienic. Also I recall very clearly how we paddled to shore and the rhythm of the brownish black paddles.

It was a high shore of some sort of rock that was not completely opaque. I do not know what kind of rock it was and though I have sought it since in museums in order to give it a name, I have never seen anything like it. It resembled a clearish blue purple glass, but with large patches of a more ruddy hue, verging on rosy pink. And there were veins in it of opaque white like alabaster. The light was taken into this mineral and reflected from within it as precious stones take in and reflect light. I was struck by its loveliness, bound and dismayed though I was.

We went close inshore and presently came into a sort of fiord winding through cliffs. Guarding this, as it were, some hundred yards or so from the entrance, was a strange freak of nature, a jutting mass of rock in the shape of a woman with staring eyes and an open mouth; a splintered pinnacle of rock rose above her like an upraised arm and hand brandishing a club; the eyes had been rimmed with white and the threat of the mouth had been enhanced by white and red paint, suggesting teeth and oozing blood. It was very hard and bright and ugly in the morning sunshine. This, I was to learn, was the Great Goddess welcoming her slaves. The savages stopped the canoe abreast of her and raised their paddles aloft in salutation. The forward paddler held up a fish, an exceptionally big one. Another savage leant back towards me, lifted my head by the hair as if to introduce me to the divinity, and then threw me back among the rest of the catch.

This ceremony observed, paddling was resumed, and after a time a a little beach on which waited an expectant crowd came into view at the foot of some high cliffs. Our steersman made a hooting noise, to which distant voices responded.

All that, I say, is perfectly clear in my mind, and so, too, is the enclosure of thorny canes into which I was presently flung. And yet upon all this memory there rests something—it is too impalpable even to call it a shadow—something, a quality in the light, that makes it all not quite credible. Even at the time I was puzzled or incredulous. I had enough of geography, in spite of the refinements of my Oxford education, to know that the Patagonians were gigantic and yellow, but I knew, too, that they were rare and lonely wanderers, living in tents of skin, while here we were approaching a considerable village. And never had I heard of translucent cliffs upon that coast, nor of any such abundance of vegetation as here presented itself. I thought that in my boyish reading I must have learnt something of all such savage and barbaric peoples as still maintained themselves against civilisation. This place, which later on I discovered was an island and not the American main-land at all, did not fit in with my scheme of known things, geographical or ethnographic, as indeed, I suppose, it will not fit into the reader's knowledge and preconceptions.

I can only tell simply and directly of these things as they came to me. At the same time they were intensely real, and they were discordant with what had seemed to be reality. Bruised, bound and in that fishing canoe, watched over by the ugly chewing steersman, and contemplating the play of the muscles of the backs of the paddlers in front of me, I could not believe I was dreaming, and yet I could not imagine this was indeed the same world with London from which I had come. Had some sudden twist of time and space carried me and my wreck into a different age or on to a different planet ? Or was the winding water channel some such river as the Styx, and these the rowers who bring in souls from their final shipwreck to the coasts of another world ?

Can one who has never died know what death is ?

Was this nightmare death ?

§ 2

THE SACRED LUNATIC

IF I was dead, there was certainly good reason for supposing I might very speedily have to die again. The bearing of the crowd when I was handed out of the canoe for inspection was full of noisome anticipations   I cannot describe in what detail they inspected me. I did my best to bear myself with dignity, but their curiosity was heedless of my bearing.

One man seemed to be exercising a sort of authority over my per-secutors. After a phase of indulgence he waved the evil-smelling crowd aside, giving cuffs and thrusts to any who seemed disposed to hinder him. He was wrinkled, squat and hunchbacked, and on his head he

wore a sort of cylindroid crown of some big leaf dried and rolled. His
voice was loud and very flat, and his arms exceptionally long, powerful
and hairy. His jaw was underhung and very heavy, and his mouth huge.
He seemed to reproach the multitude for their avidity. It was under his
direction that I was cast into the cage. I tried to interrogate him by
signs, but he took no more heed of my attempt to communicate than a
butcher does of the bleating of a sheep in his yard.

This cage was made of an open palisade of stout canes bearing thorns
of a largeness I had never seen before, bound together by tough fibrous
creepers. It was about ten paces square. The sole furniture was a stool
of the same hard blackish-brown wood as the canoe. The floor was of
beaten earth, bearing traces of former prisoners. A gourd of water and
some farinaceous roots were thrown on the floor beside the bench, and
then I was left, with a savage with a big spear guarding the door. But
the crowd, or at least the younger women and the children, remained
about me, peering in through the interstices. At first they chattered
and nudged each other a good deal, and my slightest movement created
a new excitement that manifested itself in tittering and laughter. But
after a time they calmed down to quiet staring through the spaces
between the canes. Some departed, but enough remained to encircle
my prison with eyes and gaping red mouths. Whichever way I turned
I met that same motionless bright-eyed stare. With a vague feeling of
self-protection, I squatted on the low bench with my face covered by
my hands.

Night came swiftly in that narrow gorge. Even after dark my watchers
lingered. I could hear the rustle and patter of their departure, one
group after another, with long whispering or silent intervals between.

" My God," I asked. " How can I go on living ? "

And then it was my mind rejected another of its illusions. " We do
not go on living," I said. " What is this nonsense I am talking ? It is
not our affair. We say it in that way to persuade ourselves we live by
our own act. Indeed we are just tumbled helplessly out of to-day into
to-morrow, whether we want to *go on* or not. As I shall be. And what
will happen to-morrow ? "

I tried to think of many high and grave matters, because this surely
was my last night alive. But I was too tired to think of any high or
grave matters. I thought only of those bright watching eyes and of the
malignant anticipations they expressed. I fell asleep at last. . . .

So much I have very clear.

And then a fog settles on my memories.

Perhaps I began to talk to myself or rave or sing. Perhaps I did
stranger things. Quite unwittingly I did what was best for myself.

When I strain my mind to recollection, I find vague shadows of an interrogation in a great dim cave, beneath a wooden effigy of the Great Goddess. Old men, hairless with age, make incomprehensible gestures to me. I am moved to respond with weird gesticulations. Later I lie lie naked and bound in the sun while the women scald and sear my flesh. Later still, some monstrous rite is in progress and I am confronted by bowls of boga-nut milk and blood. It is of tremendous consequence which of these bowls I shall select. I sit like a Buddha musing. I choose the blood, and amidst signs of friendship and rejoicing I am made to drink. The vegetarian milk is flung contemptuously away. The old man with the cylindrical hat plays a directive part on all these occasions.

Then I am walking through the village a free man. The children regard me with habituated respect. Much time has passed, many events have lost themselves in oblivion. I can understand most of what these people say and I can make myself understood. I wear the coarse-haired skin of a young ground sloth so that my neck sticks out of its neck and its brain-pan covers my head. Its bunch of curved claws hangs down upon my chest. The gigantic ground sloth still survives upon Rampole Island, and I have already seen a small herd of these grotesque monsters feeding on the uplands above the cliff. It deserts its young, which die and are then flayed. I carry a staff of hard dark wood obscenely carved and decorated with mother-of-pearl and the teeth of sharks. I reflect that in this guise I should cause considerable surprise to my Oxford friends, and with that thought something seems to click in my mind and my memories resume. I *was* Arnold Blettsworthy. What am I now? What have I become? I am the sacred lunatic of the tribe. I can give oracles unawares. I have prophetic powers. What is better, when I am fat and well the tribe prospers ; do I ail and its fortunes decline. I have been built a hut among the best in the village, decorated with human skulls and the leg-bones of Megatheria. I eat daintily, never asking the nature of the meat, the delicate pork-like meat, that is put before me. But generally I am vegetarian. There is much anxiety just at present because I will not accept a wife. But I will not take a wife unless she has washed, and this language has no word for washing. Moreover, the minds of these people seem unable to grasp the idea or to acquire it from any of my gestures. One projected bride has already been taken out to sea and drowned in a mistaken attempt to carry out my apparent wishes with regard to her.

So self-realisation flowed into the stream of my memory, and my impressions, and the knowledge and ideas I had acquired among the savages, joined on to my proper personality again.

It all came before me in a moment—out of nothingness. It grew plain and distinct under a sky, pale blue with a haze of nostalgia. I recalled Oxford as a sweet, clean and delicate place in which I had passed a harmless and hopeful adolescence. I remembered it now as the home of unmitigated pleasantness. I saw the great gate of Lattmeer as I had once admired it in the moonlight when I was returning from a mighty talk we had had in a man's rooms in Christ Church about the fine things to be done in the world, about the creative spirit of Oxford—as distinguished from the hard materialism of Cambridge—about Rhodes, the White Man's Burthen, English traits, and such-like noble topics. It was a far cry from that Blettsworthy to this skin-clad, bone-crowned eccentric, bearing a staff decorated in an uncongenial manner, chewing the Nut that Cleanses All Things, and expectorating according to the ritual required.

What happened to me ? What was I doing in this place ?

Before me spread the unclean village street in which a few hens were pecking. The huts were dotted along the broad path irregularly, each with its little yard in a thorn palisade. Up the street a naked yellow woman with the hanging breasts of accomplished maternity, and bearing an earthen pot on her head, paused to regard me before entering her house. She had been bringing water from the upper spring. To the right of me and before me, and to the left across the rushing river, the cliffs towered up. For it was a part of the strangeness of these people that in a land where sunshine was pleasing and grateful they were content to live in a gorge through which the wind blew rarely and in which odours brooded long. On rocky shelves to the right were the upper huts of the masterful individuals, and some scanty dwarfed trees. A path wound against the cliff face to the sunlit vegetation in the free and ample uplands above.

I walked heavily. I had contracted a sort of chronic malaria, and my movements lacked the unconscious ease of my Oxford life. There was much infection among these people, and few failed to give visible evidence of catarrhs, petty fevers, disorders of the blood, scabs, itches, parasites and the like. They were a people naturally sturdy, but infectious and contagious through their dirty habits and their fitful carelessness. That morning I felt inelastic and almost as if I were middle-aged. The skull upon my head oppressed me and the ill-dressed skin I wore, with its flat smell of decay, delayed but not arrested, and its stiffness and heaviness, chafed and weighed me down. Why did I endure this thing ? To what had I sunken ?

I stopped short, waved the flattering benediction to the woman, and looked about me at the squalid scene. I ended by staring at my fingers.

They were filthy, but in spite of the dirt it seemed to me that they were larger and yellower than I had ever supposed them to be in my Oxford days. They were now almost like the hands of any other savage.

I put my yellow hand to the dirty skull that had been clapped upon my head weeks, months, or years ago. Had I become a savage also ?

I was going to the upper table house to eat with Chit the soothsayer, and with Ardam the warrior with the splinter of razor shell through his nose, and with three old men. God knew what I should find to eat there, but this morning I lacked appetite. To what had I come, and how was it I had submitted to be the thing I was ?

I strained my mind back to that first night in the palisade.

Fear !

My soul had been white with the fear of the horror of death, and when I had realised I was not to die I had been ready to submit to anything they chose to write upon my soul. Certain things I had perceived were expected of me. How readily I had done the expected thing ! At the last moment of my trial I had turned from the milk to the draught of blood. It had been a good guess for survival, but a renunciation of my own stomach, heart and brain. And now I went about in this garb, making the proper salutations as Chit had taught them me. I did not dare fling off this half-cleaned skull or cast this stinking skin aside. I did not dare break and fling this filthy staff of mine into some cleansing fire. I did not dare. I did not dare. I looked upward, and above the darkened cliffs, touching their upper levels to translucent glory, shone the deep blue of heaven. " Out of the deeps, O Lord ! " I cried—but not too loudly, for I did not want a lot of people to come running out of their huts.

No audible response came out of that broad ribbon of blue light. But cool and clear in my heart came the answer : " Cast them down and see."

I hesitated. I trembled and blenched. I sighed. " I am ill," I said, and went on reluctantly to my eating with Chit and Ardam and the three old men.

Perhaps, I told myself, I have been given a place and prestige here for a wise purpose. Perhaps I should not throw my position away too rashly. We Blettsworthys stand for the gentler civilisation, the civilisation of infinite tact. If I talk to these people, touch their imaginations, broaden their outlook, I may win them insidiously from much of their cruelty and filth. But if suddenly, after so much surrender, I defy them, to what can it lead but the cooking-pot ?

Yet I might do something. At present it was certainly true that I was being so insidious, so Fabian, that I was doing nothing at all.

Came the sound of a drumming from among the stunted trees above. It was the dinner drum, a drum of human skin which in skilful hands was supposed to render very faithfully the borborygmic noises of a hungry Megatherium.   I quickened my paces because I was not expected to be late at the upper table.

§ 3

THE EVIL PEOPLE

I AM not naturally of a curious and inquiring disposition.   If the super-ficial aspect of things is pleasing to me I can see no reason for disturbing it ; if it is unpromising, why should I delve deeper ?   I have none of the qualities that are needed in a successful explorer or a scientific investigator.   And I lack exactitude—conspicuously.   For instance, I do not know to this day whether the Rampole islanders are dolichocephalic or brachycephalic ; my impression is that their skulls are just medium assorted.   And I am equally vague about their totemism, animism, taboos and suchlike usages.   Nor whether the language I spoke and understood was agglutinate, 'allelomorphic, monophysite, heterocercal, or whatever the proper term may be.   When I talk it to scientific inquirers, they lose their tempers.   These people I had fallen among seemed just dirty, greedy, lazy, furtively lascivious, morally timid, dishonest, stupid, very yellow, tough and irritable, and very hard, obdurate and cruel.   With that summary of their qualities the ethnologist must be contented or not as seems to him most fitting.

And it fell in with my own self-protective nonchalance that conceal-ment and falsity were wrought into the nature of these people.   Most readers I suppose would have expected a certain brutish directness from savages, but specialists in these things tell me that that is never how things are in savage communities.   Savagery, with its numerous taboos, its occultism and fetish, its complex ritualism, is mentally more intricate than civilisation.   The minds of savages are even more tortuous than they are confused ; they are misdirected by crazy classifications and encumbered with symbolism, metaphor, metonymy and elaborate falsifications ; it is the civilised man who thinks simply and clearly. And it is the same with primitive laws, customs and institutions ; there is always irrational elaboration and disingenuousness.   Civilisation is simplification.   My own experiences certainly carry out this view. Direct statement I never encountered on Rampole Island.   Not even direct address. The real name of everyone was concealed. You used honorifics and spoke in the third person. It was forbidden even to use the names of many things. They had to be referred to by complicated circumlocutions. This, I am told by ethnologists, is the common practice of savages. Everything these islanders said therefore meant something a little different and everything they set about doing they did with an air of really doing something else. So that I was perpetually haunted by the fear of misunderstandings that might do me injury, and my longing for the simple lucidity of the Oxford intelligence became at times nearly intolerable.

For example, though I have called these islanders cannibals, no allusion was ever permitted to the fact that the only possible big meat on the island, big meat as distinguished from fish, rats, mice and the like, was human flesh. The flesh of the sloth was taboo and believed to be extremely poisonous, particularly the flesh of the giant sloth. There was an excess of fish. One wearied of eating fish until the weariness amounted to loathing. I know only too well how acute the longing for good meat can be. It forced its way through a jungle of suppressions. But human flesh was never known as human flesh; it was spoken of as the Gift of the Friend, and to have inquired about either the friend or her gifts would have amounted to the extremest indelicacy. Oddly enough, and a thing in complete contrast to the ways of any other savages, there was a theory that only in warfare was it lawful to kill a human being of set intention. There was however a very exacting code of behaviour, and the slightest infringement of innumerable taboos, the slightest disregard of ritual observances, novelties in deportment, any unexpected proceeding, and even indolence and the incapacity to perform an assigned task, was punished by a blow on the head known as Reproof. As the Reproof was administered by a powerful savage, equipped with a club of hard wood weighing about two hundredweight and set with sharks' teeth, it rarely failed to slay, and the consequent body had then to be " reconciled." The scalp, bones, and less appetising viscera of the departed were put to dry up and decay on the high altar of the Great Goddess, which I found an extremely unpleasant den in consequence, and the rest of the body, no longer identified with its original owner, was placed on a lower altar for distribution among the people as the Gift of the Friend. Since everyone surviving benefited by the abundance of the Friend's gifts, everyone was alert to note the slightest breach of propriety in the community, and the visible level of morals and behaviour, according to the prevailing standards, was consequently very high. Unhappily neither cleanliness, kindliness nor truthfulness found any honour among these standards.

At least an equal reticence veiled the sexual life of the tribe. Every-thing primary in that respect was subjected to a rigorous concealment ; polygamy was customary, the first wife having a precedence over her supplementaries ; but the difficulties set to pairing for the young were enormous and the ceremonies of the first union tedious and distasteful. The candidate husband had to satisfy some rigorous tests, had to draw a satisfactory straw from a bunch in the hands of the soothsayer and had to comply with the requisite conditions for building a hut. Because of these impediments and because of the polygamy of the elders, a considerable proportion of the tribe remained perforce formally celibate, subjected to the impulses of a gross dietary and unclean habits and to the incessant vigilance of friends and neighbours alert for any slip that might lead to the high altar of the Great Goddess and the cooking pots. A hut and a wife or so went together and for that reason alone my position was ambiguous, since I had a hut which I kept even morbidly clean and refused to provide for any of the disengaged virgins of the community.

The reader, who may find my fastidiousness remarkable, seeing how much else I had accepted in my degradation, might be of a different opinion could he have seen and savoured the young debutantes in question. They used an oil made from the liver of fish to render their dark hair more glossy ; their complexions were strangely enhanced with patternings of red and yellow ochre and a scanty costume consisting chiefly of various girdles, necklaces, bracelets, anklets and nose plugs of sharks' teeth challenged the embraces of a lover. Each alternate tooth was blackened or stained with a dye the colour of madder and perpetually they chewed the Nut that Cleanses. Yet so powerfully do the passions affect the imagination that there were times by firelight or moonlight when I could find some of these oily shining statuettes not wholly wanting in allurement.

Occasionally there would be dances about a bonfire before the hut of the Great Goddess and her timber image would be brought out upon a platform to dominate the scene. Sometimes the scared little tree sloth or one of its litter, of which I will tell later, would be brought to grace the proceedings by climbing about a red-dyed perch. The youths and maidens would exhibit themselves and dance together. These festivals were conducted under a rigorous etiquette and watched over closely by the elders, and any of the young people who succumbed to the obvious suggestions of these gatherings would be unobtrusively with-drawn from the assembly for the administration of the Reproof amidst the reprobation of their friends and relatives. It became indelicate to refer to them thereafter. In this way the coarser cravings of the community were allayed under the mask of a superficial gaiety.

But that was merely one way of providing for the baser needs of the tribe. A multitude of other traps awaited the unobservant, the unlucky, or the recalcitrant, and secured a permanent edible class for the comfort and support of the higher ranks in the social pyramid. There was for example a strict taboo upon all climbing or indeed upon all talk of climbing towards the sunlight of the uplands. In this gorge these folks were born and for the greater part of them, except for those who went out for the sea fishing, life was lived from beginning to end in the gorge. It was a long, narrow world that varied in width from perhaps a hundred yards to three miles at the widest part, and above certain rapids and a great cascade was the frontier of murderous enemies. The uplands were supposed to be wastes of incalculable danger and measureless evil for the ordinary human being. Only men of exceptional magic powers might ascend there   The light, the vivid fringe of green, were insidious temptations to be banished from speech and thought. To speak of them, even to whisper to untrustworthy ears, was to come within reach of the Reproof. And so well were these restrictions sustained that I am convinced a large proportion of our tribal population went from the cradle to the cooking pot without ever dreaming of the possibility of any other sort of life.

When these things are explained the reader will understand why it was that an extremely vapid conventionality of speech and act distinguished these people and that a certain inexpressive wistfulness tempered the natural ugliness of many of the younger faces. The life of the common man was dull and spiritless to an extreme degree. It made a dismal paradox. The whole being was so taken up by the need to keep living, that there was no courage nor energy left over to make anything of life. Even upon feast days the people lurked warily at home in their huts for fear of the gladness and excitement that goeth before a fall. My imagination was particularly struck by their limited range of movement, accustomed as I was to a civilisation in which everyone—or at least everyone in a position to do so—was free to go all over the earth. It was only upon reflection that I realised that similar restrictions have been the usual lot of mankind since human society began, and that the relaxation of bounds is a very recent thing in human experience. Even in the bright world of to-day, the attraction and necessity of home increases with the square of the distance, and not to have a return ticket is for most of us a symbol of disaster. With all the irresponsible liberties of lunacy it was still only against considerable opposition that I won assent at last to an expedition to the crest of the cliffs to watch the giant sloths at pasture and gain some conception of the broader aspects of this strange world into which fate had brought me.

But of the great sloths of the plateau that sometimes even came blundering down into the gorge itself, and of their quite extraordinary biology, and of certain strange superstitions that attached to them, I must tell later. And later on too I will tell of the wars and trade of these savages with their neighbours up the gorge, and of the little old prolific white tree sloth which was supposed to be the father of the tribe. I have a little wandered from my story to give this brief description of tribal conditions.

I was telling of how I woke out of some forgotten preoccupation and discovered myself to be myself on my way to an eating with Chit the soothsayer and Ardam the warrior and the three hairless ancients who administered justice and preserved the traditions of the village.

§ 4

DISCOURSE WITH THE FIVE SAGES

THOUGH I display an ungracious disposition in the admission, I will confess I detested all these five sages with whom I was to eat. I had always considered them ugly and frightful and profoundly dangerous, and now that I remembered distinctly that I was Arnold Blettsworthy of Lattmeer and recalled all the serenities and amplitudes of the liberal civilisation out of which I had fallen to these associations, and that I had been cowed to acquiescence in these base conditions, a new indignation and resentment mingled with the hatred and aversion I had hitherto concealed. That morning I felt I trailed clouds of glory into this dingy assembly and entered in an altogether novel spirit of self-assertion.

The eating place was a round hut about a low circular slab, its roof was domed by the bending-in of long flexible reeds of which it was composed, and its wall was decorated with the frieze of human skulls, which was the normal architectural feature of all buildings of importance. The roundness of the slab which played the part of our dinner table waived the issue of who might be the most important of those squatting about it. The most striking and least offensive figure of the five was certainly Chit, of whom one spoke as the Explanation or the Light. I have already said that he was thick-set, wrinkled and hunchbacked and that he wore a great leaf made into a cylindrical roll by way of a head-dress. He was one of the brownest of the islanders, unusually big about the head and with very bright, dark furtively observant eyes. They expressed an intelligence uncommon on the Island, a watchful intelligence. He sat on his hams now with his hands resting on his knees, scrutinising my face as I entered.

I detected and disliked a sort of proprietorship in his customary manner towards me, though indeed I owed my life to him. He it was had first ruled me insane and immune from Reproof. Under his directions my position as the Sacred Lunatic had been defined. To him it fell to observe and interpret my vagaries, to indicate what were the omens of my behaviour. Occasionally he would suggest action to me. In that matter we had a tacit understanding.

In marked contrast to his alert visage was the wooden countenance of the warrior Ardam, the Honour of the tribe. It had that quality, so common among the military in all communities, of looking like a profile even when it was seen from in front, so detached and inexpressive was it. Through his nose was thrust a large razor shell and he had sharks' teeth through the lobes of his ears and large rolls of flesh cut and tormented into prominence above his large, protuberant and glassy eyes. His hair was plastered into horns tinted with red ochre, and across his naked chest, rolls of raised flesh and mysterious tattooing were further enhanced with yellow ochre and charcoal. His flapper-like hands enveloped his knobby knees, his legs were folded with extreme precision and tightness and he sucked his teeth noisily in anticipation of his meal.

The three hairless old men were the judges and assessors of the tribe. One had an enormous flattened nose and spiral tattooing on his cheeks ; the second was like a skin dried on to a skull and his teeth were coquettishly alternate red and black like a woman's ; the third, whose cheeks also were tattooed but in concentric circles, was in a more liquid form of decay and blinked and dribbled and oozed. In his old age he had given birth to scattered bunches of facial hair. All three regarded my late arrival malevolently. At the sight of them I abandoned my intention of throwing aside my unpleasant garb and talking to them freely and at once. Instead I made my habitual salutation and subdued my all too civilised legs to the squatting position on the right hand of Chit.

Ardam clapped his hands loudly and two virgins, painted and oiled, appeared and placed upon the table a long dish of wood, like a very broad canoe, in which was our meal.

We did not fall to forthwith. Etiquette forbade. We put our right hands in the dish, grasped succulent-looking morsels and waited, eyeing each other with a pretence of affectionate geniality. We must have looked like three pairs of boxers about to close.

Then, as if by a simultaneous impulse, we set ourselves to thrust the chosen morsel each into the mouth of his antagonist. So we demonstrated our unselfish preference of his enjoyment to our own. It was my habit to select as gristly a lump as possible and aim rather at the eye than the mouth, biting hard on any fingers that came too far in pursuit of the tit-bit thrust upon me. That day, however, Chit caught my morsel with the skill of a hippopotamus in a zoological garden and escaped with digits intact, wiping them neatly across my face. I reeled back but recovered my equilibrium. " Ughgoo," said I. We consumed our chunks with noisy gusto and appreciative grunts, continuing to chew for a minute or so beyond the bare necessities of the case.

" The Friend has given us of her Best," said the skull-like ancient when he had cleaned his speaking gear. We echoed the gracious words and having made this sacrifice to good manners, set ourselves to scramble vigorously for the rest of the dish. I will confess that I competed with but little vigour that day, confining myself to the roots and vegetables with which the meat was garnished.

Until the sounds of deglutition gave place to intimations of a grateful repletion, good manners prohibited all distraction of the attention by conversation, but when on these occasions the main platter was bare and a gourd or so of the fermented milk of the boga nut had been consumed, there was always a manifest disposition on the part of everyone present to tolerate talk. Then it was that the mind of the tribe became active and ideas were exchanged and toyed with. Then it was I acquired information. But to-day, now that my memory had returned to me, I was rather disposed to impart than obtain knowledge.

The moment came for conversation after the tight-skinned ancient had brought the actual eating to a ceremonial end. It was his duty to say, " Gratitude to the Friend," and demonstrate the satisfying quality of his repast.

" Gratitude to the Friend," we protested, with the like demonstrations.

" Salutations to the wise little tree sloth, the patriarch and ruler of our tribe. May he crawl about the Tree of Life for ever."

For there was a sort of cage of these creatures built among the branches of some convenient trees on a bushy shelf higher up the cliff, and there was an absurd persuasion, which most of the common people believed implicitly, that these harmless little animals were the real directors of the tribal fortunes. Chit, Ardam and the ancients were understood to be merely ministers and these queer pets of the community were supposed to whisper wisdom into their ears. It is evident that this odd convention must be the decaying vestige of some very ancient animal totemism, but with my poor powers of enquiry I was never able to get any light upon its origins. The only parallel I could think of in the civilised world was the sacred empire of the Mikado before the modernisation of Japan. In practice it relieved Chit and his associates from the detailed responsibility for many petty favouritisms, persecutions, and tyrannies. The little tree sloth, they said, had whispered it, and the instinctive loyalty of the tribe was at once aroused. Since Chit and his friends lorded it over them and devoured them, it was nice to imagine the little sloths lording it over Chit and his friends.

I echoed the customary aspiration that our Tree of Life might never be rid of its bunch of little clinging parasite masters.

" And now," said I, with my heart drumming desperately for courage, and with an affectation of casual ease I laid aside the decaying skull that had pressed so long upon my brain.

" I find it hot here in the gorge," said I. " As I came up here I saw the sunshine on the uplands and suddenly I remembered the great world out of which I came to you and the space and freedom and hope of it. Never have I told you of it. Now I can begin the telling." And I flung aside the dirty old skin that wrapped me about and squatted, a stark white Caucasian, among these brown folk in their strange garb and their honorific disguises.

I was interrupted by a simultaneous scream from the three ancient men. Three fingers pointed. " Look ! " they cried. " What is he doing ? "

The soldier did not point but he turned very red and his projecting eyes regarded me with an expression of wrathful enquiry. He would certainly have said something about my deliberate indecorum had he been able to think of anything sufficiently coherent to say. But he was a man of deeds rather than words.

Chit allayed his startled seniors by a gesture.

" This," he said, " is not a sin. For as we all know and admit, our Sacred Lunatic cannot sin. This is a Significant Happening. The spirit of the goddess is upon him. Let him do and say what he is moved to do even though it startle you. And then we—" meaning himself—" will find the meaning of what he has said and done."

Ardam grunted ambiguously.

I thanked God in my heart to find that my courage was not ebbing.

" As I came hither to-day, most high and noble brothers," I said, " I saw the blue sky. And a curtain rolled away and my mind went back to that city of light wherein formerly I studied all the wisdom of mankind. It was a sweet and gracious city. There every day one heard of new things and new hopes. There I learnt men need not live in gullies and gorges for ever but out in the free open, need not prey on the weakness and limitations of their less lucky fellows, need not go perpetually fearful and restrained."

" This is madness," said the ancient with the tattooed cheeks, and fell to picking his teeth with a gupa thorn.

" Naturally it is madness," said Chit, without taking his eyes off my face, " because you see he is mad. But it signifies. Tell us more of this land from which you came."

" World," I corrected.

" World," he acquiesced.

" There is method is his madness," said the ancient over his toothpick. " Such words deserve Reproof, mad or sane though he be."

Ardam smacked his thigh assentingly.

But now I realised the super-intelligence of Chit. " Tell us more about this world of yours," he demanded, and I saw a living curiosity in his eyes.

The slobbering old man snivelled a remark. " Everyone knows he came out of the sea. Your Wisdom taught us that. The sun shone on rotting rubbish and begot him. There is no other world but this world in which we live. How *can* there be ? "

" True," said Chit. " Nevertheless we will hear this Fable he will tell us."

" Hear him ! " snorted Ardam. " *Drill* him, say I. Let *me* put him through it and you'll hear no more of this better world of his."

" That may come afterwards," said Chit persuasively while his eyes sought to carry reassurance to me.

" The lands of the world I come from spread wide and open under the sun."

" And people walk about upside-down ! " said the skin-tight elder and was overcome by his own wit.

" Such reproof as is given does not destroy. Men live not on each other but on the meat and drink they combine to produce—like brothers."

" Blasphemy and mischief," cried the slobberer. " What is this about living on each other ? *Who* lives on anyone ? "

" It is utterly foolish," said the ugliest of the three.

Chit smiled at my incredible statement and moved his head slowly from side to side. " And there is enough for all ? " he led me on.

" Enough for all."

" But then they breed and there is not enough for all ? "

" The more mouths, the more hands. The land spreads wide and the sun shines. So far—well—yes, there has been and there is enough for all."

I stuck to that stoutly. For these savages it was necessary to simplify my facts a little. They would not understand half-tones.

So I launched out upon an impromptu panegyric of civilisation and all that it had done and could do for mankind, mixing the two a little more thoroughly perhaps than the facts justified. Adapting myself as much as I could to the outlook of my hearers I gave a highly-coloured and hopeful version of life in a modern community as I had been brought up to perceive it. I laid stress on the practical benefits accruing from the good moral tone created by fair laws and sound education. I enlarged upon the willing charities, kindly consideration and free services that met the needs of the distressed citizen, so far as there were distressed citizens.

I was surprised and pleased to note much of my uncle's optimism and moral fervour reappearing in my discourse, for I had feared that all that had been left behind me for ever. The resonance of my voice satisfied me ; I desired to hear more of it, and I pursued my argument with gathering confidence.

I spoke particularly of the cleanness and healthiness of the civilised life, of the happiness and amplitude of a state of affairs in which everyone was educated to confidence in his neighbour and of the abundance of the goods and conveniences our highly organised co-operations made available for all. I spoke of electric lighting and power transmission, public conveyances and factory inspection. I described an excursion to the sea and a football match in such roseate terms that I was even myself won over to an enhanced appreciation of these popular outings. I gave a sketch of democratic institutions and of the services rendered by the press. I contrasted our kindly constitutional monarchy with the superstitious cultivation of a breed of inferior animals, and our popular church, comprehensive enough to embrace almost every type of belief, with the bloodstained ritualism of the goddess. My vision of Oxford became like a picture of Athens painted by a Victorian artist, and it would have been difficult to distinguish my account of the Bodleian from a description of the brain of God.

As I warmed to my subject I became less aware of the hairless old men and the war lord ; they dissolved into a sceptical mist and only Chit remained vivid, close at hand, listening with marked intelligence, occasionally asking quite penetrating questions and scrutinising me closely if I did not answer pat to his point.

" Are there soldiers ? " asked Ardam suddenly emerging from the mist that had enveloped him.

" There are soldiers," I said, " men of honour whose sole aim is to keep the peace. For it is a rule of our world that if we would ensure peace we must be bountifully prepared for war."

" Arh ! " said Ardam, and a certain hostility faded from his manner.

But as I talked on Chit became more and more my sole listener. A change seemed to come over him. He remained as ugly as ever, but his strange hat became less noticeable and some subtle infiltration of delicacy civilised the intelligence of his face.

He listened, he nodded, he questioned with an increasing scepticism. His interruptions betrayed less and less of the stilted limitations of the savage mind. Abruptly he truncated my exposition.

" You yourself," he said, " know that you are lying."

I stopped short.

" I do not know why you should talk like this," he added, " about an incredible world."

" Incredible ! "

" There is no such world," said Chit. " There never was such a world. There never could be such a world, for men are not made that way."

I looked round, and the rigid face of the soldier and the ugly, cruel and foolish countenances of the three sages had become very solid and near. He glanced aside at them before he spoke again.   " You are a dreamer, you are an insane dreamer, and you are passing through life in a dream." He swept civilisation aside with a gesture of his hand. " The real world is about you here and now, the only real world. See it for what it is."

And suddenly something gave way in my heart and I myself doubted of many of the things I had been saying.

§ 5

THE DREARY MEGATHERIA

THE natural history of the Giant Sloth, *Megatherium Americanum*, as I gathered it from the Rampole Islanders and pieced it together with my own observations, is, I admit, an almost unbelievable story. Though, curiously enough, two biologists of my acquaintance find my facts more acceptable than do most of those with smaller qualifications to judge their credibility, to whom I have related them. But I do not offer this section of my book as a contribution to science. I give it here for what it is, a necessary part of my extraordinary experiences. So far as I, at any rate, am concerned, the facts given here are true and they remain true for me in spite of much disillusionment upon other matters. For the details I am unable to give chapter and verse ; I could not face the mildest of cross-examining barristers, and that the reader must bear in mind. Yet the reality of some of my impressions is overwhelming, even to matters of detail : the great flank of the beast with its long, dirty, coarse, greyish, drab hair, foul with lichenous weeds and fungi, the scrabbling claws upon the stones and roots, the peculiar *stale* smell. I do most firmly believe that in some way, though it may not be in the actual way my treacherous memory now presents it to me, I encountered these animals.

Unfortunately I cannot recall the arrangements for my visit to the uplands nor how we clambered out of the gorge. But in all my remembered observations I am conscious of the presence of Chit and of the terrified boy we brought with us as a porter on this expedition.

The reader is probably familiar with the main facts about these Giant Sloths. They abounded in the world in the days before the Mammoth and the Mastodon, the sabre-toothed Lion and suchlike monsters, and there were European as well as American species. But every variety had disappeared long before the advent of man, except in South America. In South America, which is also the last refuge of the various tree sloths, one species as big as the living elephant survived to quite modern times in the desolate wilderness of South Patagonia and Tierra del Fuego, and, if my witness has any value, on Rampole Island it still survives. A skeleton is to be seen, mounted more or less dramatically, in any considerable museum of natural history. Such skeletons are not, in the strict sense of the word, *fossil* skeletons ; they are not mineralized like real fossils, like the remains of the far more ancient Dinosaurs, for example ; they are actual bones, just as the skeleton of a horse or cow would be actual fresh bones. Remains of the skeletons of Megatheria have been found so fresh indeed that fragments of the skin with hair on and bones with adherent gristle exist. Bones have been obtained manifestly chipped by man. But, in spite of definite expeditions into these vast desolations, the animal has eluded the explorer.

Rampole Island, notwithstanding the way in which its projecting masses seem to offer themselves for examination, has escaped the search. On the charts it is a desert outline, and in our geography a name. I doubt if any white man but myself has ever penetrated its gorges or faced its inhabitants. There, protected by superstitious taboos and by other helping circumstances, some hundreds of these clumsy denizens of the prehistoric world still persist. Many of them must be of the extremist antiquity, for, like carp and some sorts of parrot and one or two other creatures, there seems to be no natural limit to their lives. No carnivora exist to prey upon them ; men will not hunt them, and Chit told me that not only to eat of the flesh, but even to get a full whiff of their decay is certain death. But that may be only a savage's exaggeration. I never put it to the test.

But let me first describe the scenery that opened before us as we came out of the gorge, because its characteristics are closely associated with the habits of these primeval ancient creatures. When I had looked up to the crests of the cliff from below I had formed an exaggerated idea of the richness of the verdure I should find up there in the sunshine, but even on my first brief emergence I had noted a peculiar broken and disturbed appearance of the trees and plants. On this second and more sustained excursion, for we wandered for five or six days, I was better able to understand Chit's explanations and to realize what had happened. These Megatheria live entirely upon fresh shoots and budding vegetation. They progress slowly over the uplands, searching the trees for growing points and nipping out every thrusting bud. The consequence is that every tree and stump, without exception, is dwarfed and crippled by them. The grass of the open spaces has been devastated, except where prickly and thorny growths have protected a bunch of blades from the destroyer. They kill all flowers they see. And the eggs of birds they consume, crushing the nests, and against any small active creatures they wage a sluggish yet surprisingly effective war. They move with such apparent slowness that often they take their victims by surprise. And on many of the lighter things of the world they seem to exercise a kind of hypnotism.

They do not rise high up on their legs like most mammals, but rather drag their bodies reptile fashion. We wandered for some time without coming upon any, though presently we struck a trail which looked as though a huge sackful of old iron had been dragged along the ground. Over the trail hung a smell as though the ultimate vilest dustman had recently passed, and Chit warned me to go discreetly because of the ticks and other nasty parasites that might be left behind. We saw our first monster towards sundown. This was regrettable, because it is not wise to camp in the neighbourhood of Megatheria—they are malignant and have no fear of fire—but my curiosity to see the brute at close quarters was so great that, in spite of the whimpering and sniffing and muttered protests of our bearer, we stalked it discreetly for some time before we struck off from its course.

Through museums and reconstruction pictures the reader has probably formed a conception of this creature; he knows that it has an enormous rump, tail and hind legs, and a head of which by far the larger half is lower jaw. But in all the imaginative restorations I have ever seen it is much too ordinary, much too like a well-groomed animal in a

menagerie, and I have never once seen it in the favourite pose of the
illustrator, magnificently reared up almost like an after-dinner speaker,
with the long claws of its fore-feet clasping a tree. It squats up, but
leaning backward on its tail and with its fore-claws flopping on its belly.
Nor does it walk, bear-fashion, as some skeleton fixers have supposed.
These experts do not seem to have noted how uncomfortably that puts
the claws to the ground. Its gait, as a matter of fact, is unlike that of
any other animal I know. It goes on what are its equivalents for elbows
and fore-arm, with its fore-claws hanging loose and rattling in front ;
its head is held low and usually on one side, and its rump is far higher
than any other part, so that it seems to cringe along. It is in almost the
attitude of an Oriental on a praying carpet. Then it is much more fleshy
about the lower lip and more snouty than the artists imagine ; it has a
great, protruding, slobbery, pink, underhung mouth, its lip and nose are
bunched together and adorned with bristles, and it has very small pink-
rimmed eyes. It can put out its lower lip like a coal-scuttle. It hears,
I know, but I did not mark and I cannot describe its ears. Its skin is a
disagreeable pink, but mostly hidden by long coarse hairs that are almost
quills, the colour of old thatch and infested not only with a diverse
creeping population, including the largest black ticks I have ever beheld,
but with a slimy growth of greenish algæ and lichens that form pendent
masses over the flanks and tail. Over the rump and tail there is real soil ;
I have seen weeds, and once a little white flower, actually growing there.
The whole body smells like rotting seaweed mixed with night-soil, and
the breath—when on one terrifying occasion I whiffed it—had a peculiar
fœtid sweetness. The beast usually moves forward in rheumatic jerks,
usually with a grunt of self-preoccupation, the front part is lifted and
extended and then the loins and hind legs, with a rather comical solicitude, come up to the new position and so, da capo. But, as I was to find
later, it can quicken this crawl to a considerably more rapid advance.
" Galumphing " would be quite a good word to express its paces. The
creature peers about it with peculiar sniffing perturbations of the very
flexible snout, and occasionally opens its mouth and emits a noise like
that of a broken-hearted calf, but louder and more sustained.

Such was the beast I scrutinized in the twilight amidst the mutilated
trees and shrubs of the island upland. It did not seem to be aware of our
presence so close to its flank. I was fascinated by this fantastic specimen
of Nature's handiwork and I might have lingered until dark, watching
it crawling and browsing, had not the persistent plucking of the boy at
my elbow, and a word or so from Chit, recalled me to the need of finding
some camping-place before night overtook us.

At the time I did not attach as much importance as they did to camping out of reach of these beasts. This one we watched seemed unobservant and almost pathetically inaggressive. But because of fresh tracks we came upon later, Chit insisted upon pushing on through the chaparral until long after dark, before he would consent to a halt. We chose a little sandy opening near a stream, with plenty of moss nearby to make us litters for the night. I had my customary skin with me by way of a rug, but I had left my official head-dress below. We built a fire of dead wood and prepared our meal of roots. The boy had brought a cooking-pot to set upon the hot ashes. I had secured and hoarded several boxes of matches from the plunder of the wreck before the savages learnt the use of them, and now, to the great terror and admiration of the boy, I utilized this treasure. We ate. The moon was rising and the night fairly warm, and for a time we squatted and conversed, while the boy watched me, round-eyed, with a newborn respect.

Chit and I naturally fell talking about the Megatheria.

" But what can they do to a man ? " said I.

Chit said they could rise up and fall upon him with their weight and crush him and claw him and tear his skin and flesh off in strips. And also it is unlucky to incur their hostility. Their malevolence had no limits. And they were very, very old and deeply cunning. And poisonous.

" Why do we see no young ? "

" Nowadays there are very few young. And they die."

I was astonished. He assured me that all the young of the Megatheria died. That was how we became possessed of their skins and bones.

I asked some further questions and his replies were so incredible that I made him repeat his assertions. If all the young of the Megatheria died, then some day there would be no more Megatheria ? But the savage mind was not accustomed to look ahead like that. Why did they die ? The Megatheria did not now nurse their young ; they were too old. The instinct had died out in them. They disliked all young things. Nowadays very few were born, if any. I blinked, for the smoke of our fire stung, and peered at my companion's ugly, earnest face under its ridiculous head-dress. I saw not a trace of facetiousness on that broad, red-lit mask. I asked for enlightenment upon some obvious points. It was hard, he said, to determine the sex of a Megatherium, nor was any heat or love-making known to occur among them. He himself believed that they were all females now, and that they conceived only when startled out of their ordinary habits of life and seriously frightened. They conceived then, he declared, and repented of it. Once, long ago, there may have been a few males. He did not know. He did not even care to guess.

" But then——? " said I, at a loss.

" They have this land to themselves. They eat. They lie in the sun. They have enough for themselves and there would not be enough for more. Why should they ever die ? Nothing hunts them. Nothing eats them. Nothing dare hunt or eat because of the poison of their blood. Here they are. Part of your madness, Lunatic, is to be for ever talking of this Progress of yours. Are there no Megatheria in your world ?— that world of yours that keeps going on and on. Does nothing in your world refuse either to breed or die ? "

" Nothing," I said, and fell into thought.

" No animal," I corrected.

He watched me for a time, smiling that sceptical smile of his. Had he not been so manifestly a savage I could have imagined he had penetrated to the reason for that reservation. His head was a little on one side, his back hunched and his huge hands rested on his knees. The boy peered up at our faces, overawed by the incomprehensibility of our talk.

" Sleep," said Chit at last, and rose up stretching and yawning to lie down. The boy, at his gesture of command, piled the fire high. I sat, staring into the smoky blaze and watching the lapping, investigatory flames conquer their way through the dry twigs and branches. For a time Chit watched me, and then seemed to come to some conclusion about me and instantly fell asleep.

I was full of the discovery that for me the understanding of life and Nature had scarcely begun. This story of the Megatheria exaggerated and made plain to me certain strange facts about my world that had long been sitting, so to speak, on the threshold of my apprehension, awaiting the fit moment for my attention. Now they came in and took possession. I had been brought up on the idea of a tremendous Struggle for Exist-ence, in which every creature and every species was kept hard and bright and up to the mark by a universal relentless competition. Yet when one came to think of it, very few things indeed were really struggling for existence and scarcely anything alive was hard and bright and up to the mark. That they were was an important part of my early delusions. I had supposed that when a species was confronted by changed conditions it set about and varied and produced an adaptation to fit it beautifully to these new conditions and survived copiously, and that nothing could defeat it except another competing species which had adapted itself still better and more promptly and was surviving still more copiously ; whereas, indeed, species under altered conditions did the queerest and most futile things like a fumbling idiot asked a too difficult question, and prolific reproduction was only one of a myriad possibilities amidst these responses. I had still to learn that most of those wonderful flowers

that are so amazingly fitted to be fertilised by this or that special moth
are never fertilised in that way. A bird has exterminated the moth
meanwhile. I had still to realise that even more striking than the survival
of the fittest is the belatedness of the fitting. I did not know then, as I
have learnt since, that all the wood anemones of a spring in the north of
England bear their flowers in vain. No seed appears, and even in the
south of England it is rare. There are endless striking instances of such
futile " evolution." And I had still to realise that such a triumphant
species as man can triumph only to convert its habitat into a desert. He
burns and cuts down the trees that shelter his life, he brings goats to
nibble Arabia into a desert, and now he sets about converting the nitrogen
of the air into fertiliser and explosive so that presently his atmosphere
may be unbreathable. As none of these things had dawned on me, these
clumsy monsters who ruled the uplands of Rampole Island came to me
as a stupendous biological shock.

I sat in a mixture of firelight and moonshine and ticked off upon my
fingers the extraordinary propositions that were breaking in upon my
intelligence.

Item the first : animals do not necessarily survive by being swifter,
stronger or wiser than others. A creature which crawls about destroying
the buds and growing points that would otherwise expand to feed a
multitude of a brighter, more active species, makes the life of that other
species impossible. Animals may survive by devastation. They may
also survive by carrying some disease in a mitigated form that will
exterminate other species. No need to outshine or defeat a more energetic
race. They may waste or stink it out of existence.

Then item the second : there is no need to go on breeding in order to
survive. You survive by being continually there, not by multiplying
there. The energy of these Megatheria wasted itself very little in breeding ; instead it went back into the individual system, so that the processes
of tissue exhaustion and decay which burn out the life of most higher
creatures did not wear them out. They had got along for a vast time
without either reproduction or rejuvenescence. They devoured the food
of the children and enjoyed a Saturnian Empire over their habitat.
Nature thrust these heaps of aimless flesh in my face with the same
indifference she displayed when she proffered me the wren or the rose
or a laughing child.

Moreover, item the third : a beast may outlive other creatures and
then itself end. The struggle for life can terminate in the triumph of
types unfit to live, types merely successfully most noxious. In nature a
relative survival of the rotten and dying is possible. And these Megatheria which have made large areas of South America a dreary desert,

have passed and are passing away—even on Rampole Island now and then, one more of them ceases to crawl and lies lax and presently swells and decomposes. So that so far from Evolution being necessarily a strenuous upward progress to more life and yet more life, it might become, it could and did evidently in this case become, a graceless drift towards a dead end.

And this was the real truth about that brisk, hard, bracing Evolution, stern only to be kind, that I had learnt to trust—when I learnt to trust so many things, beneath my uncle's valiant pulpit and at his cheerful table. I saw it now with that extreme mental lucidity which comes from dining late in the open air upon the parboiled roots of unnamed, uncertain things. I saw it as one sees things when one crouches close to a smoky fire amidst moonlit scrub and thinks to the tune of running water and the snoring of a savage.

I said, I think, that when Chit asked me whether there was nothing that refused either to breed or die in that bright world of civilisation with which I was always contrasting his squalid gorge, I had answered first " nothing " and then " no animal." What had flashed into my mind then and what returned now with perplexing force, was the idea that the laws and institutions of mankind came just as much within the scope of biological generalisation as the life of any other living being. And with one of those leaps thought takes at times across vast gulfs of irrelevance, it has occurred to me that states, organisations and institutions breed as little, have no more natural death nor any greater willingness to die, than one of these Megatheria. I found a current of notions flowing now from that instant's striking of the rock. It took on all the pallid cheerlessness of the circumambient night. My civilised world which, in the daylight when I talked to Chit, marched on assured and gloriously from one social achievement to another, appeared while Chit lay snoring, a world most hopelessly barred thereby from escaping to any peace, union or security.

I invoked the spirit of my uncle. "" Man," said I, " is not an animal, the analogy is false, and the fate of this dying species of animals is no earnest of his destiny. This Rampole Island is one thing and my great world another. For my world has a Soul. A Will."

As if to emphasise my words I got up quietly, went to our store of brushwood and replenished our fire.

Man grasps his problem and reconstructs.

I embarked upon an imaginary discourse to the unconscious Chit with that as my text.

Here of course the struggle went against hope. Here no doubt the outlook was dark and vile. At last even these beasts must perish amidst the desolation they have made. Here it did seem that the race would not be to the swift, nor the battle to the strong. The irremovables, the obstinate obstructives, won—by blocking the road and holding the fort. I granted Chit that much. Here their ultimate, belated dying would be no compensation for the buds they had consumed and all the hopes, promises, fresh beginnings they had strangled, choked and ended. They might outlive your poor tribes in the gorges who have not the heart to come up here and make an end to them and take possession of the soil and sunshine. True. But this was not the world. Man, real man—as I knew him—grasps his problem and reconstructs. He can emerge. He will set about this business in a different fashion from your poor Islanders.

Possibly I dozed. My mind certainly fell into that state of incoherence and crazy association between waking and sleep in which nearly imperceptible distinctions open to abysmal depths, and contrariwise the most disconnected things assume an air of close analogy and vivid logicality. It is curious how clearly the passing of these mere shadows of thought survives in my recollection. Perhaps the startling events which truncated these drowsy meditations served to fix them in my memory. In my fantasy Institutions had become entirely confused with Megatheria and Megatheria with Institutions, and I was organising a great hunt to clean the whole world of the lumpish legacies of the past. The world was to be born again. For man, real man, has the power of learning from his failures. There was to be a Winding-up of the Past, like the winding-up of a business that amalgamates and reconstructs. It was my reaction, I suppose, to this spectacle of huge stale beings which would neither breed nor die. I seem to remember a conference of civilised persons—with an edified Chit lying on a heap of moss as the only spectator—and how we were discussing a prospectus, a prospectus for the Voluntary Liquidation of Organised Christianity. This was to be the prelude to some inconceivable reconstruction, some religious rejuvenescence that was to make all the world happily vigorous and vigorously happy. " In order to realise," I murmured, " the good-will and other valuable assets, faith, hope and charity, still available. . . ."

I was roused from these mental wanderings by a flat loud bleating and a crashing in the undergrowth. I sprang to my feet and, peering into the dark tangle, became aware of a huge bulk against the moonlight, plunging towards me. Its little eyes reflected the glow of our fire and shone, two spots of red light in the midst of that advancing blackness. It was advancing in a succession of rapid leaps. There was nothing for it but a bolt into the scrub. I roused my companions at once. The boy was awake, I found, and bounded up at my touch with a scream. He had been cowering in terror, I believe, aware long before I was of what was coming. He darted off like a discovered rat. Chit I jerked out of his sleep in mid-snore. "Run!" said I. "Run!" and set a good example.

I took my own line.

The beast, luckily for Chit, must have come straight for me. I leapt the stream and headed in the direction in which the jungly growths about us seemed more open, stumbling and leaping and being thrashed and torn by the spikes and branches. I could feel the hot reek of my pursuer's breath on my bare back. The heavy, bounding mass was, I realised, actually gaining upon me and I quickened my pace. And now it was I realised how fast a megatherium in a mood of destructiveness could get over the ground. It sounded as if some still vaster being picked up that immense carcass and threw it at me, and then immediately picked it up and threw it again. I ran with my hearing intent upon the crashing rhythm that followed me and for two hundred yards or more I doubt if I gained a yard on my pursuer. After each leap I seemed to get away for a few seconds and then came the bound and the brute had smashed down again close on my heels.

At first I ran hardly thinking at all. Then as I saw how clear and plain were the weeds and scrub ahead of me and how my shadow ran before me up the twisted stems and branches, I realised that I was running with the rising moon behind me, plain to the great beast's view. That alone was a reason for doubling and another reason was that this heavy lump would certainly only be able to turn about in a very wide circle. Directly I saw a convenient bit of cover ahead, I resolved I would switch round it and get a new direction away from the light. But even as I glanced about me to judge the terrain, I trod on air and fell.

Some way I fell. I had gone down into a steep gully that had taken me by surprise and I lay half stunned with the nasty sensation of having knocked my jaw hard against a lump of rock. Then the blue sky above was blotted out by the Megatherium, floundering down over me. If it reached me I was done for. But it did not come right down upon me because of the narrowness of the cleft. It too had been trapped by the unexpected gully.

"Now for the double," said I, and scrambled up the stony ditch as nimbly as I could. I do not know if the beast was still trying to get me, or if it was merely entangled by this natural ditch into which we had both blundered and was trying to get back out again, but I think the latter the more probable.

I crawled clear of it for a score of yards or so, and then crept into a grateful black shadow and lay quite still. Even at that distance I could wind the thing's infinite staleness. It panted, grunted and made the most unpleasant noises. I saw and heard it gather itself up on the bank, and watched its movements intently.

It grunted and snorted and scratched the rocks with its claws. But it did not like the gully. Its first care was to get out of that and back upon trustworthy soil. Then it reared itself up on its posteriors, moved its clumsy head this way and that, and seemed to be looking about for me. In the moonlight it loomed enormous, grey-black, far bigger than any elephant.

I felt a loose rock under my hand and resisted a crazy impulse to stand up and hurl it at my enemy. " Wait," said I.

And waiting served. Not to see me was in itself assuaging to its stupid spite. I had been driven underground, my might was extinguished and honour satisfied. After a spell of bellowing the beast became still, seemed to consult itself, and then flopped down to its queer abject pose again, louted off a few score yards, listened, reared up, bellowed, made a few lumpish leaps, and then departed by degrees, sometimes pausing and rearing itself and then resuming its way. What had happened in that little brain—for the brain of a Megatherium is hardly larger than a rabbit's—I could not imagine. Perhaps I was already forgot en. Its noises diminished. At last its movements were altogether swallowed up in the faint general stir of the night.

But it was a long time before I crawled out into the moonshine, and my vain imaginations about reconstructing churches and institutions and starting the civilised world anew by common consent, were completely scattered and disposed of among the harsh realities about me.

§ 6

THE PEOPLE OF THE UPLANDS

BEFORE dawn I suffered so acutely from cold that, at the cost of several precious matches, I got myself into a steep overhung part of the ravine and made myself a fire. The little rivulet that trickled at my feet provided a refreshing drink, and I covered myself with a fleece of dried moss I stripped off a rock, and crouched and shivered until the daylight sufficed for me to return to our encampment. This was not much more than a quarter of a mile away, and it was easily found by striking back along the trail of the Megatherium. I found both my companions already there, on all fours, cooking roots in the revived ashes of our overnight flare. Neither had needed to run as far as I. The cooking-pot had happily escaped destruction, and the boy had found some ufa leaves for a comforting decoction.

Chit was evidently relieved to see me.

" He could get along ? " he asked.

I assented by gesture and grimace.

The unclean beast had gone right over my official skin and I had to wash it in the stream. Then Chit and I discussed our plan for the day. Perhaps the fine edge of my passion for this exploration of the uplands had gone, but I was still indisposed to return to the gorge. And Chit I found even more inclined to go on than I. It dawned upon me that this hunchback with the wary eyes had had other ends to serve than merely to gratify the whim of the Sacred Lunatic when he had made the expedition possible. As always, I had been his excuse. For a purpose that dawned on me very slowly, he wanted to survey the country and mark out certain routes. There was a range of hills to the south, a grey rocky escarpment that looked like weathered limestone and seemed to promise a steepness and bareness unattractive to Megatheria, and towards that we made our cautious way. We came upon nearly a dozen of the big beasts browsing and were forced into a wide detour, for it would have been excessively dangerous to get among them. We were careful to keep up wind of them.

The boy amused us by avenging his overnight terrors by a sort of dance of insult full of disrespectful gestures and a very passable imitation of a charging Megatherium. Carried away by his own inventions, he blundered into the cooking-pot he had set down for this display, and came within an ace of smashing it and scattering our supply of roots.

The limestone cliffs were all and more than they had promised to be at a distance. They abounded in clefts and shelves inaccessible to the great beasts, but the supply of wood was rather insufficient, and we followed them along the edge where they rose out of the undergrowth, and camped and made a good heap of litter and kindling stuff before dark. The boy vanished for half an hour and returned with a big grey lizard, half a yard long from snout to the beginning of its tail, which made a very pleasant addition to our stew. I found myself sitting by the fire in a mood of unusual contentment, watching the moon rise and longing for a smoke. But Rampole Island does not smoke.

I felt a wave of unwonted friendliness for my companions. I tried to describe theatres and music-halls to them, and the brisk happiness of the west-end of London about dinner-time. I sang them " Ta-ra-ra-Boom-de-ay," and several other popular songs with which I was more or less acquainted. The boy was particularly moved by " Ta-ra-ra-Boom-de-ay " ; he began to beat time in a kind of frenzy, and the cooking-pot had another narrow escape.

The next day I got my first inkling of Chit's real objective. It became plain to me that he was trying to pick up the upper gorge in order to inspect it and see something of the lie of the settlement of the savage tribe our neighbours. In response to my guarded questions he conceded as much. He was thinking of certain possibilities far beyond the range of any of our associated sages. He was thinking that we might presently be at war with these people. There had been some trouble about a girl, and there was still more trouble about our trade. War for them meant inconclusive bickering up and down the gorge, but something— my talk, perhaps, or a dream—had awakened him to the possibility of making war over these forbidden highlands. The tribe that had the enterprise and daring to do that first would get the other fellows underneath. He was taking bearings and scheming out the conditions for such a pounce out of the sky. " But all that means climbing," said I, " and even the thought of climbing is against the Law."

" Suppose *they* do it," he said in a large whisper, and then : " We can't wait for them to do it. . . ."

It was towards noon on the third day that we worked our way over a bleak, sun-scorched mass of limestone ribs and tors to the gorge again. We came upon it quite suddenly. It announced itself by the thunder of a cascade, and then we found ourselves on a great bluff with a wide oval valley on one hand, with a long scimitar of river at the bottom, and on the other a deep chasm, into which the waters poured themselves and were lost to view in steam and spray. They were on their way down to our village, and they seemed to fill the chasm so completely with their steaming, pouring haste that it was difficult to realise that there could be any paths down there, as we knew there were, between the two communities. Still more difficult was it to realise that we had been beating about the massif for two days and a half, only to return to within a few miles of our first emergence from our own settlement, and that the echoes of this same cascade whose thunder filled our ears reverberated along the cliffs and died away among the tangled trees and rocks at the upper end of our village. The scenery was as bold and fine as anything I had ever seen upon Rampole Island ; there was a gigantic quality particularly about its vertical dimensions, so that even the largest clumps of trees seemed multitudinously little. The valley to the right spread wider and shallower than did our own section of the gorge, and was far more richly wooded. There were long slopes of tumbled green. Above these an outcrop of pinkish stone made an overhanging wall of cliff that had evidently protected this abundance from the attacks of the Megatheria. Remotely presiding over the whole, a vast bluff of that same translucent rock which adorned our seaward approach played wonderfully with the afternoon sunlight. We seemed like three very little insects in the face of this easy grandeur.

" Ah ! " said Chit, with the note of one who has reached his goal, and squatted on a convenient ridge. The boy and I followed his example. Far below us, the village looked like a cluster of some insignificant fungus amidst that wide magnificence of rock and atmosphere.

For a time we sat in silence. The habitation of these up-river folk seemed to me extraordinarily similar to our own. There was the same shape of roof; the same loose scattering of the huts; the same little enclosures. We were too far off to see any of the inhabitants distinctly, but no doubt they were the same ugly, yellow, unclean beings as ourselves, with the same tattooings and the same added disfigurements. Even in peace-time we had but little intercourse with them. Trading was done by laying out goods on certain sacred slabs of rock just out of reach of the spray of the great cascade. We traded off fresh and dried fish, large oyster shells with mother-of-pearl, shark skin and sharks' teeth, and they responded with chewing-nut, of which they had a complete monopoly, pots and lumps of pottery clay, pieces of hard wood and dried fruits. Occasionally there was shouting and greetings. They seemed able to understand our language to a certain extent, and we theirs. And I was told there was furtive love-making of a sudden, violent sort between our taboo-pent young people among the rocks and undergrowth by the waterfall and rapids. The supplementary wives of our married men were supposed to be rather too willing to carry a load to the falls for their masters; it was a sly joke against them. These encounters led sometimes to the stealing of wives, and then there would be trouble.

There was also a smouldering quarrel about the exchange of commodities. We below felt we did not get enough hard wood for our fish. Our hairless sages were always grumbling that we were giving all the fish in the sea for a few pots and loads of clay. They wanted our people to be able to go up just above the falls where there was a sort of bay with banks of pottery clay, to get it for themselves and to cut hard wood as they pleased. And the up-river tribe wanted to have a few canoes in the pool below the cascades, so as to go down to the sea and catch their own fish. Their idea was that if hard wood was once cut, it would never grow again. We were getting all their nuts, wood and clay, they complained, practically for nothing. These things would be shouted above the hiss and roar of the falling water, and they made a perennial topic of after-dinner conversation at the circular table.

And always Ardam the warrior would smite the table and say : "Take."

Chit would meditate thereon. "When I was a little ugly boy," he said, "we sought to take. Many men were killed and the Goddess was generous with her gifts. Our girls grew loose and noisy. Nevertheless, afterwards things were as they were before."

"You did not smite hard enough," said Ardam. "I, too, was only a boy."

"In the world of civilisation from which I come," I began, and heard the ugliest ancient groan aloud. I had left England in the unsuspecting days before the great war and so I may be forgiven a description of Europe sanely sure of peace, held together by liberal conventions and rational explanations. I explained how we had commercial treaties and treaties of arbitration, and how in the last resort we were wont to go to the Tribunal at The Hague or hold a European conference upon the situation. There was, I explained a Concert of Europe that was speedily becoming a Concert of All the World.

"All *your* world," said the sceptic Chit.

"The great world."

"The impossible world."

"Most possible," I retorted. "If only I could bring home to you the slowly won experiences of our bloodstained Europe so that you could realise what union means ! If only you could sink this dismal feud with your brothers above the falls."

"*Brothers !* " noted Ardam in a tone of immeasurable disgust.

"You could push out of this ill-lit narrow prison of a home, upon the soil and sunshine of the wide lands above. You could make an end to the megatheria with darts and spears and pitfalls."

"He'll make an end to *us* next," sneered the drivelling elder, and toyed with the row of picked wrist-bones he had arranged on the table before him.

"You could drag the stinking carcasses away to the cliffs and tumble them into the sea, and then up there you could plough and reap and build."

"Much luck to your ploughing if you touched a megatherium," said the hairless man with the tattooed cheeks.

"Great woods would grow there, bountiful fruits and lovely flowers, There would be enough for all. There would be happiness for all ! "

"Thigh Bones of the Holiest One ! " swore Ardam. "Cannot we put this Sacred Lunatic into an eating house of his own ? "

"I pray you let him continue," said Chit. "There are omens in this talk."

" Try the Reproof upon that skullful of omens," grunted the ugliest of the three. " Then you will get the whole lot of them together and we shall eat without these sermons."

" What omens are there in this stuff ? " asked Ardam.

" Omens of war," said Chit.

" Omens of peace," said I.

" A new sort of war. Let him continue. He knows not what he says."

" We don't want any new sort of war," said Ardam. " And after I have eaten well I like to sleep. Curse his omens ! "

Many such talks we had had about the circular table in the eating house of the sages, when we had devoured the mercies of the Friend, and now they came back to my mind as we sat in that immensity and spied upon our enemies and rivals, like three little ants spying on a distant nest of emmets. It was strange, I reflected, that Chit, who was so intelligent, would admit no possibility of ending the reasonless feud between our two pitiful little clusters of human weakness. Never a gleam of that could I get from him. His mind moved within the idea of war, as Kant says our imaginations move within the ideas of space and time. For him war was an inevitable feature of human life, a necessary form of thought. He could not imagine men strongly sane enough to conquer that ancient disposition.

Three days we spent, working out the shortest and best way from our gorge to this up-river village over the shoulders of the limestone massif, the way that skirted the denser thickets and so was least likely to be blocked by wandering megatheria.

And when we had solved most of our problems we descended again into the sunless homes from which we had come. " I have had great oracles," said Chit as we came down into the dirty streets among our hovels again.

§ 7

LOVE ON RAMPOLE ISLAND

WE talked of war, but for quite a considerable time war did not come and often it seemed to me that no war could be coming. I became more and more subdued to the everyday life of a Sacred Lunatic among the Rampole Islanders. I was bored, I was unhappy, I had terrible phases of self-reproach when my soul revolted against the food I ate and the systematic suppression of other human beings that kept my dull flame of life alight, and then the slow imperatives of morning and evening, hunger, sleep and a multitude of petty natural reactions brought me back again to the common routines. I found a certain companionship in Chit and I released my oracles as they were required of me. And I persuaded myself that by talking of the uplands I was bearing my witness against the life I led.

I had queer fancies in those days that I find difficult to describe. I have told of a sort of transparency I had remarked in much of the rock that made our cliffs, and sometimes it seemed to me that this transparency extended itself to many other of the things about me. I would lift my eyes to the rocky walls above me and it would seem to me that they were pierced by phantom windows and bore strange devices and inscriptions written in letters of fire, and I would look again and behold it was nothing more than facets and roughnesses of the rock touched by shafts of the sinking sun. Or I would feel the resonance of a pavement under my feet and hear the droning of a passing street car close at hand and the warning note of its bell. But it was no more than a chance slab of rock I was treading upon and the sounds were the sound of a beetle flying from one heap of fish-guts to another and the clang of a savage beating out an old nail from the wreck into a hook for his angling.

At times as I talked of the social gatherings and amenities of civilised life it would seem to me as if I was or had just been moving among the things I described. Or I would wake up in doubt whether I was not some entirely different person from the Sacred Lunatic in his skull and skin. Such phases of confusion were bathed in the distress of an acute nostalgia. I would thrust these doubts from me, bracing myself up to the fact that I was still on Rampole Island. "This is Rampole Island," I would say; "This is Rampole Island. Do not torment me with dreams."

At first the days of my servitude upon Rampole Island had seemed endlessly long, but now, as the apathy of habitual routines crept upon me, they grew shorter and at last they began to pass very swiftly. I no longer hoped for any rescuers to come for me, and I soon ceased to imagine that with all my yarns about civilisation and progress I could make any great change in the dull inertias of the life these people led. And only when the opening uproar of savage warfare was jangling in my ears and threatening me with toil and torture was I roused to really vivid activity again. Until then my chief purpose in life was to resist the continual efforts of Ardam and the skull-faced sage to reduce me to the level of ordinary humanity by marrying me to one of the daughters of the tribe and placing her in control of the privacy of my hut. In this resistance

I had the support of Chit. It was almost as vital to him as it was to me that my prestige as the Sacred Lunatic should rest unimpaired.

Only gradually had I come to realise the extent of our mutual dependence. A Sacred Lunatic was a necessary condition to his full influence with the tribe. I was only the latest and most convenient of a series of wearers of the skull and pelt, whose overt interpreter and secret director he had in succession been. And I might be irreplacable. Without a Sacred Lunatic, he was merely the repository and interpreter of tribal traditions and all his statements and counsels were subject to the endorsement of his fellow elders. But he alone could draw omens and intimations from the utterances and vagaries of the Sacred Lunatic, and my utterances and vagaries gave him far more scope than he had ever had before. The peculiar circumstances of my arrival, my European complexion and build and the strangeness of my ideas and impulses gave me a distinction no other Sacred Lunatic had ever possessed.

Since my return to civilisation I have made enquiries about the role of the madman in savage life. I had supposed that the Sacred Lunatic of Rampole Island found no parallel elsewhere, but so far from this being the case, I gather that such strange demented figures are to be found very widely dispersed, playing the part of, what shall I call it?—a *rocking* influence, among the complicated balances of the savage and barbaric community. They enable little wedges of innovation to be driven into the tight mosaic of custom and precedent. In some parts of the world they are the familiars of medicine men; in others they themselves are witches and prophets, treading their eerie way amidst familiar things. There is a summary of this subject published by one of the anthropologists of the Smithsonian Institute of Washington: " The Eccentric Individual in Primitive Society," I think it is called. The writer connects the Sacred Lunatics of Patagonia—for it seems they are known on the mainland also—with the wide-spread worship of sacrificial kings, and so shakes down a mass of ripe and rotting fruit from the *Golden Bough*. He links this cult of the madman not only with witches, but with the Lords of Misrule, who were given power during the Saturnalia, and with the Jesters and such-like privileged fantastics of the Middle Ages. There I am told he is on firmer ground. And he brings down his argument very strikingly to our treatment of the man of genius of to-day, with his remarkable privileges of unorthodox suggestion and his conspicuous immunity from responsibility. No doubt, he says, eccentrics have always been made use of by people more deliberate and cautious than themselves, but who are also, after a different fashion, in revolt against established authority. It is interesting to find my life in that dull and heavy gorge, linked with and enhanced by so much that is interesting in sociology, and I note it here for what it is worth—repeating my warning to the reader that this is the story of a personal adventure and not a contribution to science.

My predecessor in office had been an atavistic idiot who had died from a surfeit of offal and in the days before my arrival Chit must have had a dull and subordinated existence. If the hairless ancients contradicted him, he could produce no omen in response. Precedent ruled unchallenged. In the interim he had tried to throw the glamour of incalculable imbecility over a young man whose sole genuine abnormality was a squint, and had failed completely. From a partly inaudible story told one day by the slobberer, I gather that the claims to insanity and immunity had broken down and Chit's protégé had been found guilty of blasphemy and had terminated his brief career under the Reproof. The unfortunate pretender to dementia had been betrayed by his wife. He had affected to have trances and visions in seclusion during which the Great Goddess had honoured him with peculiar favours and, in a moment of jealous mortification that no credit for the revelations came to her, his wife had exposed this pretence.

" That almost made *Chit* squint," squeaked the aged narrator, and choked with reminiscent amusement.

The defeat had been a serious one for Chit. He could establish no fresh defective. There was a hunchback or so about the village and one deaf and dumb girl, but they were all malignantly sane and moral. Nothing would tempt them to conspicuous behaviour. The four sages had contemplated a blissful future of authority unchallenged by any fresh revelations, with Chit's interventions waning towards his ultimate Reproof, when chance or heaven sent me to rehabilitate him. I was so queer and astonishing that even my detractors more than half believed in everything he claimed for me. My craziness lay along lines beyond their penetration. They hated the sudden restoration of decisive power to Chit, but they faltered and went cautiously in their attempts to undermine it. The belief of the common people in my sound and unquestionable madness was absolute.

My enemies assailed me therefore with an appearance of solicitude ; they professed to desire nothing so much as my comfort and honour. The chance that a wife would undermine me had the attraction of a successful precedent. They were shocked, they said, to see me sad and alone, in such melancholy contrast to the rich satisfactions of their own lives. So gifted and precious a creature should have wife and appetising handmaidens, rich with sharks' teeth and mother-of-pearl, brightly painted and dripping with fish oil, always about him. They had so much faith in the destructive power of matrimony that they even extended their proposals to my associate. Chit also was a lonely man, they remarked, living too austerely; he had two wives and each by some queer mischance had bitten off the end of her tongue and went speechless and discreetly about his household. He too would lead a more seemly and happier life had he also the harem of chattering handmaidens affected by other leading and influential men. Why was he so silent and secretive?

Now I must confess that in this matter I was assailed by enemies within me as well as without. Like most people of active imagination and acute sensibility I was sometimes stirred by great gales of physical desire and sometimes tortured by a loneliness in which any response, however coarse, would have been a relief, and as I have told already, my religious beliefs which might otherwise have assisted me, had been greatly strained by my misfortunes. So that there were lights and times when these savage women stole a magic out of the depths of my own tormented being, with which to adorn their fishy greasiness, and when the false promise of a smile or even a steady tranquil gaze could storm my heart. The deepest self reproach in these memories is to think how little I sustained the attitude of a superior person among these Islanders. Time after time I had to hold myself back, and I did not always hold myself back, from snatching at the tawdriest, most filthy lures.

The feelings of men for women and of women for men upon Rampole Island were far harsher, crueller and more dishonest than anything I could have imagined in the days of my Wiltshire upbringing. Their relationships were infinitely more tortuous. I was repelled as violently as I was attracted by these Island women, and enlightened by my own reactions, I detected a similar see-saw between desire and repulsion in most of the male savages about me. In that clean and civilised world out of which I had fallen, love was normally a pretty and gracious business, very fruitful of happiness. My own first mischance and its revelation of the dark fountains in my own being, had come as something monstrously exceptional. The common way in that better world was the happy development of a pleasant preference and companionship into an ardour of mutual and equivalent desire and the establishment of a life of the completest confidence, helpfulness and self-sacrifice, upon the basis of its consummation. But these Islanders were fierce, greedy and mistrustful. They feared and resented the physical attraction that drew them together.

As I have explained, because of the difficulty in building and finding huts and because of various taboo systems, which I never completely understood, there was rarely any really free mating. The man found himself drawn towards women in general but thrust towards one or two in particular, and with the girls the selection was even more restricted than with the men. The pick of the girls, whether they liked it or not, was with the sages and then with the headmen, executioners, ceremonial assistants, steersmen of canoes, net and hut makers, moral guardians and other leaders of the tribe. Polygamy prevailed, as it must do wherever the light of Christianity has never shone. The higher a girl could find her protector in that hierarchy, the safer, save for his displeasure, she felt from the Reproof. She would be torn between a natural desire for some friendly and gallant, if oily, youth, and the practical advantages of some tattooed ancient's prestige. The thought of the Reproof would always restrain her from any freedoms with the youth, but a rankling dissatisfaction would fill her with a thirsty desire to see her elderly conqueror uncomfortable and ill.

The love story on the Island, therefore, was never the free and pleasant thing it can be under civilised conditions. It was saturated with insincerities, poisoned by reluctant submissions and tempered satisfactions. The lover distrusted the motives that brought his mistress to him, and she watched warily to ensure the full rewards of her surrender. Of all this I was acutely aware. At the torchlight festivals I would find some panting young beauty pressing herself against me, supple and slippery with oil, gay with gleaming nacre and every charm enhanced with lively scarlet, and looking into her eyes I would discover nothing but fear, distaste and the compulsion of circumstances beyond her control. I would glance at the dais under the red perch of the little tree-sloth, and there I would see Ardam and the tight-skinned elder with their heads together watching their decoy at her work.

I would smile my firm refusal to her mute interrogation, and involuntarily her eyes would go to the dais for some intimation of her next move in the game.

An odd minor result of this struggle to preserve an effective chastity was that I gave up eating fish and redoubled my efforts to keep my person sweet and clean. I perceived that once my nose became tolerant of the reek of rancid fish oil I should have lost one of my main defences against this persistent siege.

§ 8

THE WAR DRUMS BEAT

WAR, which had been hovering over the gorge for years, like clouds that gather upon the mountains and disperse and gather again, came at last very rapidly. Suddenly it had banished every other topic from the round table of the sages, and War Dances and War Incantations swept all thought of torchlight merrymakings before the shrine of the Great Goddess from our minds. It was the up-river folk who were the final aggressors. Instead of the customary chewing-nut, timber and fireclay they had requited our last trade of fish—a not very generous offering, I understand—with objects and symbols of the most offensive character. Our people, shocked and aggrieved, had responded still more grossly, but the honour of the first insult rested with the enemy and rankled very sorely.

Directly war was declared, Ardam, by law, custom and necessity, became the supreme master of the tribe. He seemed to expand physically forthwith. He assumed a novel state, inserted two pieces of razor shell in his upper lip under the nose fragment, dyed his nose scarlet, cut a large fresh gash over each eyebrow, and flanked himself at meals with two richly adorned guards, with nose spikes, clipped ears, hair in long red horns, and vast spears, so that at last he occupied a full half of the circular table, and the other five of us had to be content to subtend no more than an angle of thirty-six degrees each. " It is war," he said simply.

He affected a profound preoccupation with hostilities, so that we others talked among ourselves and addressed him in vain, but sometimes he would intervene magisterially. Outside the eating hut we had great war drums beaten by relays of old men ; they were made out of the skins of former heroes and sustained a tiresome booming roar day and night. Even now, at the thought of it, the rhythm of that dreary reverberation echoes once more through my brain. The drummers seemed to be perpetually dozing off and then waking up to a new storm of energy. All the men and women of the tribe, all property, it was now Ardam's right to requisition for the common security. And he made himself felt by us to begin with, in preparation for the inflictions that were to subjugate our enemies.

All the young men were enrolled as warriors, and in order to harden them for conflict they were severely tortured and mutilated ; their ears clipped, their flesh hacked into raised folds, and a peculiarly idiotic way of walking, with the chin thrust forward and the tongue protruding, was imposed upon them. All the girls of the tribe were also at our War Lord's disposal, and they were instructed to sustain the courage and fierceness of the fighting sex. Nearly everything, until the supplies of colour ran out, was painted red. Every few days there would be orgiastic War Dances, in which slaughter and victory were rendered with great animation, or there would be Howling Meetings against the enemy.

These gatherings were supposed to keep up the spirit of our people. In them the sages and leaders of our tribe denounced the vices and crimes of our antagonists amidst the applause and indignation of the tribe. The sentences of the speakers were punctuated by violent howling, and it was extremely unwise to betray any slackness in these responses.

In the tirades of our speakers three main accusations constantly recurred, our grievances against our foes, their master crimes. The first of these was that they were cannibals. This charge never failed to evoke the most impassioned indignation. The speaker would lean over and ask impressively : " Do *you* want to go into these up-river cooking-pots ? "

Their second offence was that they were uncleanly in their persons and habits. The third was that they kept a family of loud-croaking bull-frogs as their mystic rulers, a thing all our people found incredibly disgusting and degrading. The offensive noises made by the parental bull-frog and his loud-splashing leaps hither and thither were contrasted with the louse-like movements and inoffensive gentleness of our own dear tribal totem. And then, adopting a more practical tone, the speaker would demonstrate that in no other way was the danger of war to be avoided excepting by carrying this war to a successful finish, and finally he would dilate on the abundant chewing-nut, clay, timber and fruits we would have when at last our enemies were trampled underfoot. As there was already a serious shortage of the Nut that Cleanses, this stirred our most inveterate cravings. We would remove the bits of wood with which we solaced ourselves for the want of chewing-nut, howling together very heartily, eyes and ears alert for anyone who seemed remiss in the howling.

Meanwhile the war made remarkably little progress. As I have explained, the frontier was near the great cataract, and the path on either side of the fall was extremely overgrown by thorny shrubs and precipitous and narrow. Above it, the cliffs rose sheerly for, I should say, a thousand feet or more towards the forbidden uplands. It was a place in which a mere handful of men could hold back an army coming from either direction. Our outposts had pushed up beyond the trading slab and lurked hidden amidst rocks and bushes, armed with slings and long beams of wood. These latter were used to push an antagonist off the path into the water. Our sentinels had also trapped and netted the path beyond their ambuscades. The enemy watched from above the fall. Their command of good wood gave them a supply of longbows, which we had every reason to envy. They could send a shaft a quarter of a mile down the gorge, and their marksmanship was decidedly respectable.

Neither side betrayed any appetite for close quarters. Now and then one of our people, who had shown himself inadvertently on our lines of communication, would be picked off, and once, at least, one of their fellows slipped on a loose rock and fell into the torrent and was drowned. We tried to get a few of them by throwing them poisoned fish, but it is doubtful if that succeeded. So that as far as the region of contact went the war degenerated into mere hiding, sniping and petty assassination, to the incessant hum and rumble of our war drums and the sharper yap, yap, yap of the wooden clappers with which our foemen supplemented their drumming. It was in fact a deadlock war, and the best part of the excitement went on above and below the actual front.

I do not think that Ardam ever took his tremendously decorated person within range of the up-stream arrows, but in the village his activities were prodigious. Long before dawn he would turn out all our sore-eared levies, fasting and limping, for hours of marching to and fro, chin out and tongue protruding ; should one faint, he was kicked and prodded until he revived, and if he fainted again he was meet for the Reproof. The people were for ever being assembled before the shrine of the Goddess to hear of some new proclamation that Ardam fathered upon our master the little tree-sloth. Now it was that we, his faithful subjects, were not to chew the Nut that Cleanses, even if we could obtain it, before the stars were visible ; and now it was that, except by express command from Head-quarters, streaks of red paint must not be put on the body vertically but only horizontally. There also began a sort of inquisition for poor wretches supposed to be sympathetic with the enemy.

And now, at the table of the sages, Chit, using my name much too freely for my peace of mind, began to talk of the possibility and advantage of a flank attack upon the enemy over the plateau. This suggestion, because of its implicit criticism of the deadlock war, was received very badly by Ardam, and Chit betrayed a warmth of feeling for his darling idea and a satirical conception of the current campaign that greatly stimulated Ardam's resentment. The argument developed rapidly and easily into a noisy quarrel in which the hairless elders were invoked for judgments they were not in the least disposed to give.

With a gathering apprehension I heard Chit being asked what he and I were doing in the war except to make difficulties for the military authorities, and where it was we had really gone when we had pretended to watch the megatheria on the uplands last year. In fact, with a great bang on the table, let us know where we were ; were we or were we not " sympathetic with the enemy " ?

The hairless ancient with the tight-drawn skin intervened with hoots of remonstrance ; the snuffler snuffled, " My lords ! my lords ! " and Ardam was persuaded to reduce his accusations to a vague complaint of tepidity. But he left us both gravely scared. It was clear we had to drop the subject of the upland offensive and that it behoved us both to display more war zeal than we had shown hitherto. Chit put two shark's teeth through his ear lobes and adorned his leaf head-dress with fierce patternings, and I painted my sloth skull red, added two violently squinting eyes I made of balls of clay, and cultivated the habit of keeping my hardwood staff of office close at hand wherever I happened to be.

In spite of these efforts, Ardam complained of our unserviceableness. He demanded that I should have my ears cut off and my skin tattooed and slashed like any other young man, and that I should be sent right up to the front in my skull and pelt to gesticulate and intimidate the enemy. The Sacred Lunatic of the up-river folk, it seemed, stood at the head of the great fall, and cursed us very effectively. Why could I not do the like ? Their archers missed more often than not. We resisted these suggestions, but at the price of feeling still more outcast and endangered.

We did not want to incur suspicion by prowling alone, but we were kept so distinctly out of things that we were almost obliged to prowl alone. Sometimes we went together, but not often, lest we should fall under suspicion of plotting against the wisdom and leadership of Ardam. Throughout all this phase of my story Chit was extremely cautious in what he said to me, but on one occasion at least, he betrayed a distinctly treasonable thought. We were wandering in a sort of undercliff, a patch of country made by great rockfalls in the past and now overgrown with scrub cut up by channels from the main torrent, and dotted with deep pools of water. From a patch of rising ground we got a distant view of the cataract. " I suppose their soldiers *are* as stupid as ours," brooded Chit. " They would be as little inclined to listen to a reasonable idea.

" All soldiers are alike," he said, generalising from his limited experience. " Here we are ! If we went over the uplands we could finish this war in six days—and twist Ardam's nose for him. . . ."

Even now, at the thought of that Island warfare, the feeling of brooding detachment from my own kind returns and once more I am wandering in moods of acute solitude amidst the tumbled hillocks and lonely turns of the undercliff, homesick for a civilised world, with the sense of being watched and in danger, and with that infernal idiotic drumming for ever beating in my ears.

" What have I done ? " I asked, " what have I done that my brief portion of life should run to waste in this barbaric land ? Surely I was given my little scrap of strength, my desires and my possibilities, for some better end than to be a counter in the game of Ardam and his idiot friends ! Am I to be cast aside amidst this wilderness of warring fools, am I to be silenced and useless, and is that to be my all? Am I never to see the great cities of the world I had promised myself, nor add one little scrap of decent work to the achievements of life? Am I to miss love and equal friendship, and continue a pretender, an observer of laws and customs I despise, a mockery of manhood, until the end? Why was I born, why was I ever made?"

Little did I suspect the strange mutations that Fate was even then preparing for me.

§ 9

THE CAVE AND THE GIRL

THE undercliff which was my lonely rambling ground during these dreary months, had a wild beauty of its own of tumbled ground, pools, marsh and wild flowers. There was an abundant plant like the English sun-dew but very much larger and more active in its gripping movements. It made great carpets on the damper places and I never once ventured to walk across the prehensile leaves it spread so hungrily. Its sticky, hand-like leaves captured not only flies as the English sun-dew does, but lizards, efts and small birds. Their little shrivelled skins and bones lay everywhere on the morass. There were also thistles of an intense blue in dense pyramidal masses, and a bramble with very large berries. And there were many sweet-smelling herbs and flowers. Always there was the background of towering cliff, bare and bright or veiled above with delicate haze. Much of that scenery, when during a brief interval in the afternoon the sun pierced down to it, made me think of a disorderly heap of vividly-coloured silks at the foot of a limitless Gothic shaft. And in its deep and enclosed pools I sometimes bathed.

One day I chanced upon a discovery that kept Chit and myself active and hopeful for some days, for it seemed at first to promise a second way round towards the conclusion of the war.

This was a huge fissure in the mountain. I had passed several times by a sort of funnel arch whence there came a little rivulet of sparkling water, without thinking of its use as a hiding place. Then one afternoon when the menaces of Ardam were heavy on my mind, I came upon it and was struck by the possibility it suggested of a hiding place. I set myself to wade and crawl up it and was rewarded for my enterprise by discovering a cave of very considerable size. I advanced discreetly and was very soon in what I could feel was a large airy darkness. I kept my feet in the stream because, if I stuck to that, there could be no possibility of my falling into any abyss ; manifestly where there was running water I must be at the bottom of things. I struck a match and produced a fantastic storm of startled bats which had been reposing amidst the stalactites above. So far as I could see amidst the swirling wings and bodies the cavern was very great indeed, and adorned very richly with stalagmitic sheets and pillars.

I did not care to waste matches and I had not thought to bring anything that would serve as a torch, nevertheless I went on with my exploration in the dark, trusting to the guidance of the trickling water and knowing it would warn me by an increasing splash and spatter, of any shelf or fall. Presently, at a very great distance, I saw a pale light and made my way slowly towards it. It filtered down from above and as I approached it, the fact became clearer that this great cavern was really a huge fissure which even reached at times to the sunlight above. Its floor, the torrent bed, which slanted upward, was like a railway track in hill country which passes alternately from tunnel to cutting and from cutting to tunnel. But it is necessary to qualify that comparison by noting that the vertical dimensions were colossal in proportion to the width of the cleft. I saw hardly any blue sky because of the bosses and bulges on the cliff faces that leant over towards each other, and the endless reflections the light underwent in its descent, seemed to rob it of all its vitality and to attenuate it to the complexion of moonlight. Everything about me was pallid, with a sort of phantom clearness, even in the brightest places, and water dripped from untraceable origins upon the face of the rock. The rock shone in that twilight an alabaster white.

I brought Chit to see my discovery next day. We made torches of thornwood from the thickets and pushed our explorations as far as the caverns permitted, but we found no way either round to the up-river folk or up to the plateau. We poked about for days, very reluctant to admit that this hopeful rift was merely a dead end. We did find some interesting caves and a supply of fungus that was not unpalatable, and in the upper parts our efforts to scramble out led us up to some high ledges on which were the nests of sea birds and many eggs. Even if we had not found a way round we had discovered a very practicable hiding place if presently the war mania should threaten us too urgently.

I cannot now recall how long it was after this that the decisive adventure which was to release me from Rampole Island occurred, for my memories of those dreary war days lie so to speak in a heap with no proper sequence between them. I had been prowling in the afternoon in the middle part of the district, and I was sitting on a rocky slope above one of the largest and deepest of the lonely tarns. I sat brooding, vaguely and aimlessly as a purposeless and unoccupied man must needs brood, I became aware, first from her reflection, of one of our girls wandering on the opposite shore, knee-deep in deep green weeds. Her shining slender yellow body caught my eye and my imagination. I followed her undecided movements with a quickening interest.

Her presence recalled a myriad possibilities not only of delight and excitement, but of companionship and reassurance. Suppose that slip of life over there should prove to be no evil-smelling savage, but some strange miraculous escape from the world of my youth and hope ! The hunger of my soul and body could evolve and play with even such fantastic impossibilities as that.

She seemed to be looking for some point of vantage at the margin of the water and presently her search came to an end. A big boss of rock stood out into the lake and to the end of this she went, stood for a moment thoughtful and then, flinging up her arms, cast herself into the water. I sat on for a moment like a spectator at a cinema show, and then all the ancient traditions of the Blettsworthys stormed up in me ; I flung aside my skull head-dress and skin mantle and ran headlong for the water. You must rescue drowning people, though you drown yourself in the process ; nothing is more sacredly imperative. I had never attempted nor rehearsed such a rescue before, but in I dived and swam across to her.

To get a frightened, struggling, able-bodied young woman out of deep water from which she is not disposed to be taken, is really a very difficult and dangerous undertaking. As I struggled with that buoyant yet vigorous floating body and gripped and was gripped and pulled under, as I swallowed water and rolled over and kicked, I did my best to recall what I had read and heard about such work. I had an impression that I ought to stun her and aimed one or two blows at the back of her skull, but I only succeeded in smacking her face. She was sufficiently greased to make a hand-hold difficult and for some time she created needless difficulties by clinging with both hands to my ankle. The water made a strange thunder in my ears, like the shouting of people and the hissing of steam jets. I heard a sound like a hooter. A phantom boat, all hands, went by me. The illusions of exhaustion were, I suppose, beginning. For a time the affair ceased to be a rescue and became a rather aimless fight, and then when I was already half insensible and more than half drowned, my feet as we sank together touched bottom. We had drifted inshore. We were in our depth. With one last desperate effort I freed myself from her, stood up, spouted water like a Roman fountain, took a deep breath, and then clutched her by an arm and hauled her in to me.

We stood shoulders out. She was dazed. She thrust back her wet black hair, stared at me in amazement and collapsed in my arms.

" Get out of it ! " I choked and bore her to the bank.

She had fainted. I pushed her out of the water, and it was no light task, for the bank was steep, clambered out—and with an excess of zeal, dragged her some few yards up the slope through the sweet-smelling herbs. Then I dropped her like a sack and fell into a sitting position beside her, panting and sick and unable for some moments to do anything more. I seemed to be breathing air that changed most uncomfortably to brackish muddy water in my throat. " My God ! " I said, " this isn't like they do it in books."

I had a queer impression that we were not where we were but somewhere else. I rubbed my eyes and stared about me to see again the green foreground and the lonely pool, with the palisade-like cliffs behind it. I coughed up water and spat it out. My breath and strength returned. I considered what I had to do with my inanimate companion.

And I cannot now retail clearly what I did do. I seem to remember the words, " methods of resuscitation," floating over my mind, and I tried pumping with the arms ; they were pretty arms ; and much rubbing and slapping of the chest and body with the herbs about me to restore the circulation. The fish-oil was rubbed off her and the air was filled with an intense smell like the smell of lemon verbena.

" Let me die," she said. " Oh, let me die."

" Nonsense," I panted.

" They'll get at me again ! "

" '*They*' be damned ! " said I. " I'll help you."

" I don't want to trouble anyone. I'm done."

She conveyed to me that she had been pursued and tortured by Ardam. " I cannot love him. I am terrified. How can one obey his wishes when one is frantic with terror ? "

There were bruises upon her arm and some weals across her shoulders. " He will get me killed," she said, and her terror was so manifest that I took her in my arms and carried her towards a more sheltered spot among the bushes. There very gently I lowered her to the ground again and put myself beside her, and my hygienic rubbing changed by degrees to reassuring caresses. I realised that she was very pretty.

She had held to me and seemed reluctant to be released. And seen so closely I found her face and neck and body warmly beautiful. She had level brows, she had a tender and exquisite mouth. Suddenly the brief afternoon sun smote down the gorge and lit our lurking place to glory, and in that instant our eyes met and mutely we searched each other's purpose.

Once before in my life, far away in Oxford city, I had seen that same expression in the eyes of a girl. But this time I did not fly the challenge of the occasion.

§ 10

FUGITIVES

So the tenor of my life was changed. The story I have told is told as I
find it now arranged in my memory. I have described my journey out
from the crowded confidence of common life—to utter isolation in a
savage and dangerous world. Then suddenly my destinies turned about.
It was as if I was baptized to a new life when I plunged into the water.

And then in an eddy of scent and sunshine, I found other flesh that
was flesh of my flesh, another heart beating as if it were beating in my
body, fears and sensations I could share ; a living mate whose eyes
followed my movements with acute participation, whose dangers and
hopes and body were mine also. We two had come to that tarn one and
one ; we left it linked fast together.

And we needed all the help we could give each other, for now we faced
frightful dangers of torture and death. Wena, for that was my companion's name, belonged to Ardam and, by all the rules of island law,
she would have to be given up to him to do as it pleased him best. I too
had inflicted an intolerable outrage upon the dictator. Wena was all for
flight and hiding or suicide together, but the gift of this girl to me had
roused a new anger and fierceness in my soul, and I could even contemplate for a time the possibility of an open conflict with the War-lord.
" No," said I, " we will not hide. You come to my hut as my wife.
I am the Sacred Lunatic, and all I own is sacred and taboo." I put my
head-dress straight and flung my cloak about me and stalked back staff
in hand towards the village, with Wena following in an ecstasy of terror
and admiration.

We came to the beaten track between the cascades and the village and
presently met Chit. He was aghast to see us. I told him with a newborn
lordliness of my intentions and the changed spirit of my life. He protested in the profoundest dismay. Ardam would raise the whole tribe
against me ; I retorted I would raise the whole tribe against Ardam.
But Chit knew the tribe better and implored me to go warily. " She
shall hide in my hut," I said.

" Go there now," said Chit.

The tribe was holding a Howling Meeting outside the hut of the
Goddess and the path down to my quarters was deserted. I can still
hear the droning voices of the speakers from the open place above,
punctuated by the disciplined howls of the tribe, as we followed our
lonely way on the lower path. Chit left us to hurry back to the war

gathering and see what Ardam was doing there. " Into my hut ; into your home," said I, and held back the reeds at the entrance, and then in the dark of my refuge, I took her in my arms.

Could I have dreamt a thing like that ? Could I have begun the world afresh in a fantasy and a dream ?

It was wonderful to be in that loneliest of places and no longer to be alone, to be caressed and waited upon by this other human being I had made my own, to see her handle my ordered possessions and prepare a common meal. But presently comes Chit from the meeting, eager and urgent. " They are looking for Ardam's lost maiden," he says. " They say the enemy has stolen her. I implore you, get away from here and take her to the cave we found. Now you have got her, why should you want to die ? "

He vanishes. He has gone outside to listen. Presently his broad face comes back into the opening of the hut.

" There is a canoe below. You can go in it up to the falls before the searchers come here. I cannot be found here. Later I will see you."

We hear him retreat through the bushes behind the hut. I draw my woman to me. I am for a tremendous fight in the doorway of my hut. But not she. " I want to live, oh, my master ! " she says. " Now, very greatly do I want to live. Let us escape even as Chit has counselled."

I too discover that I want to live.

Then we are creeping down the steep place below the hut to Chit's canoe. Twilight is darkening to night and the village is alive with the moving torches of our hunters. Voices call. Bells sound, and a shrill whistle pierces the stillness. We are in the canoe and I have seized a paddle. There is a sudden outbreak of strange lights. Immense green glow-worms that wax and wane pierce the deep blue obscurity, and the water makes a noise like the traffic of a great concourse of people and reflects the flares perplexingly. We paddle swiftly for a time and then we are held up by a swirling rapid, we hang motionless and then thrust forward again. That struggle goes on for immense periods. Slowly the roar of the great cataract towers up over all other sounds. We scramble ashore and run, bending low, to find the tarn and the tunnel that leads to the cleft. Something strikes me hard on the shoulder and bears me to the ground. A great arrow from up-river has pinned me down. Then she has tugged it out and helped me to my feet. She strokes my shoulder and her hand is covered with blood.

" The cave," I say, " the cleft."

The sweet scent of lemon verbena is strong in my nostrils. I see a blue ribbon of stormy sky reflected in the tarn. Far behind us there is a tumult of pursuit.

But now we are near the point where the waters gush out of the cliff.

The great cave is cool and safe and dark, but a sudden weakness comes upon me. " Keep your feet in the stream," I say, as I stumble and fall.

My feet are dragging in the rivulet, and she is carrying me. Comes a blankness, though surely I must have directed her. And now I am lying on a litter of sweet-smelling leaves and branches and she crouches beside me, giving me food out of a basin. It does not strike me as strange in any way that she should be feeding me out of a basin. It is daylight and the cave is less like a cave than a commodious, pleasant room. And under my head is a pillow. Our eyes meet.

" Eat some more," she says. " It's good for you."

I take a spoonful of the stuff and then sit up abruptly. My shoulder is bandaged and painful and stiff.

" But where is this ? " I say.

" Our home," she says. " And——"

She puts her cool hand on my forehead. " The fever has gone ? Do you know me, Arnold ? "

" You are Rowena," I answer. " But tell me, where am I ? "

" Brooklyn Heights. . . . Have another spoonful."

" New York ? "

" Sure,—New York."

CHAPTER THE FOURTH

Of the Strange Transfiguration that happened to Rampole Island.
How Mr. Blettsworthy came back to Civilisation. How he played his
part manfully and was wounded and nearly died a hero in the World
War for Civilisation. Of Rowena his wife and his Children. How he
found an occupation and of a Great Talk he had with an Old Friend,
Leading to those Reflections upon Life in General promised on the
Title Page.

CONTENTS OF CHAPTER THE FOURTH

CHAPTER THE FOURTH

§ 1

ROWENA

I GAVE it up for a time and finished my soup.

She put her hand on mine and said again : " But your fever has gone ! "

Mutely I sought to get up and mutely she assisted me. I sat on the edge of the bed. I was perplexed because the place was certainly the cave in which now for weeks she had been feeding me, tending me and guarding me. And also it was a room.

" What is the matter with my shoulder ? " I asked.

" That was hurt when you were knocked down by the taxi-auto."

" Taxi-auto ? An arrow."

" No. A taxi-auto. I dragged you out of the gutter." I ran my fingers through my hair. I considered another difficulty.

" You are wearing civilised clothes," I said.

" Why not ? We can't always be making love."

" But you are the woman I love, all the same ? "

" Don't you doubt it."

I explored my poor muddled memory. " I saved you from drowning ? "

" In the Hudson."

" The Hudson ? You were no end of trouble to get out of the water. . . . But you were worth it."

" My poor puzzled dear ! " and she kissed my hand as she had done a hundred times before, with the same mixture of devotion and indulgence.

I stared about me. " The way that ceiling takes the light from the window. It used to be a great limestone slab. And those cliffs outside, those tall, grey cliffs, they are great buildings ! "

I sniffed the air. " Somewhere," I said, and my eyes searched the room. Upon the window-sill were three flower-pots containing, I knew, lemon verbena.

I stood up and she supported me, for I seemed to be groggy on the legs. We went across the room to the window, and I looked upon a scene that was at once strange and familiar. Over the busy water with its traffic, the mighty masses of lower New York towered squarely up to the sky, softened and etherealised by the warm light of late afternoon. Her arm about me, protected me and sustained me as I looked out.

" Have I been delirious ? " I asked. " Have I been in a dream ? "

Her arm about me tightened and she made no reply.

" This is New York. Of course—this is New York."

" There's the Brooklyn Bridge."

" This is not Rampole Island ? "

Mutely she shook her head.

" This is my own civilised world."

" Oh, my dear lover ! " she whispered.

" And Rampole Island and all its cruelty, barbarity and hopeless stupidity was a dream, a fantastic dream ? "

But she was weeping. Perhaps she was weeping with happiness because my delusions were lifting from my mind.

§ 2

DR. MINCHETT EXPLAINS

A THIN veil of doubt seemed to be falling across the first brightness of my world restored. I turned from the window, sensible that I was still very weak. She helped me to sit down in a little arm-chair, which had, I felt, a castor out of order. " So all that dreary frightfulness," I said, " the war, the cruelties, Ardam, it was all no more than a dream."

She did not answer. Her face was turned from me towards the door. Came a rap, for which she seemed to have been waiting. " Come in," she cried, and a man appeared with a brown and broad face, that might have been the face of Chit the soothsayer, washed and brushed and adapted to the standards of Brooklyn Heights. He stood in the doorway considering us. It was Chit and not Chit. I knew he would speak with Chit's familiar flat voice.

She addressed him joyfully. " He's ever so much better. We're no longer in a cave. See ! He's been looking out of the window He knows New York."

The new-comer, squat and broad-shouldered, advanced and scrutinised me with Chit's eyes. " You find yourself in Brooklyn."

" I find myself a little uncertainly."

" And you know who I am ? "

" I've called you Chit."

" Short for Minchett. Dr. Aloysius G. Minchett, at your service."
He walked past me to the window and stood looking out. He spoke
over his shoulder at me as though he did not want to disconcert me by
speaking to me too directly. " How often have I told you that this
is the real world ! And how often have you answered it was Rampole
Island ! Until I lost all hope for you. And then this young lady does
all that I and all the other alienists of New York have failed to do.
She brings you back to your senses by pitching herself into the Hudson
River up above the Palisades, just as you were wandering along the
bank alone. And here you are—both of you—if I may say so—clothed
and in your right minds."

He had turned and smiled at Rowena as he said the last words, and
now he faced me.

" Well ? " he said to assist me. He perched himself on the edge of
the table with the air of a man who has time to spare.

" You must forgive my mental confusion," I said at last, weighing
my words. " I do not know how I came here. I want to know how
I came to be here, looking at Manhattan Island, when I thought I was
far away from all the world on a quite different island off South America.
My mind, I know, plays strange tricks. What trick is it playing
now ? "

" It's ceasing to play tricks," said Dr. Minchett.

" Have I been—abnormal ? "

" The abnormal," said Minchett in the exact manner of the Island
Soothsayer, " is only the normal disproportioned."

" The abnormality amounted to—insanity ? "

" Not—how shall I put it ?—structural. There was, there is, no
lesion. But your mind is *exceptional*. Very sensitive and rather
divided within itself. And I happen to be in that line of research.
You have afforded me peculiar opportunities of study."

I looked from him to Rowena. Her expression encouraged me to
go on. I turned to him again with a question.

" Was I your Sacred Lunatic ? "

" You were more or less in my care."

" But where was I in your care ? "

" Here—in the State of New York. After you were brought here.
Yonkers chiefly. The Quinn mental clinic."

" But about Rampole Island ? "

" There is a place called Rampole Island. You must have caught up the name when you were rescued."

" And I have been there ? "

" Possibly you went ashore for an hour or so. In the boat that took you off the *Golden Lion*."

" You are certain this is not Rampole Island ? "

" No, no," said Rowena, " this is the real world. Hard reality."

I turned to her and considered her. How fragile she was and how pretty ! " Which you were doing your best to leave," I said, trying to piece things together. " You were trying to drown yourself. *Why* were you trying to drown yourself ? "

She came to me and sat on the arm of my chair and drew my head close to her breast. " You saved me," she whispered. " You jumped into the water and saved me. You jumped into my life and saved me altogether."

For a moment I seemed to get hold of things, and then I realised I had hold of nothing. A score of riddles baffled me.

I turned to Dr. Minchett again and apologised for my mental haziness. I asked him to explain the situation more clearly and then, feeling suddenly giddy, I went back to the bed and sat down on it. " I'm a case, I suppose. Tell me the history of my case. Tell me why I have leapt suddenly from Rampole Island to New York."

He considered the heads of his subject.

" It's good to be able to talk to you plainly at last," he remarked. " I'm all for letting you know."

But he did not begin forthwith. He swung off the table and paced to and fro, the width of the room.

" Well ? " I said at last.

" He's got to say it properly," Rowena excused him.

" Do you remember you were on a derelict steamship, the *Golden Lion* ? Do you remember that ? "

" Right up to the end. The captain had left me to drown."

" Left you to drown ? "

" He slammed me in a cabin when the boats put off."

" H'm. Never knew that before. He slammed you in the cabin. You must tell me of that. Anyhow, you were found on that ship by a boatload of men from the steam yacht *Smithson*, collecting various scientific data in the South Atlantic and Tierra del Fuego. That's where *my* story begins. Two of our sailors found you asleep behind the funnel and when you woke up you screamed and went for them with a hatchet. You were—to make no bones about it—stark, staring mad."

" But——" said I, and then : " Go on."

" You were, regarded as a specimen, rather large and unwieldy for the *Smithson.*"

" Wait a moment," said I. " How long ago was this ? "

He did a little sum in his head. " Nearly five years."

" My God ! " I said, and Rowena gave me a sympathetic squeeze.

Dr. Minchett held to his course. " You were, to put it mildly, a very inconvenient specimen indeed. The Director of our expedition handed you over to me, me being a mental doctor by profession, and I did what I could to adapt you to our circumstances. You must understand I was there in the capacity of ethnologist. I'd had worries of my own, and I was making the voyage for a holiday. I knew the director. . . ."

He reflected and seemed to be selecting his statements from a great wealth of material.

" You were some handful," he said. . . .

" They took you into a creek in Rampole Island, and that's all you ever saw of the place. You were raving that you had lost your world and that we were all bloody savages and painted cannibals. They brought you aboard the *Smithson* and I was detailed to tone you down, or keep you locked in a cabin. I was interested in you professionally from the outset. My idea was that you weren't, in any physical sense, mad ; nothing wrong, I mean, with your cells and tissues. You'd been treated badly in some way, and were still badly frightened. Also you had got mentally disconnected. I suppose if I'd let them do what they wanted to do and lock you up in a cabin to batter the door, it would have about finished you. You had a real horror of being put in a cabin. Do you remember about that ? "

I searched my memory. " No."

I hesitated, and said less surely, " No-o."

Some dim memory of trying to get out of a cabin returned to me. But that had been on the *Golden Lion.*

" You had to be humoured," he recalled. " And you weren't popular. You just hated all mankind for a lot of dirty savages and— Well, you were tactless about it. They would have dropped you out of that ship almost anywhere if it hadn't been for me, but I said you weren't merely a vexatious human being ; you were my one scientific specimen, and that made you respectable. So they brought you all the way home. I wanted to get you back for intensive study at the Frederick Quinn Institute at Yonkers. Europeans are hardly beginning to suspect yet how good our observational and experimental work on mental states is

over here. We get such a variety of types. I've had difficulties with
the Immigration Authorities and difficulties with your old guardian
in London, but I've kept them both more or less squared, and I've had
you under observation at Yonkers or in New York ever since. Your
guardian is a good sort. He sent people to look you up, and when he
saw what we were doing he did me the honour of giving me a free hand
—and paying up. We put it through. You've had some legacies and
you're fairly well off. I've got all the accounts in order. It took me
two whole years to establish you were not really dangerous either to
yourself or to others, and get you released under my guarantee, in a
flat of your own."

" This one ? "

" You've moved in here, since you picked up with *her*."

" It's *my* flat," whispered Rowena. " You took it for me and gave
up your own."

I reflected. " That is all very well as far as it goes. But why do I
remember none of these things ? "

" Some of them you remember in a different fashion. But you're
what I insist is a type case of Interpretative Reverie."

He waited for me to say " Go on," and after a momentary pause I
realised and did what was expected of me.

He came to a stop in front of me and stood, hands in pockets, and
became—to use his own phraseology—a type case of university teacher.
" You see," he began, clawed at nothing with his left hand, and began
again. " It's like this."

But I will not attempt to reproduce the tattered fabric of his exposition.
Let who must, suffer from the university teacher. This is a printed
book. His theory, or his explanation, whichever you like to call it,
was based on the idea that our apprehension of outer reality is never
exact and uncritical. We filter and edit our sensations before they
reach our brains. Even the least imaginative of us lives in illusion,
protected and given confidence by this mitigation of exterior things.
All minds are selective and admit what may prove humiliating and
disagreeable as little as possible. We continue to edit and revise long
after events have been apprehended. What a man *remembers* about
yesterday is not what he actually saw and felt at this or that moment
yesterday. It has been touched up and expurgated, cut about to fit
his convenience and his self-love. Imaginative types and people who
have been brought up protected from the more violent buffetings of
reality, can, in perfect good faith, misinterpret the world extraordinarily,
colour it, impose superstitious laws upon it, clothe it in fancy
dress.

Now that, he explained, coming close to me in a friendly, half-apologetic way, was where I was so interesting. For I was *most* interesting. He was good enough to say that. Had I heard, he asked, of double personalities, of the fact that in the same brain it was possible for two or even more systems of association to exist side by side, so independent that it was almost as if two different beings possessed a head in common. I admitted I had heard of such cases. Nowadays, I suppose, everyone has heard of them. And that, he declared, was what was the matter with me. I had a main personality which had been so wounded and shocked at its first onset on life, that it had taken refuge in the fiction that such rudeness and hardness as had struck me were really only qualities of a remote and secluded corner of the earth. It clung obstinately to the idea that the world of fair illusions it had lost, still existed as the main world of civilisation, out of which I had fallen and to which I should presently return.

I considered these propositions and made him repeat them. I gave a guarded consent.

In that consoling reverie, he said, I had been mainly living for the last four and a half years, while a minor practical personality I was only too anxious to ignore, kept me going about, avoiding obstacles, observing meal-times, even doing business when that was necessary. This poor minor personality, this practical self, went about, it is true, with a pre-occupied air, like a man in a brown study, as people say, lost in its dream, but still acting sanely and intelligently—even if slowly. It read the newspapers ; it had its moments of commonplace conversation ; and all the while it was nothing but a detached part, a hewer of wood and a drawer of water for the main romancing complex of my brain. It gathered its memories only to have them ignored. The main reverie would have nothing of this side of my life, or accepted suggestions from it only to alter them profoundly. "All of us are a little like that," said Minchett. "The interest of you is that you are so obstinately, persistently and completely so."

"Yes—yes, it is very plausible," I said, "but—listen, Dr. Minchett. I knew Rampole Island by taste and smell. I've seen that land as vividly as I see the faded places of this worn carpet. What negative memory, refusing realities, could have evolved what I have seen, cliffs and mountains, feasts and pursuits—and Megatheria ? I have stalked Megatheria and had one after me. Hard after me. Megatheria—great land sloths. I doubt if I had even heard of them before I was cast away."

"That's easy," said the doctor. "The *Smithson* had been looking for Megatheria. It was a main part of our job. If there was a Megatherium left alive we wanted to get it before the British. The whole

ship was keen on those Megatheria. We were always talking of them.
Our zoologist and our spelæologist talked of nothing else. They showed
you drawings. They had got the skull of a young one and bits of skin
and droppings. And I remember now ; one day you embarked upon a
wonderful dissertation about their habits and breeding ! An amazing
invention ! Extraordinary stuff. So you think you saw Megatheria ? "

" Were there none on Rampole Island ? "

" We never observed any."

I sat baffled.

" You mix in dreams with your memories. A thing more common
than many people suspect."

I bowed my head between my hands and then sat up again.

" I'm not tiring you," he asked.

" I'm drinking it all in," I answered, " though some of it is hard to
follow."

" I give in half an hour the results of four years and more of patient
observation."

" Chit," said I, " was always a patient watcher. . . . But I wonder
where I got that head-dress of his from."

The doctor knew nothing of his remarkable head-dress and let my
question pass unheeded. He was too preoccupied with the tale of his
research. " It has been fascinating to dissect out the threads of your
personality."

" Glad it amused you," I said.

" For example——" He resumed his pacing. " I found out you
are of very mixed origin ; good English on one side, Syrian, Portuguese
and Canary Islander on the other. There was an extreme break in
your life as a child. First came a passionate childhood in Madeira ;
then a healthy boyhood in Wiltshire, with scarcely a link between the
two sets of experiences. Even your language changed. You lost all
touch with Madeira, yes. But—— Something eager, stormy, self-
centred and intense, pessimistic, lay hidden beneath your English self,
formless and indefinite, outwardly forgotten. In your—your Rampole
Island dream, was there—I am guessing—an abundant sub-tropical
vegetation ? "

" The trees and plants," I reflected, " were rich. The mountains
steep and fine."

" The real Rampole Island is a bleak desert," he said.

I turned my eyes to Rowena's.

" He has been very clever," she said.

" He is very clever," I agreed.

" We have argued it out so often," said Dr. Minchett.

I stared at my knees, in faded, pale-blue pyjamas, and at my bare feet. I felt for and met and pressed Rowena's hand. I looked at the pots of lemon verbena and then at the open window.

"You are very clever," I said, "and it all seems very real here. But so does Rampole Island. Still. So does the food I ate there, the food that was the life of other people. So does the howling and the war. Tell me, how do I get what I eat and live in this world here? Are there no Gifts from the Friend in this world? And what was that war, that insane and dreadful war that at last towered up over all the rest of my dream? What was all that tumult of war? The drumming and howling. Was that nothing? And why did you, my dearest, throw yourself into the water? There my dream and your reality met. You see, he has not shown and you have not said and I do not feel, that that was a dream."

"No," he said, and came to anchor again. "There was—a basis—for that."

"And the war?" I said. "The war?"

"Dearest! dearest!" murmured Rowena, as if she sought to restrain something that at the same time she did not understand.

"She was in trouble," said the doctor reluctantly. "She had no money."

"And Ardam the warrior?"

It made his announcement none the less impressive that he answered only after a long pause.

"Nearly all the world," he said; " —the real world—is at war."

"Ah! now I begin to see clearly," I said. "Now one memory can join on to another."

"Yes," the doctor agreed. "These are high and tragic times. And now at last you can brace yourself to face the real world."

"This is the real world?"

"Surely."

"The real world," I echoed, and stood up and faced the window which framed the tall, fierce buildings of the mightiest of living cities, red in the sunset light and with ten thousand reflecting windows hotly aflame.

"I begin to see," I said.

Minchett watched me closely for my next words.

"This is the real world and I admit it." At that he looked relieved. "And also," I added, "I perceive that it is Rampole Island, here and now! For, after all, what was Rampole Island, doctor? It was only the real world looming through the mists of my illusions."

§ 3

THE WAR DRUMS ROLL AGAIN

It is perhaps remarkable that I have never questioned my wife closely about her life before that attempt at suicide which brought us together. An instinctive aversion on my part has conspired with her own reluctance to recall particulars. There are things upon the pages of the Recording Angel at which we shall flinch when the truth is read out. We shall be in your company perhaps. Who among us who has lived thirty years does not need to put a brave face upon some inglorious phase of lost control and dismal self-discovery?

My wife, who is so dear, so fine and so essentially brave, and who is also sometimes quite unwise and sometimes quarrelsome and perverse, came from the little township of Allan Lane in Georgia. She ran away from her home. She was the child of one of the poorest Everetts of that state but her father was a Nisbet. They tried to bring her up in a simple, old-fashioned Protestant way, but they were prevailed upon to send her to Reid College in Cappard, and she had an insatiable curiosity and habit of reading. She read everything and became excessively a rebel. She was brilliant and the intellectual standards of Cappard were low. That and Southern gallantry gave her an exaggerated idea of her power over men and things.

Partly to escape the consequences of an escapade and partly to conquer the world, she ran away to New York, being rather helped in the process by a young lawyer from Manhattan who had been advising upon the financial entanglements of Reid College. He held very advanced views in an unobtrusive way, and his relations to Rowena were fearlessly romantic at first rather than discreet. But in New York he broke back towards discretion and left her to fight her own battles. She was armed with several manuscripts of short stories and a first novel, that had seemed " better than lots of the stuff they publish " in the friendly air of Georgia. I won't meet the sentimental reader halfway and pretend that even technically she was a " good " girl. She was as egotistical as most of us, as greedy and as vain. She had tried to use her pretty animation, and she was very pretty and animated, as a man uses his strength, for personal ends. I doubt if she was really in love at any time with her lawyer and she was far too proud to pursue him when he turned away from her. I rather think he contrived things so that the breach came imperiously from her.

Her idea of turning men to her purpose soon involved her in an affair with a high official in the police organisation—no need to name him to those who know New York and no use in naming him to those who don't. Her poor little intrigues threw him into a fury of malicious jealousy, and he hunted her with all his influence and power. In the final stages of that hunt she had thought the river the least distressful way out of New York.

I suppose this wife of mine will be judged a naughty and unlucky little adventuress, but I cannot endure that judgment because I know better. Or, granted that she was all that, she was also something much more and much better. I know what lovely things, what possibilities of courage and tenderness were still alive in that brain, while the body it belonged to struggled in the swirling grey water. I could tell a happy history of their abundant increase. And my mind can stretch back over the series of ugly, unknown incidents in her " romantic " phase that do not matter now, to the dusky child playing in the Southern sunshine, full of the clean urgencies of life and rich with laughter, to the girl in the window-seat for ever poring over a book, to the girl kneeling on a chair to write again the wonderful discoveries that every budding writer makes, phrasing her first sarcasm and her first purple patch. I understand her vision of success and social triumph and her dream of the wise and subjugated Prince-Companion who would at last share her culminating glories. And she met rebuffs that left her stunned with amazement and her hopes and pride were not so much defeated as kicked aside.

It was a friendless failure and a hunted thing I pulled out of the water. And also it had in it, locked away and untouched, that treasure of gratitude, possessive love, loyalty and tenderness I have found inexhaustible. I thought her pretty at first, and still I find new beauties in her fine and sensitive face. Her dear and sensitive face.

She gave herself to me in a passion of gratitude and took me into her life so soon as she realised the isolation of reverie in which I was living. For it is the supreme function of the lover to come between the beloved and the harsh face of reality. Both of us needed to be screened a little from reality. Minchett had the sense to grasp the benefit of our relationship and was liberal-minded enough to let me go to the only human being who had broken through the crust of reserve that had thickened so dreadfully about me. We saved each other for life.

For a long time she wouldn't let me marry her. She was a " broken potsherd," she said, it was a phrase she had recalled from some book about fallen and unlucky women, and it was good enough for her to be let retain me and nurse me and save me until I was fit to return to normal life and let her go her way. She would efface herself then in some way not specified and I could marry a " good " girl, she said.

Normal life was very abnormal in these days and I realised that for me, the peculiar distortion of normality to which I had to return was the role of a British soldier in the Great War. The war drums that had been rolling louder and louder through my illusions of cliff and torrent, rolled still more urgently when I awoke.

No doubt I had thought vividly about the onset of the Great War and watched its swift development from day to day, but my real memories of that time are all overlaid or distorted into details of my reverie. My mental state sustained my own indisposition to enlist, and it was actually in the woods above the Palisades and in Riverside Park that I did most of the lonely wandering in which I came to realise my widening isolation from the war-busy multitudes about me.

But now the issue of my sanity was being decided, and with that the question of my deportation from the United States and my entry into the British army became close and urgent. Steadily and clearly Minchett unfolded the details of my circumstances. We sat while Rowena prepared our tea and all three debated what I should do if my recovery proved to be permanent.

" I'd like to keep you here," said Minchett, " and at a stretch I could give you certificates. But we're an excitable nation and if America comes into the war, things may change about you."

" One thing I do right now, as soon as it can be done ; I marry Rowena."

" *No*," she said, stopping short between pot and kettle, kettle in hand.

" If you refuse me, you desert me," I said.

" We'll break down that No," said Minchett.

" And how will you do that ? " she asked.

" I'll prescribe *you*. I'll turn you from a pretty girl into a medicine. I'll make a wife his treatment."

" I'll go crazy again the moment you leave me," I said.

" What good is marrying if it means you are taken for a soldier ? "

" Because nothing can touch me if I'm thinking of coming back to you."

" Coming back," she said and pondered the implications of the words.

She stood hesitating with the kettle in her hand. She decided to replace it on the stove. Then like a woman who is sleep-walking, she came and stood close to us. She was beginning to see clearly what had happened to us that afternoon. She sank slowly to her knees between us. She put a hand on my knee and spoke to Minchett.

" I've been happy for nearly an hour, Doctor. Just an hour. Because he'd come back to his senses. And now I see what a fool one is ever to be happy. As happy as I was. This war is calling for all the men in the world. Oh ! . . . Keep crazy, my darling ! That's the way out for us. Keep him crazy, Doctor ! I don't want to marry him. I don't want him to be sane to marry. I want to go on as we were. I've cured him to kill him. I just don't want him to go. . . . Go back to your dream, Arnold. This is still our cave on Rampole Island. Indeed it is. Look outside there ! Rocks and stones I swear ! It's just a curious resemblance they have to houses. And we will hide from the soldiers and stay here always. Until we can get out of this place altogether into that civilisation, into those Great Spaces of which you used to talk for hours and hours. Don't you remember those Great Spaces ? Under the sun. We'll wait as long as that—together. . . . Here . . . Patiently . . . No hurry."

§ 4

THE WAR DRUMS THUNDER LOUDER

I DO not know whether it was wise or foolish or right or wrong to go back to Europe for the war. But I am telling the story of a mind and not judging either myself or the world. So it was things came to me and so I acted. This very Rowena who implored me not to go to the war had worked the miracle that made it natural and necessary for me to go back to the war.

I was still " under observation for recovery," as Dr. Minchett phrased it, when old Ferndyke the family solicitor, my distant cousin on his mother's side, appeared in New York. He had come over, part of a commission that was discussing the question of Allied finance. And as my guardian he made it first among his unofficial duties to lock me up. Minchett brought him to Brooklyn to see for himself how things were with me, and the old gentleman was gravely polite to Rowena and immensely sympathetic with the position and he would say nothing about the war except as a problem in financial adjustment. The actual fighting he evidently considered too indelicate and brutal a business to mention. He admired our view immensely.

" Will they take Arnold ? " said Rowena, as he stood before the window.

" Oh ! no, no, no ! " said Mr. Ferndyke.   " How can they *take* him ?
And even if he wants to go——"

" He doesn't want to go," said Rowena.

" If he *wants* to go," repeated Mr. Ferndyke, looking over his glasses
at her with the mildest of reproofs in his eyes, " I doubt if it would be
possible to train him and equip him and send him out before the whole
business was over."

" He won't go," said Rowena.

" Why raise that issue ?   In certain eventualities, it might be a very
useful gesture to seem to begin to want to go."

" I don't want to lose him."

" That wouldn't be loss," said Mr. Ferndyke.

Towards the end of his call he turned to me in the most casual fashion
and asked me to go up town with him to his hotel.   He had all sorts of
little things to tell me about, several papers to sign ; we could sweep it
all away in an hour or so and then if Miss—Miss——

" We'll call her Mrs. Blettsworthy," said I, " for that's what she has
to be."

" I congratulate my client," said Mr. Ferndyke, and shook her
hand.

" It's what *he* says," she apologised.

" If the prospective Mrs. Blettsworthy will join us for dinner——
Just a dinner-jacket occasion, Mrs. Blettsworthy.   Nothing elaborate."

So he carried me off alone, dropping Dr. Minchett down town for
William Street.

" It's very delightful to see you again in this recovered state," said
Mr. Ferndyke.   " The last time I saw you, well——"

Delicacy made him pause.

" You called me the hairless elder and said you would not have me
subjugate your soul.   Am I so hairless ? "   He beamed through his
glasses at me.   " I suppose that now we can forget all that. . . ."

He repeated his expressions of pleasure in his hotel sitting-room.
" The last time we were able to talk together on equal terms was in
London when you started out upon your well meant but most unfortunate
sea voyage.   It was the worst of luck that you were left on that
wreck. . . ."

" Did the crew and captain get away ? "

He told me how after grievous hardships they had arrived at Bahia
and in return I told him of the captain's attempt to murder me.   " Tut,
tut ! " said Mr. Ferndyke and, with a lawyer's instinct, played for a while
with the idea of bringing home that five-year-old crime to its perpetrator.
He pointed out the absence of confirmatory evidence, the crew scattered,

the details confused in the men's minds. " Nothing doing," he summed it up and shook his head.

" And that," he said abruptly, " brings me to the very present question of what you are going to do."

" The war," said I.

" The war," he echoed. " After all you must remember you carry a very good English name."

" I want to marry and secure the advantages of that for Rowena."

Mr. Ferndyke sat back and reflected on my Blettsworthiness and his own. " I think, I have always thought, and the war has done little to alter my opinion, that the British are the substantial part of the world and that a few such families as yours, Scotch families there are as well as English, going on from generation to generation in honour and discretion, with discretion and honour, are the substantial part of Britain. One does not say so much to our Allies, but here between ourselves one may confess oneself a little. No doubt many of our best strains are here also—I am not excluding America. . . . But this young lady ? "

" Good southern stock."

" Her past has been a little—undesirable."

" I want to make her future desirable."

His expression became broadly liberal. " There has been a certain courage, I must admit, in several Blettsworthy marriages. The strain has never failed in courage. Sometimes it has been delicate courage, but courage there has always been."

" Once or twice, sir, my heart has failed me badly. It's just that I'm most ashamed of."

He readjusted his glasses in quite his old fashion.

" I saw a ship's boy grossly ill-treated. I said nothing."

" You probably didn't know what to say. Put it like that. But I'm told you went straight into the water after this girl as a Blettsworthy should. And I admit I like your spirit in the matter. The girl seems fine in texture. She has the gentle voice of a lady. Sometimes over here, women's voices—have you noticed it ?—are apt to be strident. She may have touched pitch but I do not see that she is defiled. I like the way she moves. I think the way a woman moves is sometimes more important than the things she may or may not have done. She is probably warmly affectionate and if I may guess, as an old observant man—not without a temper of her own."

" Yes," I considered. " Yes. She has that."

" So many attractive women have. Quite a large proportion. But I see no reason why she should not go over to England, when this war is finished and take her place in your proper world. If you do all that is demanded of a Blettsworthy in the present situation, that is. And for her sake, even more than your own, you have to be a Blettsworthy now."

He stopped short and his magnified eyes interrogated me.

" This war," I reflected by way of answer, " is a very stupid war. Ugly and monstrous on both sides."

" I'm inclined to think. But not altogether. . . ."

Mr. Ferndyke seemed to consult some internal partner. " I would like," he said, " to go a little into—what I might almost call the *philosophy* of this business. You say this war is stupid. I agree. It was preventable ; it could have been warded off. Probably ; if things had been different. But as they were not different it had to come. The stupidity was a cumulative stupidity, here a little and there a little. It was all over the field and I don't see anyone in the business quite enlightened or quite benighted. We, you and I, were in that stupidity system, making, we don't quite know what contribution of our own. Or failing to make some contribution that might have helped to prevent this outbreak. This world, with all the threads of stupidity there are running through it, is the world that bred us and has in a fashion fed and educated us and given us our opportunities. The British Empire sheltered us, gave us foundations of confidence and pride. Then suddenly it and Europe swung into this frightful war. We can't suddenly ask to get off the ship. It's a muddle, but we can't let the old Empire be smashed with nothing else hopeful in sight. It's always been the tradition of your Blettsworthy breed to tolerate imperfection, take a hopeful view of imperfection and play its part—upward."

" But the war—— ! "

" There are millions on our side who believe this is a War to end War."

" And on the other ? "

" Not so large a proportion perhaps. On the whole I think that now that this disaster has happened it is best that the storm should end with German Imperialism down."

" And for that ' *on the whole* ' I, with millions of others, have to turn in all my possibilities, all my hopes, everything that was fine in my life——"

Mr. Ferndyke interrupted with the innocent professionalism of a solicitor taking his instructions. " *What* was so fine in your life ? " he asked, and waited with his eye on the opposite wall.

I found it hard to define, but at the same time I felt that Mr. Ferndyke had asked me an unfair question.

" If," said Mr. Ferndyke, " many people and more and more of them came into this war saying and believing and making other people believe that it is the war to end war, it may really become a war that will end war."

" We fill the ditches on the road to peace ! "

" If they are effectively filled," he said and left me to complete his sentence. " All over the world Blettsworthys have died in the cause of civilisation. We have salted the earth with our dead. If *we* die, our race, the civilisation that made us and sustains us lives on. Lives on because we die. Why should *you* not do your dying in your turn ? "

" And," he went on with a sudden change to a manner more professional than ever, " it does not even follow you will have to die."

Difficult old gentleman he was to answer.

" I put my point of view," he said in the pause.

" If you think the question whether civilisation is to survive or fail enters into this war," I stipulated.

" Confusedly but surely—yes. After this war, nothing perhaps will seem settled and nothing will be settled. The dead I admit become a vast multitude. Everyone is touched. My partner has lost his only son. My only nephew is badly wounded. My neighbour three doors away has lost a boy. It is frightful. But this way we have to go, if there is any way we have to go. And when the full reckoning comes, the world will be found a great way nearer peace and unity. As the dust clears away. Because of this war and through this war. It will have made a stride, a vast stride forward. Indeed ! If I did not believe that, how could I go on ? But we have to go on."

He stood up. " What is the alternative ? " he asked. " You'll stand out from the main stream of life. You'll be strange. . . ."

" What else," he thrust at me, " is there to do ? "

A page at the door arrested our conversation. " Mrs. Blettsworthy," he announced.

Rowena came in and stood still and scrutinised our faces. Our eyes met. She nodded her head like one who finds an expectation confirmed and turned slowly from me to Ferndyke.

" You're an old devil," she cried. " I can see it in his eyes. Arnold is going to the war."

§ 5

MR. BLETTSWORTHY IS DISCIPLINED

I WENT but I was not convinced I ought to go. I went doubting and unhappy and if I had refused to go I should have remained doubting and unhappy. I was much less assured than Mr. Ferndyke of the balance of goodness in favour of the war but I could not see any effective way of going on with my life except by going on through the war.

It was impossible to ignore the war in those thunderous days. It was the frame of all contemporary reality. It swallowed up the world. If one was not to be a combatant, then one would have to face the drive of all the millions who were, as the phrase went, " doing their bit." It was an opposition altogether too immense for me. It was to face a stampede of millions. It was like thinking of reversing the rotation of the earth by pushing against it. With nothing even to use as a lever for one's feet. For me at any rate, out of touch as I was with anyone else of my way of thinking, there seemed nothing for it but acquiescence and enlistment—unless it was mere hiding, a confessed evader, until Ardam's emissaries found me.

It complicated my difficulties that Rowena set her face passionately against my going. The infinite gentleness and self-subordination of her attitude to me broke to reveal a much more vigorous aspect of her character. She scolded the war, she scolded Ferndyke and most desperately she scolded me. She scolded resourcefully and comprehensively. She felt my sanity was hers and that to take me away from her without her approval was the cruellest robbery. I was inordinately distressed to see her disappointment and anger but the forces that turned me eastward were far too strong for either of us. But I stipulated that I should marry her before we sailed and that Ferndyke should wangle a passage to England for her, no small thing to do in these years of the submarines. In England she could qualify for hospital work and feel herself as close to me as possible. I could see something of her during my training and I could be with her on leave. And I saw to it that my property was secured to her should I be killed.

I went into the ranks. It was a great regiment with very old traditions. Mr. Ferndyke was for getting me a commission, but that seemed to me to be too definitely supporting the war, and my mental history, I saw to it, stood in the way. It seemed very improper to Mr. Ferndyke that I should be a common soldier. It was not in our tradition. I doubt if there were many Blettsworthys in the war without tabs or stars. But if I came into this war at all I preferred to take the harsher side of it. I preferred the more fundamental discipline of the private.

I had missed the first onset of the war with its storm of brilliant enthusiasm. Nearly a million English volunteered when the war was still, upon the face of it, a " war to end war." That was all over when I joined up. Conscription was already upon the British, a people who had never before known what it was to be forced combatants. My English world had entered upon an unheroic phase. The old army had gone, the volunteer new armies were shattered. The English are an inventive and bold people, but no inventiveness nor boldness had a chance with Ardam's gang. The British generals, too professional, obstinate and dull-witted to use the tanks more intelligent men were thrusting into their hands, had wasted those bright lives of the opening phase, by the hundred thousand, slaughtered them lavishly in the hope of escaping the indignity of relearning warfare from men not of the military caste. They fought the new sort of war in the old fashion. The faithful multitude obeyed their foolish orders and learnt too late the fruits of obedience. 1916 was a year of failure for the Allies everywhere. Upon many miles of front the unburied British and French still lay in swathes of khaki and horizon blue, where they had been sent to be mown down by the German machine-guns. Later on I too was to fight my way over those battle-fields and see the multitudes of our unburied dead still lying many of them in line as they fell, others in the holes to which they had crawled to die, horribly mutilated by their wounds and now far gone in decay, contorted grotesquely, rotting, rat-eaten, robbed, in tattered uniforms with the pockets inside-out, their faces, or rather what had once been faces, seething masses of flies, amidst smashed equipment, dud shells, wire, and splintered trees. No one will ever convey the horror of those fields of death. I saw dead men like a tramp's washing hanging in rags on wire entanglements. I breathed the air of Britain's putrefying patriotism. My God ! did these pink-faced, intriguing generals of ours never dream of nights ? Had they no inkling of the colossal agonies their little jealousies, their petty professionalism, their habitual and protected ignorance, inflicted upon those generous lads who put themselves in their hands ?

But through those defeats Ardam got his conscription and our mankind was now all his slaves.

What a squalid slavery it was !

At the thought of it the chill of a bleak morning returns to me and I am back in my squad upon the parade ground facing my enemy the sergeant instructor. The air is broken into a crazy uproar of shouting, yelling, snarling, cursing, the " smart " slap of hands on accoutrements and the tramp, tramp of feet. I haven't, he considers, kept my eyes to the front and he is informing the world that I am a filthy bastard, a bloody blotch on the face of the army and so forth and so on, raising his tenor voice to a scream and making feints of striking me that may cease at any time to be feints.

He puts his red cad's face two feet from mine and bawls to deafen me. I have done nothing to deserve this but something has annoyed him this morning.

If I hit him back I shall be marched off to the guard-room and put through a process of torment that may break me physically and mentally. I have seen that happen to a fellow soldier. Over this vile ruffian no authority is set that would even listen to a complaint. I have been given to him. So presently he hits me as his mood requires and I must brace myself up not to stagger.

There is no factor of dream-reverie in that shameful memory which still burns red and sullen in my brain.

To-morrow he will be cadging for a half-crown—with a threat behind his cadging. I'll be damned, I resolve, if he gets that half-crown, be the consequences what they may.

I went through my training with great bitterness of soul. I cannot be sure how far my conception of Ardam is due to that life of insult and humiliation. My queer memory, so strangely mobile, which will let nothing rest unchanged, which embroiders and breeds and rearranges in a perpetual search for a logical and consoling presentation of life, may have thrust back a myriad impressions from this latter phase into that visionary experience before my sanity was restored.

I became an insulted slave. I had to listen submissively to the vilest exhortations, to obscenities that did not merely befoul me but touched my mother and my wife. I was put to toilsome and degrading tasks in order that I might bribe my persecutors to escape from them. I was wearied unspeakably. And all this was to so break me in that I might not presently refuse to face a needless death, when some floundering general, playing his obsolete and futile war-game, decided to send a few battalions of us to attempt the impossible. And to that at last I came.

My mind through all these days of soldiering was like a fugue in which two thoughts chased and interlaced : " What a fool I was to come," and " What else could I have done ? " I had known it would be bad but I did not anticipate the half of the evil, the foulness and degradation of the training of a private soldier. It is a story unknown to the new generation of civilians. Ex-soldiers will not talk of it ; it is too shameful. Many men, finding these memories intolerable, expel them from their minds.

Yet as that grinding down of my soul went on I must confess that the tender excessiveness of my egotism also was subdued and changed. I am telling the story of a mind, I am not explaining it and above all I am not sentimentalising it. So it was.

§ 6

WAR OVER PIMLICO

" I am still upon Rampole Island," I said, " and there is no hope here. That fair and kindly civilised world I dreamt of in my youth was a childish fairyland. In this gorge we must live hatefully, driven by ignoble stresses, and in this gorge we shall presently die."

Rowena had half a mind to agree with me and then for my sake and her own, she would fight against our despair. There were moments of sunlight and beauty, she insisted, and that was a promise, there were gleams of good faith in the darkness and she loved me more than herself. No world is dead if love can live in it.

Did she love me more than herself ? For a time my soul was helplessly dependent upon hers and if this woman who was weak, irritable, easily bored and foolishly generous had in some obvious and primary manner failed me, I think I should have failed altogether. If my life was full of indignity, overstrain and impotent anger, hers was full of the negative and far more intolerable hardships of solitude, waiting and fear. She had no friends in Europe at all, and my not always too accommodating relations found her such few acquaintances as she had. She took rooms as near to the training camp as possible, but we met very little and inconveniently, because I would not risk murder by bringing her within the range of the gallant impertinences of the lance-corporals and ser-geants, my masters.

When presently I came up to the reserve battalion in its London barracks, she got apartments in Pimlico. In London the discipline was not so rigorous and we saw each other more frequently. It became a matter of passionate interest to me that I should not go over to France before she became a mother.

Now in the retrospect I see those Pimlico nights of ours as very beautiful. The streets of London in those days were greatly darkened because of the German air raids ; the houses became portentously tall, all the vistas were exaggerated and athwart the dark-blue sky a strange silent drama of search-lights and mysteriously drifting stars played perpetually. The rows of tall brown-black houses with their pillared porticoes were darkened, or they betrayed by thin cracks and lines of golden light the hidden illuminations behind their blinds and curtains. The Embankment which overhung the shining black river was very still, with an effect of always waiting for the magic incantations of the search-lights to bear their fruit, and the minutest red lamps upon almost invisible craft crept up and down the stream. A few people would go by, or a taxicab purr past.

We would wander, whispering. She would cling soft and warm to my arm; her dear face would be close to mine and my heart would go out to her.

" This war will go on for ever," she would whisper.

" It cannot go on for ever," I would comfort her.

The banging of maroons would warn us of the coming of a raid and we would hurry home to her rooms and I would sit with her in my arms amidst the din of anti-aircraft guns and crashing bomb explosions, and stay until the latest possible moment before my return to barracks. And sometimes by wheedling and bribery I would so fix things that I could stay with her all night. When I was with her she was happy; it was only gradually that I realised the fears and interminable solitudes of her days between.

Until the coming of the child was close at hand, she worked with a woman's organisation under Lady Blettsworthy of Uppingminster, making bandages in the galleries of the Royal Academy. And her landlady was a grimy kindly soul who manifestly loved her.

Occasionally I would commit a grave offence against discipline. I would hurry early to her rooms, have a bath, and change into forbidden civilian dress. We dared not walk in the streets after that, but presently she would go out and call a taxi and we would make off to a very pleasant and discreet restaurant in Wilton Street—Rinaldo's it was called, but whether it still exists I do not know. They seem now to be rebuilding all that part of the world. There we would have a little table for two in a corner, with a red shaded lamp and flowers and all the trivial, pleasant luxuries of the occasion, and there at times I could almost forget the parade ground and she the war.

Our child did come before I was warned for the draft. But three days after its birth I was marked with the tab sewn on my shoulder that showed I was for the front. Rowena bore her child without any very great suffering, but she was very weak and I visited her twice before I told her that I had to go. I saw Ferndyke and make all the necessary dispositions for her welfare. I passed the doctor for service abroad and got my new kit for the front. She took the news bravely, lying back on her pillows and pressing my hand. " My dear," I said, " I know I shall come back."

" I know it too," she said, " but all the same I must weep, my darling, because I am so weak, my dear, and because I love you so."

There was no sense in leaving her and our little baby son in dark and foggy old Pimlico, exposed to air-raids and all the strains of a bombarded town, and I managed to get leave and take her to a healthy farm-house lodging found for me by the wife of my cousin Romer near her own home at Chalfont. Romer was away in Egypt ; she too had a little child, and the two women had a sense of liking at the first encounter. I was glad to leave those two within call of each other since leave I must.

The train service was not very good for me, I found myself back in London with an hour and a half to spare before I returned to the cage. An impulse took me to old Rinaldo's again and I got unobtrusively to my old corner. A man was sitting and eating there, but the place was crowded and busy and I made that an excuse for taking my customary seat. I had not been there in uniform before but Rinaldo knew me, greeted me with a friendly smile and made no comment on the fact that I had suddenly become a private soldier.

I ordered a dinner that was exactly like one Rowena and I had eaten together. Then and only then did I glance at the individual who was just commencing to nibble at his *hors d'œuvre* opposite to me.

§ 7

UNTIMELY OPPORTUNITY

RECOGNITION came very slowly. Where had I seen that thick-set frame, that square sandy head before, and why did he move me so strangely ?

He was wearing a naval uniform but with wavy gold stripes instead of the straight ones that distinguished the permanent naval men. He was an officer in some auxiliary marine force.

Then my mind and body seemed all atremble together. Suddenly into my preoccupations with Rowena had leapt that great occasion which had seemed to me—how many ages was it ago ?—the supreme objective of my life. Here in the hour I had appointed for the tenderest of thoughts, I sat face to face with revenge. The captain of the *Golden Lion* was before me, seated in Rowena's chair. My brain seemed to be spinning round and round in my skull. Until it ceased to rotate I could say or do nothing.

The captain betrayed no sense of my presence. His attention was divided between a dish of radishes and some olives. Then he drifted to potato salad.

How should I set about him ?

I was astonished to discover how little I was disposed to set about him. I wanted to think of Rowena and not of that old, old story. Confound him for intruding his ugly face here and now ! And what could I do to him ? I could not kill him suddenly as he sat where Rowena had sat and whence she had signalled love to me with every glance of her dark eyes, hardly a month ago. Yet surely one could not be so faithless to one's past as to leave this meeting uneventful.

My dinner was to begin with *consommé*. It came as the waiter cleared away the captain's *hors d'œuvre*. I filled my soup plate slowly. His soup when it came was some thick creamy fluid. I watched him tuck his serviette into his neck in the old familiar fashion and seize his spoon with his freckled hand. I had an inspiration. Had he learnt anything since those days upon the *Golden Lion* ?

No ! He still drank soup with the same loud indraught. I took my spoon and followed suit with a perfect imitation. Phantoms of the first officer and the engineer became almost visible about us. He put down his soup spoon and stared at me just as he had stared at me five long years ago. Scrutiny gave place to recognition.

I had to subdue an undignified impulse to laughter. " Queer place this is for meeting people," I said.

" Damn' queer," said he.

" You know me ? "

He considered the position. His memory was evidently still vague. " I seem to know you somehow," he admitted with hard eyes on mine.

" You ought to know me," I said, tapping on the table. " Seeing that you murdered me."

" Ah ! " said he. He had taken up his soup spoon again but now he put it down to make a spreading stain upon the tablecloth. " Yes. *Now* I got you. I never expected to set eyes on *your* face again."

" Well ? " I said.

" You, that young feller. Eh ? "

I did my best to be cold, hard and ominous. " The man you drowned."

He drew in the corners of his mouth and moved his head slowly from side to side. " Not it," he said. " I don't believe in ghosts. Not in ghosts that imitate their betters eating soup. Now, *how* did you slip out of that room ? You got on the other boat, I suppose."

I shook my head.

By all the rules of the game, that ought to have puzzled and disconcerted him, but it did nothing of the sort. " There's chaps," he said, " you *can't* drown. If this war hasn't taught me nothing else, it's taught me that."

" You did your best."

" It was one of them antipathies," he said with the faintest flavour of apology.

He laughed grimly and prepared to finish his soup.

" Gods ! " he said. " How sick I got of that face of yours at meals ! Sick isn't the word for it."

By this time I was altogether disconcerted.

He made an amiable gesture with his soup spoon, inviting me to proceed with my meal. " I'll stand it for once," he conceded, and finished his soup with his soul apparently quite unruffled.

" You bloody old ruffian ! " It was undignified of me to say it.

" Not *it*," he said, and really enjoyed his last mouthful.

He pushed back his soup plate and wiped his face with his serviette, drawing it across to and fro several times. This cleansing duly done, he addressed me with unwonted friendliness. " You're in khaki," he said, " like the rest of the world. All that gentleman business is over ? I'd have thought though, Mr. Blettsworthy, they'd have made *you* an officer."

" I didn't choose."

" No accounting for tastes. And you've got your ticket sewn on there —that red label."

" I go over next week."

" I couldn't stand the trenches," he said. " I'm glad I haven't come to that."

God knows what had become of our situation. It had vanished into thin air. We were talking like old acquaintances who had met by chance. His disposition to let bygones be bygones was overpowering.

" What do *you* do ? " I asked.

" Mystery ship," said he. " Submarines with a bit of mine-dredging. We get 'em all right."

" You like it ? "

" *Like* it ! After being a damned van-boy leaving parcels all over the world ? I love it. I don't want this war ever to end—leastways not until they've blown me sky-high. . . . I could tell you things. . . . Only I mustn't."

He decided to confide. He leant over the table so as to be close to me, and whispered hoarsely : " Got one last week."

He leant back and smiled and nodded. He had become quite a genial person. " Came up within fifty yards of us. They'd been following us an hour and putting up their periscope, and signalling. We shot an old rifle at them, desperate like, and then hauled down our flag. He went round us twice to peep at us, and then came up. Greenhorn ! But we certainly looked an innocent lot. We got a gun, with a canvas mask in

front of it painted like the rest of the side—we don't roll it up or anything, we just shoot through it and make a new one each time, and the
first they know of it is when they're hit. Little solid steel shell that
pierces the skin of the boat, you know. Lord ! he *did* look surprised.
One minute Lord of all he surveyed, got his speaking-trumpet in his
hand to give us orders and everything, and the next minute she'd gone
bubbling down under him like a stone and he was kicking about in the
water. Our canvas always catches fire and has to be put out, and that
flare-up distracted him, and he didn't seem to grasp what had happened
or what was happening. Thought perhaps we'd blown up something
and caught afire. Even when he went right under he was staring. The
water just came up to him and the air out of his damned boat blupped and
blobbered all about him. Laugh ! I haven't laughed so much for years."

He didn't laugh now at any rate, but he seemed uncommonly well
satisfied with himself.

" I could tell you a lot," he said, and proceeded to tell me a lot. His
indifference to me except in my passive rôle of hearer was complete.

He talked of the crazy tricks and treacheries into which the submarine
war had degenerated. He stuck his forearms on the table and held knife
and fork erect as he recalled this and that savoury item of the wonderful
anti-submarine story. And I realised more than ever I had done, that
Rampole Island had indeed now spread out and swallowed all the world.
I hadn't a word to say for civilisation in the face of that self-satisfied flow
of homicidal knowingness. I sat appreciative of a mentality whose one
clear delight was triumph—the coarse male triumph over a woman's
submission, the bought woman's submission, or the triumph over an
outwitted adversary going to his death. Was he or I the human being ?
Was I or he the abnormality ?

We parted outside Rinaldo's door with an unreal cordiality. " So
long ! " said he.

" So long ! " said I.

" Good luck to you ! " he wished.

" Good luck," I said, but whether I wished it for him or the next
torpedo he had to dodge I did not search my heart to learn.

I was so amazed by this absurd inversion of all my expectations that
I went back to barracks as if I was under a spell, dazed by my renewed
realisation of the cruelty of creation. This man long ago had robbed me
of my last confidence in life, had toppled my reason into the fantasy of
Rampole Island and my present realisation of the evil in things, and here
he was again, when I was soft and tender from parting from all I loved,
to assure me that even Rampole Island was no better than a mild carica-
ture of the harsh veracities of existence. How far away was that God

my uncle had evoked to comfort my soul in its tender years ! That night it seemed to me that in the remote, dimly bestarred blue sky, above the shadowy façades of the Buckingham Palace Road, a God must rule with a face as implacable as the face of the old captain, a God of brutish triumphs and implacable insistence. To batter an incompetent cabin-boy to death would be altogether in the spirit of such a God. Under that God, who knew no pity, that God of Hate, I had to leave my dearest and our weak little wailing child, and take my chances in those dark massacres that passed for battles in France.

And suddenly, as I loitered reluctantly towards my prison-house, the maroons began to bang their warnings of an air-raid, and far away to the east the hullabaloo of the anti-aircraft guns arose, and spread out to encircle me and creep in upon me and beat upon me until all heaven and earth were filled with threats and concussions.

People seemed to vanish from the pavements by magic, and I walked on, neither hurrying nor loitering nor sheltering, but talking to some vaguely apprehended adversary.

" You'll have to kill me," said I, " for I won't die of my own accord. I'll stick it, you Brute. I'll stick it to the bitter end. And if you touch my Rowena again—you who hunted her to death—if you so much as send a germ at her or our child——"

I stopped short at a loss for a threat, and stood shaking my fist at the windy stars.

Three hours ago Rowena's arms had been about me and we had whispered together. It seemed incredible that in this thudding, crashing, malignant universe Rowena should be sleeping, with her eyelashes still wet perhaps from the tears of our parting, gentle and yet courageous, and our little child, warm and safe in her embrace.

§ 8

MR. BLETTSWORTHY IN BATTLE

THE day came when I scribbled my last uncensored letter to Rowena, and our draft was marched through the streets to Victoria Station, band playing brassily, and girls and women thrusting into our marching ranks. There was no one to see me off; but about me was a storm of emotion, and I waved farewells to strangers, was kissed suddenly by some unknown woman, and shouted " Good-byes " with my fellows. So by quay, pier, steamship packed like a sardine-can, thundering gangways, lumbering trains, a base camp, and a long road march towards the front.

We were moved about behind the front in the darkness of blinded trains—their windows had been put out and replaced by sheet-tin—and finally we were poured out, to bivouac in a drizzle upon a bleak upland and listen to the loutish muttering uproar of the guns to which we were presently to be offered up. Ardam had got me after all. I was beaten, and Ardam played with me now as it seemed best to him, in the lunatic chess of modern war.

With a slow inevitability I was thrust forward, through a land that was continually more horribly desolated. There were halts, rests, fresh advances.

Trees, houses, churches, factories in this land of man's supreme effort became at last mere splintered stumps and rags ; ever and again an insane activity of trench-making and barbed-wire distribution had occurred, and the ground was more and more broken by the craters of shell-bursts, and littered with rusty, smashed and abandoned war material. Across this desolation went trains of supply lorries and food-carts, and a per-petual dribble to and fro of troops. We saw ambulances coming down, litters, walking wounded men, prisoners.

There was a halt and a lightening of our equipment. We were being put into the front line.

Presently we were in the zone of fire and could learn, if we chose to do so, the various screams and whines of shell and what these noises might mean for us. Shells burst about us, sending up massive pillars of red-black smoke, that seem to stand still for a long time, boiling up within themselves, and then blow away. We began to whiff the sweetish smell of gas and put on our stifling masks which made our faces like the faces of hogs under our helmets of painted tin. Then came a whirring aeroplane that peppered us with machine-gun fire, killed two men close to me and left three others wounded on the ground. One of them wriggled and screamed very disgustingly, and suddenly, suddenly, out of the evil in my heart, I found I hated him. For the cruelty of the universe was in me as well as about me, and my nerves were on the defensive.

After a halt to wait for the protection of night, we resumed our progress to the front. The impact of the great guns was heavier and heavier, and we stumbled and cursed our way over the broken, uncertain ground. Once we came near to an unsuspected gun-emplacement, and were nearly deafened by the blow of sudden gunfire close at hand. Shells came at us, specially at us, they found our track as easily in the dark as in the daylight. Red flares lit the desolation horridly, betrayed our knots and groups to distant machine-guns and showed many crumpled dead about us.

We were now going up to an intensely contested part of the front. Whiffs of human decay became frequent. Then for a time we struggled through a place thick with unburied enemies and our own all too lightly covered men.

I fell over a dead body alive with maggots ; my knee went into the soft horror. There was a place where all of us were obliged to trample our dead. Through such circumstances as this I toiled to a trench, where I was given a bomb to throw and told to wait for my captain's start at dawn. Meanwhile we squatted in the dirt of that trench, ate beef and jam with such appetite as we could summon, smoked cigarettes, winced at the flight and whizz-bang of shell about us, and reflected upon life.

" Rampole Island," said I, " was sanity to this—a mere half-way house to reality."

And suddenly it came to me with overwhelming force that I should be killed and that Rowena would be left in the world without me, exposed again to all the treacheries and cruelty of mankind. A trick of that sort would be just after the Captain's heart. Our confidence in my safe return had been the confidence of fools.

I stood up suddenly. " My God ! " I said—quite inappropriately. " What am I doing here ? I'm going home, out of all this cursed foolery. I've got serious things to see to."

My captain was a little shop-man sort of fellow, a temporary gentleman, as we used to call them, of about my age and type. He held a revolver in his hand without either menace or concealment. But he knew how to restrain me.

" It's foolery all right, old chap," he said, " but you'd better stick it now. The way home for all of us here, is over the top and east. You won't last a minute if you try going back out of this trench. It's just suicide for you."

" Well, take us over soon," said I, and subsided.

The waiting seemed to go on for ever.

" Why did I come from America ? " I repeated.

He kept beside me and studied his wrist-watch.

" Ready ? " he said presently.

I fiddled with the emergency ammunition in my bandolier.

" Time," he said, and we scrambled out of the trench together. It was already quite light and the eastward sky in front of us was red. The world seemed to broaden out to a vast exposure. The azure skyline ahead exploded with rockets and guns at our emergence. Our shells made whirling pillars of smoke and dust amidst that blue indistinctness.

Our charge was a plodding walk over tumbled ground and under a heavy weight, towards an unseen enemy. Our men were so heavily burthened they did not look like men charging. They staggered along, hunched and despondent, looking as though they were running away from something rather than delivering an attack. They made a sort of pattern of bluish-khaki figures, repeated endlessly in the cold morning light. As they dodged along amidst holes and mud puddles they lost alignment, and here and there they bunched.

My little shop-man captain, who had kept by my side for a bit, ran ahead and turned towards a knot of men. By his gesticulations I could see he wanted them to open out. For a moment there were five soldiers moving forward and an officer waving an arm beside them. Then something seemed to drop out of nothingness among them and flash blindingly with an immense stunning detonation.

Something wet hit me. The five men had vanished. There was nothing there but a black source of unfolding smoke and dust. But all about me were bloody rags, fragments of accoutrements and quivering lumps of torn flesh that still for a moment or so moved as if they were alive. I stopped aghast. My knees seemed to lose their strength. I staggered, and then I was physically sick.

I stood on the battle-field, stunned and sick and sobbing. Dully the maxim came back which the captain had printed on my mind, that the only way out of this lay eastward through the enemy lines. I went on. I do not know for how long I went on. I believe I was blubbering like a miserable child.

Suddenly my legs were knocked from under me and down I went. It was as though I had been struck on the shins by an iron bar. " Damnation ! " I said, " I'm killed," and felt our hopes had cheated me.

My childish desolation changed to rage. I rolled to the bottom of a slope cursing God and fate, and found myself in a basin-shaped cavity, with the helmeted heads of men passing onward just invisible over the basin. It was D company; our second wave. They passed and were gone.

I have a strong suspicion I fainted and came-to again. I seemed to be just out of things in that hole, the battle skimming past a foot or so over my head. Ever and again the earth on the brim of my basin flew up in little puffs. · I rolled over on my back and, after a careful estimate of the depth of this sheltering hollow, sat up to examine my wounds. One calf was bleeding, but not excessively, and the other leg had a bone smashed. And I was not killed.

I contemplated my situation. I seemed to contemplate all my life.

For this moment I had enlisted. This was the end of my active service. For this I had been brought over from America and drilled and equipped. The foolery of it! Far away above the battle the sky was flushing towards sunrise and a little line of horizontal clouds shone like burnished pink-gold.

I felt scarcely any pain at first, except for a sickening twinge when I moved the broken bone. My heart was hot with rebellion. To be born for this! To live for this!

I addressed the universe. "And you, you Idiot," I said; "what next before you've done with me altogether?"

§ 9

MR. BLETTSWORTHY LOSES A LEG

WHAT happened next was a day and a half of anger and suffering in that hole. I remember only a little of those interminable hours of thirst, pain and fever. At the time, they were, I am certain, endless. I suffered for eternities and sank into insensibility and was born and lived again.

Presently a badly wounded man from D Company crawled in beside me. He had been shot through the shoulder and afterwards hit several times by machine-gun fire, as he struggled to find some shelter. He scrambled and fell into the hole, his strength already spent. He worried off his gas-mask and asked for water but he was too weak to swallow what I gave him, and slowly he bled to death. He was grey in the face and inert and did not answer when I spoke to him, but ever and again he would whisper hoarsely, "Wa-er." His coat darkened with the spreading stain of blood. After a time he choked in his throat once or twice and sobbed and then ceased to move or speak. He just lay still. He lay silent with his mouth open, I heard no death rattle, and I do not know when he died.

Afterwards came another of ours whom I knew slightly, and he was scarcely wounded. He dropped in on me and crouched breathless, mopping his face. He stared at the dead man's face for a time and turned away from it. "A wash-out," he said. "Half our fellows are done for."

He mentioned some names. "Never saw a blasted Jerry," he said.

We winced as a shell burst near at hand. We crouched silent for some time as though it might still come after us.

"I'll help you out after dark," he promised, when I had shown him the nature of my injuries. I think he was glad to have an excuse for skulking there and for presently going back. Theoretically he was still

bound to advance. He was very fraternal to me and helped rather skilfully to bandage my broken leg. But that night the Germans kept No
Man's Land so lit by flares and so swept by machine-gun fire that we
did not dare come out of our cover. He made a faint-hearted start and
came back.

We suffered greatly from thirst. I had already poured out a half of
my water upon the lips of the dying man who was now dead and stif-
fening beside me. My living companion talked of getting a water bottle
from some of the dead in the open but he did not dare go out.

The next night came a lull in the fighting and we made a push for it
and got back to the trench from which the advance had started. Both
my legs were useless and when I tried to bend the one which was un-
broken it bled. So I dragged myself along with my arms and whenever
a flare came over I lay still and shammed dead for fear of some observant
German marksman or machine gunner. My companion kept by me,
aiding me but little except for the sense of human company he gave me.

We got to our old trench at last by the purest accident, I tumbled
myself down into it head first before I realised it was there and was
nearly bayoneted for a German raider. There we found water to drink
and men to help us. They were the ninth Downshires relieving what
was left of us.

In the morning a stretcher was got for me and I began a dreary and
painful journey back to a saner world. I set my teeth and fixed my mind
on Rowena. Whatever I suffered I resolved I would hold on to life for
her sake. I was bundled along trenches, carried over the open, set down
by the roadside to await an ambulance that took half a day to come.
After years of suffering I reached an advance dressing station and was
patched up for the further journey. Then by ambulance, collecting
station-clearing station and slow-crawling, shunting, lumbering, agonis-
ing train I made my way to the hospital where, none too soon, my leg
with the smashed and splintered bone was amputated at the knee.

And so at last, crippled and wasted, back to England and Rowena.

§ 10

PAIN IN THE NIGHT

WHEN the body lies for hours that seem endless, tethered to pains in a
leg one no longer possesses, when ease and sleep seem ten thousand years
away and the prospect of a limping life too tedious to consider, the mind

wanders with an extraordinary looseness through the vast universe God has vacated. For now, it seemed the last lingering echo of my uncle's personality had gone from me and I had to square myself to live in a system of things that from the pus and poison in my wound to the utmost star had neither benevolence nor purpose with regard to me. I was not alone in my disillusionment, for faith of that sort has, I perceive, faded in all the world about me. I belong to a generation that has never really believed. But circumstances have conspired to make that fact exceptionally clear to me.

There is no kindly Human God, no immanent humanity in this windy waste of space and time. That, it seems, we have all decided upon.

And yet there is goodness.

There is this something that is between Rowena and myself. It may be impermanent and vanish. That will not alter the fact that it has been between us and about us. It was neither her nor myself. It had nothing to do with any gratification. It was better than either of us. It was and it still is love.

At times also there comes a quality upon things seen and things heard that lifts them, or seems to lift them, above pain, cruelty, stupidity, fear or discretion. There are certain moments of visible beauty and there is something in great music, that makes the Captain at his vilest and most terrible seem small and defeated. I, even I, poor thing that I am, have seen the world transfigured and know the glory of the vision.

And also I am not yet disposed to die. I am not at the end of my courage, and surely out of something good but altogether imcomprehensible to me and altogether beyond me that courage must come.

Love, beauty and courage. I clenched my fists and set my teeth for the sake of them in the hours of my utmost pain.

The mind wanders with an extraordinary looseness through the universe in these long hours of solitude and endurance, but it is apt to come home at length empty-handed and nevertheless sit down as though its quest was done.

Will there ever be any other end to such explorations ?

§ 11

THE FRIENDLY EYE

IN the convalescent hospital near Rickmansworth I became aware that an Eye observed me continually.

It was a reddish brown eye. It looked out from a system of bandages that also projected a huge shock of brown hair upward and a great chestnut beard with a red conversational mouth below. Upon this eye it was manifest I exerted an irresistible attraction. The body which carried it about was in the same ward with me. It was always hovering towards me and making little futile conversational advances while the Eye watched me with the illuminating but expressionless detachment of a head-lamp. In the night I would discover this patient sitting up with his bandaged head turned round so that the eye could watch me across the intervening beds.

I responded to his conversational approaches. The patient was not one of our graver cases. He was really getting better. A fragment of shell had skinned most of his forehead and taken away an eyelid, wonderfully enough without any grave injury to the eye, the unimportant eye that was now bandaged out of sight. A time would come quite soon when it would look out safe and sound and mitigate the glare of its fellow. Its owner's arm was also in a sling. The same shellburst had got his right hand. At present that was still only a surgical triumph and it might never regain its old flexibility. Polyphemus, for that was my private name for the man, was earnestly trying to write and make sketches with his left. He showed great perseverance. "And it will be great to shave all this," he said, " when the time comes." He was very confident that we wounded men would be the recipents of the gratitude and devotion of mankind for all the rest our lives, but he did not want, he said, to live for ever as a dependent. He had already, I gathered, discussed the possibilities of a partnership in an advertisement agency with another man at the base hospital. It would be very important in that event to write and make little sketches.

We talked together quite abundantly but always at the end of our talks he showed a curious indisposition to break off. He never said anything of great importance after our first exchanges of experience but always he had the air of having something quite important unspoken on his mind.

One day Rowena, who was now very frequently with me, brought me our child for me to see. I was up on crutches that day and very full of the promise of a mechanical leg which, they said, almost defied detection, that had been promised me. It was to be the costliest sort of mechanical leg. So subjugated was I now to my misfortune that I had the brightest anticipations of pride and triumph in my use of this contraption of springs and cork, which of course never came anywhere near these expectations. I showed Rowena the special drawings they had given me.

It was a very happy afternoon. Rowena was looking sweet and gentle, and anyhow war and the mischances of life had still to come within the scheme of things for our utterly healthy and triumphant son. They might not come for years. He was already leaving the baby stage and attempting friendly conversation of a monosyllabic assertive type. He was adorable and enviable. He was intensely dear and funny. He seemed to have stolen my egotism from me and centred it in himself. We sat about on the veranda and I was so loath to let them go that I crutched it with them down to the gate.

When I returned to the veranda to collect various books and papers I had left there, I found the Eye awaiting me. During all the visit Polyphemus had been in the offing observant. " Who is that man ? " Rowena had asked. " He's the Week-day *Observer* and the *Sunday Observer* too," I had replied. " He collects any little crumbs of fact the Recording Angel drops."

" I don't mind his watching," Rowena had decided, " if it helps him along a bit."

Now she was gone he came up to me and remarked ; " It's good to see you so happy, Blettsworthy."

" That's kind of you," I said appreciatively, for sympathy in happiness is rarer than sympathy in misery.

" It does me good—real good."

" I'm glad to do anyone good."

" Indeed it does," he stuck to it. " I have, you see, very special reasons for wishing you well."

I assumed the interrogative defensive.

" I owe you a great deal—in one way and another."

There was something familiar in his gesture and intonation.

" Three thousand pounds, not to mention the interest."

" Lyulph Graves ! " I said.

" Well ? " he awaited my response.

" Three thousand golden pounds and my golden girl. I forgive you the last anyhow."

" Well you may," said Graves with a gesture towards the hospital gate through which Rowena had departed.

The old revengefulness had gone on his account also. I realised I was a luckier man than he and that there was no sense in pursuing him further.

I extended a hand over my crutch head and shook his left. "How fiercely young I was ! " I said.

" And I with enterprise like a disease. I got a lesson."

We surveyed each other.

" Look at us now ! "

" Look at us."

" And what have we learnt and what have we got by it all ? "

We stood a little awkwardly while I watched his likeness returning faintly through the disguises. He had the same poise—drilling hadn't altered that. By tacit consent we sat down on the veranda for a talk. And prisoners together in that hospital as we were, we were bound to go on intimately as well as amicably now or quarrel and cut one another. That last would have been a great bore.

" You went to the Gold Coast," I asked.

" I was making good with Crosby and Mitcheson all right," he said, " when the war came to disorganise us all. I had some skill in marketing—I have it still—and I found it paid to advertise even in the West African jungle. New to the old firm—but it paid."

" And then ? "

" Enteric at Salonika. Propaganda job in Italy until I was passed for active service again. Then all this—three days before the Armistice."

He went on to give me some details of his war services and his post-war prospects and as he talked he bacame more and more like the Graves of six odd years ago. I was astonished I had not recognised him before in spite of his swathings. His activities in Italy had been peculiarly important, he explained. He had learnt all sorts of exceptional and advantageous things that he might turn to use later. Now he was pining to get out and set about affairs again. They had told him he was not to be disfigured.

He had the same light hopefulness as of yore. He thought the world was full of opportunity now ; he had always thought it full of opportunity. He was all for " vigorous effort " and so he had always been. Even the devastation of the war seemed to him a reason for cheerfulness. " We rebuild ourselves and the world." He seemed so unchanged that I marvelled to think of the change that had happened to myself and I was amazed when he remarked that I seemed to have altered scarcely at all ; he had recognised me directly I came into hospital. " The façade may be much the same," I said, " but all sorts of things have knocked me about inside."

He had been chary of asking what had happened to me in the interim and he knew already from previous talks the regiment in which I had served and the nature of my wound. For a time we had both skirted any mention of our Oxford days. But he had had them on his mind and now he broached that tender issue.

" I was in Oxford," he remarked, " two months ago. Before my last operation."

" How did you find it ? "

" Smaller. And more disturbed than I should have thought possible for Oxford. A lot of post-war undergraduates with tooth-brush moustaches. . . . I saw your Olive Slaughter."

I made a mildly interrogative noise.

" She's married. Her mother's still in the old shop. Olive married the pork butcher at the corner of Lattmeer Lane within a few months of—your departure. Perhaps she always meant to. It was mother I think had her eye on you. Oh ! I don't know. Anyhow she's married the pork butcher. Curly headed, pink-and-white chap in bright blue aprons and a shop of marble slabs and pink sausages. Her tastes were always simple and I'm sure he's made her far happier than you or I could have done. He took her as she was."

He paused. I laughed. " I didn't," I said. " Go on. So she's married a pork butcher."

" She's quite nice about it. Whenever he kills a pig, she told me, she *has* to put her fingers in her ear."

" You talked to her ? "

" Oh, yes. She's in the shop behind a sort of rail, doing the bills. And she was quite pleased to see me. No resentment about—anything. ' Lots of our old customers come in to see me,' she said. And had I been to see mother ? "

" Had you ? "

" No. Never fancied mother."

" Children ? "

" Three or four. She and an uncle ran the pork butchery during the war and hubby used to come back on leave, kill a pig or two and so forth. Very nice children, they looked, Blettsworthy, pink and gold. Wholesome as the stock. But not little lumps of feeling and hope like that young gentleman of yours."

" But she *was* a lovely thing, Graves."

" She's plumper now. If you tried to idealise her to-day, Blettsworthy, you'd find it heavier work."

" She was quite friendly ? "

" She asked after you. ' Your friend,' she said, ' who started that shop with you.' "

" Do you think she told her husband about us ? "

" Not a word. It was too complex a business to explain and her tastes were always simple. Probably she never quite understood what happened herself."

" She hid it all ? "

" She forgot. She simplified and forgot all about it because it was too troublesome and perplexing to remember. Except as a possible source of misunderstandings with her husband, it had no practical importance for her at all. She had probably wiped most of it out of her mind before you departed from Oxford."

" They tell me the mind is as selective as the stomach," I said.

" Life offers far too much experience for such minds as ours," he went on, " and that's the truth. We must all of us refuse the larger part of our possible cargo. Some day perhaps by a sort of trepanning we may be able to grow larger brains and carry more. Carry it all ; who knows ? I'm told that's quite a possible thing—in the future. But as it is with us now the simplifiers are the practically wise people. As she was and as she is and as she will be. If you don't reject the difficult things you must adapt them and dress them up and cover them over. They complicate and hamper. . . . What is the good of that ? And where does it get us ? I'm a practical man at bottom, Blettsworthy. We must still follow our *petit bonhomme de chemin*— whatever load we have on our souls. What does it profit a man if he thinks of the whole world and loses his little business ? And those larger things, the excess of cargo ; at the best does it give anything more than vague vast desires that are bound to turn at last to discontent and unhappiness ? "

" But if one hasn't the sort of mind that rejects——? "

" Yes, I know. That I admit is a difficulty."

" If one *must* recognise and try to get things square altogether——? When you reject things, then even if they do not trouble you in your mind for a time, they are still round about you, moving against you or at any rate moving without any regard for you. Perhaps they are not so completely out of the picture as you suggest. A bullet might have ticked off Mr. Pork-butcher or a bomb dropped into the nursery in Lattmeer Lane. You followed your *petit bonhomme de chemin* on the Gold Coast, but when the war came what happened to that hopeful little track ? I was troubled about the universe even before the war, scared and rebellious, and you, you say, ignored the trouble like a sensible simplifier——"

" As far as I could."

" Yet all the difference in our fates is the purely accidental difference between an eyelid and an arm on the one side and a leg on the other."

" But what did *you* do before the Great War ? "

" I travelled far. I went a good long way beyond your Gold Coast. And at any rate I went into the Great War with my eyes open."

" We won't discuss the advantages of that," said Graves.

And thereupon, assisted by his questions, I began an account of

Rampole Island and the adventures I have been telling in this book. It was not perhaps the account I have given here, because it was my first attempt to tell it and I can assure you it has been no easy story to tell. Perhaps I should never have told it if it had not been for Graves. I should have left it to sink back into oblivion as millions of other such stories have done even though the men who lived through them are still alive among us.

§ 12

POST WAR RESUMPTION

I FOUND it pleasant, I found it stimulating, to have resumed my acquaintance with Lyulph Graves. There was I realised a natural interchange of interest between our minds. Subconsciously I had missed him. We had both grown, we had both been violently ripened by experience and misfortune, but we still had that contrast and complementalness of characteristics that had sustained our former friendship. I was as responsive and unoriginal as I had always been ; he was still obsessed by the idea of his immense practicality and still as wildly enterprising as ever. It was quite characteristic of him that he could think of the removal of the human brain-case as a possible undertaking to release the human will and intelligence to ampler achievements, and expand his experiences of marketing sewing machines on the Gold Coast into plans for the systematic economic organisation of all mankind. He was particularly vivid with his projects for marketing not only books now but all possible human produce on new lines and I listened with a revived appreciation of his quality, making only one unobtrusive determination, that my own capital was not to be involved in the experimental stages of any such adventure.

The leisure of my final weeks at Rickmansworth while I was making the acquaintance of my mechanical leg and preparing my present home at Chislehurst with Rowena were passed in long discussions with him. I found I could open my mind to him extraordinarily. He had the queerest knack of understanding me and then firing himself off like a Verey light to illuminate aspects and considerations I should never have discovered for myself. He agreed with me essentially, and differed from me profoundly. The world was Rampole Island, yes, and civilisation a dream, and then he went off without even taking breath to discuss how we could make that dream a reality. He was a Stoic just as much as I was a Stoic, but never in anyone else have I met with such an aggressive Stoicism.

Meanwhile he was evidently very hard-up. He was full of hopeful, immediate plans for the development of an advertising and propagandist business in automobiles, luxury hotels, air-transport, canned commodities and compact folding bath-rooms for small houses—the particular application of his organising abilities varied from day to day—and these schemes mingled very agreeably with projects evoked under the stimulus of my comparative pessimism, for a complete recasting of the League of Nations, the defeat and chaining up of Ardam for ever and ever, and an effective restatement of religious ideas. He seemed incapable of doubting that all the Megatheria in the world could be not only killed, but disposed of in an entirely sanitary manner, and all the malignant Captains and stupid ancients, hunted down, laid by the heels or slain.

His face had come out of its bandages, which had been replaced by an extensive green shade, and his arm was now in a simple black sling. He was more and more like the former Graves, except that a large artificial red scowl spread across his once candid forehead, and was likely to remain there for some years. It contrasted oddly with the optimism of his lips.

Occasionally it became advisable to assist him with small sums of money, and he was always very punctilious in his acknowledgment of these advances, adding them on to the larger debts between us. " One of these days, Blettsworthy," he would say, " you will give me your receipt for the last halfpenny of this, with four and a half per cent. interest up to date. Then you shall stand me a bottle of the best champagne then current, and when we drink that together will be the happiest moment in my life."

He had few connexions to help him in these difficult days of reconstruction after the war. I, on the other hand, was able to appreciate the advantages of a widespread family. My wife had been a social success with Lady Blettsworthy of the bandages, and she had made a friend of Mrs. Romer. Romer came back unscathed and a colonel ; he had done great things in the final drive to Damascus, and he found the firm of Romer & Godden almost guiltily rich through the chances of war. Other cousins had had very parallel experiences. The desire to behave well to a wounded hero was prevalent in the family. My relations, and particularly the Sussex Blettsworthys, had lost several of their sons, and I found myself almost automatically a junior director of the century-and-a-half-old wine and brandy firm of Blettsworthy & Christopher. The days when English families had younger sons to send abroad have come to an end. There is a home demand for them. My establishment in business seemed to me as undeserved as my misfortunes, and I tried to accept it with the same inner stoicism and the same outer civility.

I saw to it presently that Graves got a chance with our marketing, and he did quite brilliantly for us, suggesting our present popular brands, the Mars, Jupiter and Old Saturn labels, that are already familiar names wherever men find themselves in need of vigorous, sound, or ripely-seasoned brandy. He continues our marketing adviser.

§ 13

OLD HORROR RECALLED

ROWENA thinks that if it were not for Graves I should forget about Rampole Island altogether. It is her conception of our relationship that she has to obliterate all that complex of memories and ideas. Everyday is, I admit, a powerful bleacher of irrelevant realities, but certainly everyday is not so powerful that it can bleach out as much of myself as that. True it is that routines are closing in on me, routine behind routine, the routines of a new phase of my life in which I shall now soon be a middle-aged, outwardly contented figure. Wife and children, this pleasant home we have made at Chislehurst, the business I must attend to if our comforts are to be ample, friends and acquaintances, exercises and amusements all close in on me ; this tangled skein of immediate interests holds and busies my waking attention for the large and increasing part of every day. Yet still I feel the shadows of the gorge lying across my spirit, and still the memories of the lad crying out in the night upon the *Golden Lion,* of the dead upon the battle-fields, of my wounds and my despair refuse to vanish before the reassurances of our new security.

I scent the whiff of Megatheria in the London air more often than I confess, and time and again I feel the Captain going about his implacable cruelties behind the thin screen of this post-war world. So far from forgetting Rampole Island, it is this sensible world that sometimes threatens to vanish out of my consciousness, and I have to exert myself to keep my hold on it. Once at least I have had to summon all my strength to do so.

However much my fellow-mutilated may forget the war and the

ugly face life turned upon them then, I do not forget. For all Rowena's manifest desire, I doubt if I want to forget. If some mental specialist made me an offer to clear every trace of that interpretative reverie out of my mind, if he assured me that this present life would lose its translucency and become completely real for me and safe in appearance as the life of a young animal seems safe to that young animal, certain I am that I should not accept. I have read that men who have nearly died in the desert, or men who have passed as explorers through the indescribable hardships of an Arctic winter are for ever afterwards possessed by an irrational craving to return to the scene of their endurance. It has made common life trivial for them, it has enslaved their imagination by its intenser values. So it is with me. Rampole Island calls to me in much the same fashion. It is as if I felt my real business was there, and that all my present swathings of comfort and entertainment were keeping me back from essential affairs. I have never to forget Rampole Island, I feel, I have to settle my account with it. Until that account is settled, the island lies in wait for me. For that I was made to feel ; for this I exist.

For some years, it is true, I did my best to co-operate with the psychiatrists and thrust away these visions of reality altogether, lock them off from the main currents of my present existence so that presently they would die. In my love for Rowena there seemed that possibility of beginning life anew. But now I realise that of all things the least possible is to begin life anew. To both of us indeed there came that same elusive promise. She too is haunted, though less consciously than I. She is a little exacting about our present happiness because to her it has a compensatory quality. It is hard enough, she thinks, that we should both have to make the best of my amputated leg. My recurrent brooding on the grimmest presentations of life has for her a quality of real ingratitude.

So Rampole Island lies like a shadow between us and keeps us from that unlimited understanding and openness of mind we both desire. To her it is an entirely evil obsession from which it is her rôle to release me. She does not understand the nature of its fascination. To have failed to obliterate it is her defeat. And that is why she singles out Graves from all my friends as an antagonist. Her quick instincts tell her I talk to him of this that I conceal from her, and she will never understand that for me to talk to him is not a renewal but a relief. He spoils her picture of our life. He exposes its falsity. She sinks beneath her normal dignity in regard to him. Her effort to be civil to him is only too manifest. And behind his back her hostility is undisguised.

" You say that man swindled you and disillusioned you," she argues,

" and still you make him your friend and put business in his way."

" He does it very well."

" He ought to," says Rowena. " *Think* how he has injured you ! "

And after my silence. " I cannot understand men : the things they will tolerate, the things on which they will not yield ! "

It was to Graves alone that I was able to tell of the hidden crisis through which I passed, because of the long accumulating stresses upon my mind produced by the trial, the appeals, the prolongations and delays, the re-trial and the execution of Sacco and Vanzetti in Massachusetts. I will not recapitulate that case here. Everyone has heard their story. It is quite possible that the truth of that affair was very different from the affair as I saw it in my mind, but this is a history of my mind and what I have to tell is not what happened in the Massachusetts Court House, but what happened inside my skull. I am one of that considerable number of people who are compelled to think these men were innocent of the crime for which they suffered, that they were tried with prejudice and upon a wrong charge and that the revision of their sentence was one of those issues that test the moral and intellectual values of a great community. If I err in that judgment, I err with men like Frankfurter of Harvard, and Thompson the eminent jurist, who have scrutinised every detail of this enormously long and complex legal process. And I was impressed beyond measure by the unimaginative hardness, the poverty of sympathy, the vindictiveness against " Radicals " and reformers, displayed by great masses of comfortable and powerful people throughout the world. I was less concerned with the rights and wrongs of the trial than with the way people thought and spoke and wrote about those rights and wrongs. This troubled me more and more. It kept me awake of nights. It became monstrous in the night. It is unreasonable that this should be so, but so it was.

Gradually as I brooded over the intricate developments of this case the sense of Rampole Island resumed its sway in my brain. The world's transparency increased. The tall cliffs and the ribbon of sky above, appeared more and more distinctly through the dissolving outlines of surrounding things. I would sit behind my morning newspaper in the London train and hear the comments of my fellow business men, and it would seem to me that the rattling of the train was the noise of the torrent in the gorge and that I sat once more at the round table in the upper eating-house while the ancients delivered judgment on the safety of the state.

I fought against the return of that old obsession as well as I could. I did not want to forget Rampole Island but I did not want it to arise about me with this power of conviction and swallow me up again.

I had no specialist in England to whom I could go for effective help.

I did my utmost to conceal the trouble in my mind from Rowena's observation, for I had a horrible fear that she might take sides against me. She might have regarded Sacco and Vanzetti as her enemies and mine, and have felt called upon to defend me from their villainous appeal to my sympathies. We might have fallen into arguments and she might have betrayed that hardness of heart that comes to women on combatant occasions. That I could not have endured.

I managed to carry on with business and kept touch with practical things throughout. But to fall asleep, to sit alone, to walk with an unoccupied mind, was presently to pass right out of England completely into that familiar gorge of reverie. I would find myself talking aloud to the Islanders and snatch myself back to my real surroundings by a great effort. I would exclaim suddenly. I startled my secretary several times when she thought I was musing over business issues.

The scenery of Rampole Island was still exactly as it had been before the war. But Chit had gone and no longer did I enjoy the immunities of a Sacred Lunatic. Though the war was over, Ardam was very much in power, he was now very busy developing the ideas of Chit that he had once dismissed with contumely. In the next war there was to be a great march over the uplands in a particularly idiotic special equipment invented by Ardam and with the sacred tree sloth leading us. The circle of the Ancients had been reinforced by various judges and lawyers and strange, strong-jawed biters of cigar-ends and chewers of gum. This time I seemed always to be jostled in a crowd, the brown unsavoury crowd of the tribe, denser crowds than I had known before ; always I craned over heads and shoulders, watching events unroll before me. I never got into the foreground. And those two men perpetually on their way to execution I saw in the likeness of two commonplace, luckless, excuse-making visionaries, who had come to the Island as cheap, ill-trained missionaries from some source unknown. My fancy dressed them in shoddy clerical garb. Sacco looked puzzled and dark and sullen, but Vanzetti had the mild face of a dreamer and his eyes were fixed on the lip of sunlit green between the cliffs and the ribbon of sky. I saw the pair of them very plainly. If I could draw, I could draw their portraits even now as though they were before me.

To me they appeared always to be marched, marched continually, for six fateful years, through these dense crowds of hostile men towards the Reproof and their doom. If there was no hurry there was no respite. The people cried out upon them. They got very little sympathy, but in the throng sham sympathisers made mischief for ends of their own. Always as they went past me, the Administrator of the Reproof went before them with his club upon his shoulder and a file of Ardam's minions marched behind.

" What have they done ? " said I.

The answers were various but the spirit was always the same.

" Come to teach us this gorge isn't good enough. Come to start a hunting of the holy Megatheria. Come to persuade us to eat no more of the Gifts of the Friend. How could we live without the Gifts of the Friend ? "

" Revolting ! " I said, with my heart sinking at the thought that I too shared their guilt. This was a lesson then for all who would climb beyond the gorge.

" We'll teach missionaries to come here, setting us against the life we lead ! Look at their nasty clothes ! Look at their pale faces ! Why they don't even smell rich."

And in my fantasy it was like this, that when these two were at last executed we all killed them, all of us, they were torn to little fragments, handed out, and their flesh was eaten by everyone who acquiesced in their fate. " Eat," said a voice, " since you could not save them ! " Such is the cruel over-emphasis of these visions ; they magnify verities into monstrosities. I was thrust and compelled to the open place before the temple of the Goddess, where the killing and tearing to pieces was done, and the portion that was given me to eat was exactly like one of those quivering fragments I am always trying to forget that were scattered by the shell-burst just before I got my wound. " Eat, since you belong to this affair ! " The thing repeated itself over and over again. First very swiftly came the killing, and then interminably that hideous sacrament. Always one shared. Everyone shared. I came to a mental crisis. In the night I shouted loudly, " I will not eat ! Oh ! I will not eat ! " and awoke.

I got up presently and hopped and blundered about my room, afraid to lie down and resume this dream which went on and on, always the same and always proceeding, saturated with an ever-deepening horror. Rowena appeared silently in the doorway.

" Nothing," said I. " A touch of indigestion."

" What have you been eating now ? "

What had I been eating in my dream ? No good to speak of that.

" God knows." I invented an explanation on the spur of the moment. " My old stump is sore again."

" Those doctors ! You ought to bring an action for damages against every one of them."

" I doubt if the stump would benefit."

" You take that so tamely."

I turned my back on her and stood staring out of the window at the night. Little she dreamt how that darkness teemed for me. Once more I drew near to the temple of the Goddess. Once more the moment of killing drew near. I saw Vanzetti looking towards me. I was so lost I started when my wife spoke to me.

" Poor old darling ! "

I turned a guilty face to her and watched her as she got me some sedative and did her best to soothe me. . . .

But in a little while I was up again, moving very softly and cautiously for fear of disturbing her afresh. . . .

In that fashion I passed the night when Sacco and Vanzetti died.

Next day I had business with Graves and I opened my tormented mind to him. " Things like this trial and execution happen every day," said he. " It is not the monstrous event you think it is. It is as natural as a man stamping on a mouse. It is a stupid social system defending itself against a real though feeble attack. You think in metaphors and visions that distort more than they emphasise. . . . After all you are not so certain those men were entirely innocent. And all mankind was not against them. There were long reprieves and they found advocates and supporters. If cruelty and prejudice triumphed at last it was only after a long struggle. Think of the crucified gladiators on the road to Rome after the servile war. What friends had they ? Or come with me to the Zoological Gardens. If you knew more of history and nature, Blettsworthy, you would be less distressed by current things."

He drew me into an argument. He forced me to re-translate the glowing horror of my vision into arguable propositions. We disputed late and as we disputed the power of my hallucination declined. That night I slept and the crisis passed. I awoke in the morning sad but sane, and talked easily to Rowena of everyday things.

§ 14

SANGUINE INTERLUDE

A LITTLE while ago Graves and I spent an evening together.

He has been prospering lately and he wrote and asked me to dine with him. He is becoming a figure in what he calls the world of post-war marketing. He has had several successes with novel commodities, he has become an influence in the Rotary Club movement, he gives addresses to gatherings of business men anxious to study and adapt themselves to post-war conditions. He writes articles and he is the author of two thoughtful, original and able books on current economic and political development; they have been seriously reviewed and discussed. I believe he is the first, but I feel sure not the last, who will enter the field of literature by way of writing advertisements. Nowadays he is stouter than he was, his right hand can hold and use a pen, his restored eyelid merely gives humour to his expression, and his scar which was fiery red is now only a declining pink. He has reduced the chestnut beard to the David shape. The world, I learn from him, is threatened with a return to beards.

My dear Blettsworthy, he wrote, *I talked to you long ago of repaying all I owed you. You smiled I remember. You shall smile some more before the end. I could pay back two-thirds of the principal now without a strain, but I want it in my business and there it shall help to earn the odd thousand and balance the interest account. We are to have champagne on that great occasion. Come and dine with me at the old National Liberal Club. This time of year they put out an awning on the terrace and tables al fresco, and one can sit and watch the L.C.C. trams lit up and admire the lights through the plane trees and watch the reflections under that dear dark brown old bridge all these damned artists and people want to replace by some monstrosity of modern Renaissance—while I have plans of my own. It has to go, but that corner is too good to Berlinise as these people want to do. The quality of the N.L.C. dinner is a little uncertain, the service is intimate rather than stately, but I can answer for the champagne. Thursday at eight.*

Yours ever,
Lyulph G.

He was looking well and in easy possession of himself. He greeted me with eyes of friendly scrutiny. "You're getting over Sacco and Vanzetti," he remarked, and led the way to this terrace of his. I admitted its pleasantness.

"This club amuses me," he said. "I like to think of the political traditions of the 'eighties looking out at the railway bridge of the 'sixties, and imagining themselves still in the van of progress. It is a symphony in mist and summer twilight, with the trams of yesterday doing their best not to make a noise as they go by. Do you notice that all about us are grey heads, brown men from the unchanging east, Jews of the most orthodox conservative type, and the perennial young person? Down below in the gardens young couples sit and whisper. Need I say that they whisper the old, old story?"

He insisted upon sherry with the soup and then disinterred some excellent Deutz and Geldermann of 1911.

I found his manifest gaiety infectious. My spirits rose. It was not the first time that Graves had done me good. He talked for a time of the supersession of Liberalism and he contrived to make that particular ebb and failure of human hopefulness not so much tragic as encouraging and amusing.

" Here this club stands, a banner of progress that someone has forgotten to carry on. It has said all it had to say, and it sticks here like an old-young Megatherium, merely because it doesn't know how to get off the stage or where to go if it did."

" Liberalism dead ? "

" Not Liberalism. That is immortal. The undying repudiation of the thing that is. But this venerable party, its organisation, its party traditions, its Gladstonian tricks and John Bright postures." He dropped his voice and glanced at an adjacent table. " It's fallen into the hands of the Old-Clo men. They've cleaned it up with naphtha and go about offering the poor old formulæ as the latest thing in progressive wear. Have an olive ? "

Then Liberalism he thought was alive ?

" In your blood. In mine. In every living thing with intelligence and capacity."

" The gift you have for hoping ! "

" The gift you have for neither looking through things nor over them ! "

" I could see Rampole Island through the things about us."

" And I. But I can see the sky overhead."

" Tell me, Graves, do you believe mankind will ever leave the gorge ? "

" If our sun does not burst or blow out—if nothing hits our planet—yes."

I shook my head. He leant across the table and regarded me very earnestly.

" But tell me, Blettsworthy, do you believe that things will go on for ever as they are ? "

" Change is not progress. Is human life anything more than an air with variations ? "

Graves paused. There was some shifting of plates and the waiter hovered round us. The remains of our asparagus went, and something else came, I forget what.

" There are things one can't say to everyone," Graves began, and left that to sink in before he spoke again.

" You know me fairly well. A bit flimsy and headlong, eh ? Not altogether reliable. At times somewhere near a cheat."

" Never quite."

" I thank you for that. But here I am. Silly—I can't measure it— vain, fond of my own voice. You know you're a sounder man than I am. Yet even a man like I am may see better than he does. May sometimes have something to tell a better established man—as you are."

" Call me a Stick-in-the-mud."

" I call you a stabler and steadier man than myself. But you lack my enterprise. You lack enterprise or any faith in enterprise. I tell you this world is full now of enterprise. Confused, conflicting, disorganised, aimless, if you like, but it is here. And it is getting clearer-headed than it was. It isn't so conflicting as it was. It isn't such a rotten character. Knowledge grows, a collective purpose grows, power accumulates."

" Prospectus-maker you are and will be to the end of things," I inter-jected, but I wanted him to go on.

" You know your Bible ? " asked Graves.

" I did."

" A certain man called the Preacher visited your Rampole Island, twenty-odd centuries ago. He said men were living not in a gorge but in a cavern, without a hope, without an exit, without the gleam of a star. Vanity of vanities, all was vanity. But nowadays even you have to admit a very clear view of the sky. You talked to the hairless elders of the civilisation that might be, and to talk to men of a good thing that might be, is half-way to bringing it about."

" If I could believe that ! "

" Certain things since the war have hit you hard. That is an in-dividual tragedy. But——" He considered how to put his point. " Need a man nowadays measure the value of things from the standpoint of the individual ? "

He broke off.

" I wish," he remarked in parenthesis, " when I talk of what I really think and feel, I hadn't this feeling of being, so to speak, Baalam's Young Ass."

" I don't see why we shouldn't think what we think—even if we haven't the beards and foreheads that justify our thinking. Go on, Graves."

" You and I," said Graves, " may have ideas it is quite beyond our power to realise. But stronger and better men may come along and get the same ideas. Where a straw spins to-day, a windmill may grind to-morrow."

" My trouble is that I get no glimpse of these stronger and better men."

" Even so. Blettsworthy, you and I, multiplied by ten thousand thousand, begin to have the effect of a force of stronger and better men."

" That I don't altogether accept. No. There is a certain level of effectiveness and below that a man is not even a contributing fraction. He is *nil*. For example—let me talk for a minute, Graves—this question of war. But before I come to that, let me remind you of that poor little start of ours in Oxford, the blue façade, the chain of shops that was to spread knowledge, thought and culture through the world."

"To this day," said Graves stoutly, "I maintain that was a sound idea."

" We failed."

" For want of capital. Financial and moral. I was a grabbing cad and a wasteful fool. I was disgusting. Nevertheless someday, someone a trifle better than a greedy, ill-balanced adolescent will take up that old idea and make a great thing of it."

" My trouble is," said I, " that I doubt the moral and material capital available for this great advance of mankind which you assume so readily. In particular this question of war. All our generation surely saw Ardam for what he is. And what have we done, what are we doing to restrain him ? Some flimsy schemes."

" Under-capitalised, so far. Half-hearted, tentative."

" And where will you find the needful capital ? Man is a coward, perpetually stultifying himself. Do you see a gleam of anything more hopeful ? Here on this terrace we picnic amidst the ruins of Victorian Liberalism. The owl and the bittern entertain their friends at adjoining tables. Yet this Victorian Liberalism was an inspiration in its time. It liberated slaves ; it educated to a certain level ; it cherished freedom. What appears, better and stronger, to take its place ? The question at issue between you and me, Graves, is precisely this question of available capital. I think of the misfortunes and disillusionments of my own life. Some indeed I ascribe to the indifferent quality of nature, which heeds man no more than a tapeworm or a falling rock. Nature has given me good and bad——"

" Stars, mountains, sea and flowers," Graves murmured.

" But the greater part of my distresses I owe to the incurable insufficiencies of man."

" *Why* incurable ? " whispered Graves.

" He blunders into life, he blunders through life. He is cruel, destructive, ruthless, stupid, frantic and dangerous in his panics, jealous of all life but his own."

" There are things to his credit."

" But that is the balance of the account. So he has been. So he will be."

" *No*," said Graves.

" All history is for me."

" History is the study of what is over and done."

He broke off to make some decision about coffee. When he took up his parable again, we had cigars and had turned our chairs a little away from the silver finger-bowls and bright debris of dessert upon the table. We looked out through a lattice of maple leaves and branches upon the deep blue immensity of a July night in London ; the thundering bridge and an endless coming and going of lights weaving a broad and brilliant selvage to its lower edge. For a time we had been sitting in silence.

" Blettsworthy," he said, " you do not know the mighty adventures that are close at hand for mankind."

" Do you ? "

" I dream of them—and feel them coming near. . . .

" You and I, Blettsworthy, are very ordinary men. There is nothing in our brains that cannot be in the brains of thousands of other people. You haven't been alone in your visit to Rampole Island. Thousands, millions perhaps, have been there. You and I think rather figuratively, rather ineffectively, of getting out of the gorge. The movement hasn't really taken shape yet, and second-rate people like we are hang about afraid of the plain conclusions of our own brains. But hundreds of thousands must think and feel as we do. It's absurd to suppose there are not many more people, more decisive than you and I. They are feeling their way ; making their plans. It's just that sense of the other people which is needed to start the whole thing going."

" It *is*," I said with quiet emphasis.

Graves seemed to consider whether he should answer that and anyhow did not do so.

" The war," he said, " *was* a war to end war and it will end war. There will never be a war so huge and silly as that last war again. We just carry on with the old things for a time, the old governments, the old arrangements. The war exposed and damned them all, but we carry on. The real reconstruction of human affairs isn't to be done in a hurry. No need to worry about trial reconstructions and transitory failures. The real reconstruction, Blettsworthy, the *real* reconstruction is afoot. It's launched now just as certainly as progressive experimental science was launched in the seventeenth century. We must begin with promotion companies—exploratory operations. Naturally. Everything begins with sketches and incomplete suggestions. No hurry, but no delay. To alter all this we want expenditure on a scale far beyond the scale of the Great War ; and the job may take a few lifetimes. Great propaganda campaigns. Great educational campaigns. They will

gather and come. Watch what happens now. First the statesmen have
to get the courage to ask for the outlawry of war. A phrase you say, but
is it only a phrase ? When they are used to that idea and when they have
accustomed people to that idea, then, Blettsworthy, then, first timidly and
then boldly they will begin to discuss the next stage towards that inter-
national control of the collective interests of mankind, without which
this blessed outlawry is obviously absurd. These steps are being taken
—now."

" But consider the human beings we know and measure them against
the magnitude of the task ! Think how they quarrel, cheat, fail and
dribble away their lives."

" The hairless ancients who misrule the tribe are all on their way to
the grave. Thank God for death. Megatheria *can* die. Properly assisted
they can die quite rapidly."

" And what replaces them ? " said I. " Only a new crop of similar
weeds. Only a fresh variation on the theme of human futility."

I looked across at my host. His face regarded the old railway bridge
with a serene confidence in spite of all I had said. For a time he pursued
his thoughts in silence. Presently he turned to me.

" Blettsworthy," he said ; " nowadays we begin to have some idea,
a dawning idea, of what man can do with the physical world—flying,
submarines, wireless, the abolition of distance, modern surgery, sanita-
tion. . . . Hardly any of us as yet have more than a dim suspicion of
all that may be done to the mind and motives of mankind. In quite a
few years. Teaching is still at the mule-track stage and we base our
morals and religion on creeds that are absurd to a boy of fourteen. Do
you think matters are going to stick at that ? "

I made my expression obdurate.

" Look at *our* lives. Have we been used—to the tenth of our full
possibility ? The efficiency of the educational machinery of mankind
isn't one per cent. The rest is fuss, neglect and misdirection. What a
raw, silly, greedy, gaping undisciplined thing I was when I led you into
trouble at Oxford ! And I had had the best of education England has
to offer. Not one in a thousand had been worked upon as I had been.
And you——"

" I was a bit of a gaper too," I said.

" What might not have been done with the lives of even such second-
rate material as you and I, if we had had an education that was an education, and grown up into a civilised world instead of into a scramble
seasoned by cant. Even nowadays education spreads. In matters of
conduct people—quite ordinary people—understand their own moods
far better than any generation did before, they watch themselves for

irrational angers, they question their cravings and animosities, they release tensions and they are infinitely franker. That is only the beginning of enlightenment and intelligent self-control—in the place of dogmatic discipline. Customs and institutions broaden out to keep pace with the spread of ideas. People seem to imagine a love affair is just what it was a hundred years ago. It's absolutely different. And hate affairs too. In business people are less grabbing, distrustful and competitive. The quantity of spite per head of population isn't a quarter what it was in the days of Dickens and Thackeray. Read them if you don't believe me. Read the snobbishness and meanness in a volume of *Punch* of fifty years ago, and read the social jokes to-day. And what I am telling you is just the first slow movement towards a psychologically intelligent life. Merely the first steps. It has still to be taken up—massively. You know as well as I do that seven-eighths of the cruel and bad behaviour in life is due to fear and suspicion, ignorance, haste and bad habits. Every one of these things is curable in whole or in part. Do you think people will know these things are curable and not set about curing them? And to cure them you have to give people clear ideas of what, as a whole, they are up to. If we could come back here in a century's time do you think we'd see the same sort of crowd as clusters out there to-night? I don't. We'd see a crowd better grown, better dressed, better mannered and with far less drift and far more definite purpose in its movements. The people in towns nowadays look to me like things that have just strayed in, as ants and flies might come into a kitchen—in search of casual food and drink. My dear Blettsworthy, do you think that this sort of thing "—he indicated London by a sweep of the arm—" is going on for ever? Do you even think it is going on for long?"

" But where is this new age of yours beginning?"

" Within a mile of us—in a thousand skulls. And everywhere."

" Graves," I said, " you must write another book and call it ' The Prospectus of Mankind—Unlimited.' "

He knocked out the glow of his cigar stump in the ashtray at his elbow. He seemed to be considering the proposition. " Why not?"

" And for our individual lives?" I questioned.

" Stoicism—creative Stoicism. What else can there be? And it need not be even stern. Admit, Blettsworthy, there are endless lovely and exciting things in life and that for all our frustations, you would rather have lived than not."

" I'm not ungrateful. A summer night like this alone is worth living for. But I wish I had lived and I wish I lived now to more effect."

" Your discontent even may be effective, and after all, Blettsworthy, you're barely forty. There is still a lot of living for you to do. Things may begin in earnest. . . . The individual life isn't everything. Human beings have overvalued their individual lives and cared too little for their kind. This can be changed without any change of nature ; merely a change of direction. . . . Oh ! I know you think I am slipping out of my individual problems when I talk of the general advance of mankind. I read that doubting smile of yours so well. Perhaps you think I say to myself that it doesn't matter much what I do personally or how I get to my ends ; good or bad I shall be carried along by the stream. I don't say that. I don't feel like that at all. On the contrary, I get myself away from all sorts of mean impulses by thinking in these large terms. I've become honest, more honest anyhow. I've got near to generosity lately in one or two small sffairs. Among other things—as our dinner here is meant to witness—I mean to pay you back all that I took from you."

" Is there any need for that ? Why burthen the future with the blunders of the past ? I'm quite willing to wipe off all that. For the sake of what you and I have taught one another."

" I shall never feel satisfied until I have paid you back."

I queried that mutely.

" Let me be exact to please you. I shall never feel satisfied until I am persuaded I am surely going to pay you back."

I smiled at that characteristic correction and his face brightened with a responsive smile. " I shall pay you, nevertheless," he said. " You are the doubter—always. Take my word for it—it is your Rampole Island that will pass away, and I who will come true."

THE END

CHRISTINA ALBERTA'S FATHER
H.G. Wells

978-0-7206-1939-3 • PB • 416pp • £9.99

With an introduction by Michael Sherborne

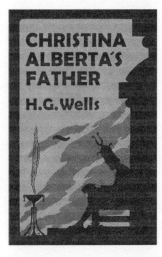

'Surely one of the best books you have ever written.'
– letter from Karl Gustav Jung to H.G. Wells

'H.G. Wells's imagination is of that flashing and creative kind which illuminates common objects and situations with all the time-effacing and place-escaping beauty of pure art.'
– *Spectator*

Christina Alberta is a thoroughly modern young woman of the 1920s. Independence, short skirts, progressive politics, even extramarital sex – she seems to meet all the requirements of a Jazz Age flapper. But Christina Alberta has an eccentric father who refuses to fit any kind of stereotype. You never quite know what Albert Preemby will say and, worse, what he is ultimately planning to do. Is he a madman? Is he the prophet of a new order? Is he even her real father?

This wonderful comic novel is an even-handed satire on society between the two world wars and on the idealists who tried to challenge it. An overlooked gem in the canon of H.G. Wells, it redeploys the humour and themes of *The History of Mr Polly* to explore the fine line between insight and madness. Make the acquaintance of Mr Preemby – or should that be Sargon, King of Kings?

Published as a companion volume to
Mr. Blettsworthy on Rampole Island

H.G. WELLS
ANOTHER KIND OF LIFE
Michael Sherborne

978-0-7206-1391-9 • PB • 424pp • £14.99

With a foreword by Christopher Priest

'A brilliant portrait of the man and the writer . . . sympathetic but clear-eyed . . . packed with facts and discreetly witty.'
– *Sunday Telegraph*

'Authoritative . . . Michael Sherborne has an unrivalled command of the writer's diverse output . . . He writes with bemused detachment and great clarity.'
– *Times Literary Supplement*

'A valuable contribution to Wells studies.'
– *The Wellsian*

'Authoritative, comprehensive and crisply written.' – David Lodge

When H.G. Wells left school at the age of thirteen he looked destined for obscurity. Defying expectations, he became one of the most famous writers in the world, creating such classic science-fiction as *The Time Machine*, *The Invisible Man* and *The War of the Worlds*, reinventing the Dickensian novel in *Kipps* and *The History of Mr Polly*, pioneering postmodernism in experimental fiction and haranguing his contemporaries in polemics which included two best-selling histories of the world. He brought equal energy to his love life, with a series of affairs with well-known authors such as Dorothy Richardson and Rebecca West, the gun-toting travel writer Odette Keun and even a Russian spy. Until his death in 1946, Wells had artistic and ideological confrontations with everyone from Henry James to George Orwell, from Churchill to Stalin. He remains a controversial figure, attacked by some as a philistine, sexist and racist, praised by others as a great writer, a prophet of globalization and a pioneer of human rights. Including material from the long-suppressed correspondence with his mistresses and illegitimate daughter, renowned Wells scholar Michael Sherborne sets the record straight in this authoritative and entertaining biography.

SOME AUTHORS WE HAVE PUBLISHED

James Agee • Bella Akhmadulina • Tariq Ali • Kenneth Allsop • Alfred Andersch
Guillaume Apollinaire • Machado de Assis • Miguel Angel Asturias • Duke of Bedford
Oliver Bernard • Thomas Blackburn • Jane Bowles • Paul Bowles • Richard Bradford
Ilse, Countess von Bredow • Lenny Bruce • Finn Carling • Blaise Cendrars • Marc Chagall
Giorgio de Chirico • Uno Chiyo • Hugo Claus • Jean Cocteau • Albert Cohen
Colette • Ithell Colquhoun • Richard Corson • Benedetto Croce • Margaret Crosland
e.e. cummings • Stig Dalager • Salvador Dalí • Osamu Dazai • Anita Desai
Charles Dickens • Bernard Diederich • Fabián Dobles • William Donaldson
Autran Dourado • Yuri Druzhnikov • Lawrence Durrell • Isabelle Eberhardt
Sergei Eisenstein • Shusaku Endo • Erté • Knut Faldbakken • Ida Fink
Wolfgang George Fischer • Nicholas Freeling • Philip Freund • Carlo Emilio Gadda
Rhea Galanaki • Salvador Garmendia • Michel Gauquelin • André Gide
Natalia Ginzburg • Jean Giono • Geoffrey Gorer • William Goyen • Julien Gracq
Sue Grafton • Robert Graves • Angela Green • Julien Green • George Grosz
Barbara Hardy • H.D. • Rayner Heppenstall • David Herbert • Gustaw Herling
Hermann Hesse • Shere Hite • Stewart Home • Abdullah Hussein • King Hussein of Jordan
Ruth Inglis • Grace Ingoldby • Yasushi Inoue • Hans Henny Jahnn • Karl Jaspers
Takeshi Kaiko • Jaan Kaplinski • Anna Kavan • Yasunuri Kawabata • Nikos Kazantzakis
Orhan Kemal • Christer Kihlman • James Kirkup • Paul Klee • James Laughlin
Patricia Laurent • Violette Leduc • Lee Seung-U • Vernon Lee • József Lengyel
Robert Liddell • Francisco García Lorca • Moura Lympany • Thomas Mann
Dacia Maraini • Marcel Marceau • André Maurois • Henri Michaux • Henry Miller
Miranda Miller • Marga Minco • Yukio Mishima • Quim Monzó • Margaret Morris
Angus Wolfe Murray • Atle Næss • Gérard de Nerval • Anaïs Nin • Yoko Ono
Uri Orlev • Wendy Owen • Arto Paasilinna • Marco Pallis • Oscar Parland
Boris Pasternak • Cesare Pavese • Milorad Pavic • Octavio Paz • Mervyn Peake
Carlos Pedretti • Dame Margery Perham • Graciliano Ramos • Jeremy Reed
Rodrigo Rey Rosa • Joseph Roth • Ken Russell • Marquis de Sade • Cora Sandel
Iván Sándor • George Santayana • May Sarton • Jean-Paul Sartre
Ferdinand de Saussure • Gerald Scarfe • Albert Schweitzer
George Bernard Shaw • Isaac Bashevis Singer • Patwant Singh • Edith Sitwell
Suzanne St Albans • Stevie Smith • C.P. Snow • Bengt Söderbergh
Vladimir Soloukhin • Natsume Soseki • Muriel Spark • Gertrude Stein • Bram Stoker
August Strindberg • Rabindranath Tagore • Tambimuttu • Elisabeth Russell Taylor
Emma Tennant • Anne Tibble • Roland Topor • Miloš Urban • Anne Valery
Peter Vansittart • José J. Veiga • Tarjei Vesaas • Noel Virtue • Max Weber
Edith Wharton • William Carlos Williams • Phyllis Willmott
G. Peter Winnington • Monique Wittig • A.B. Yehoshua • Marguerite Young
Fakhar Zaman • Alexander Zinoviev • Emile Zola

Peter Owen Publishers, 81 Ridge Road, London N8 9NP, UK
T + 44 (0)20 8350 1775 / E info@peterowen.com
www.peterowen.com / @PeterOwenPubs
Independent publishers since 1951